SPIRIT LEVEL

SPIRIT LEVEL

Richy Craven

eriu

First published by Eriu
An imprint of Black & White Publishing Group
A Bonnier Books UK company

4th Floor, Victoria House,
Bloomsbury Square,
London, WC1B 4DA

Owned by Bonnier Books
Sveavägen 56, Stockholm, Sweden

Twitter – @eriu_books
Instagram – @eriubooks

Paperback – 978-1-80418-492-9
Ebook – 978-1-80418-585-8

A CIP catalogue of this book is available from the British Library.

Typeset by IDSUK (Data Connection) Ltd
Printed and bound by Clays Ltd, Elcograf S.p.A.

1 3 5 7 9 10 8 6 4 2

Eriu is an imprint of Bonnier Books UK
www.bonnierbooks.co.uk

For Shell
Without whom, this book wouldn't exist.
So she's to blame

Chapter 1

Danny woke to the sound of moaning. A deep, sorrowful howl echoed through the flat, the lack of any real furniture and terrible build quality working together to create acoustics that Dolby could only dream of.

He stared at the ceiling, figuring out what he could do next. He could hide in his room, trying to make shapes out of the water stains on the ceiling, hoping it would go away, or he could confront whatever was making the noise. Option A was obviously the most appealing. Unfortunately, he had been trialling this on a *pro-tem* basis for the past fifteen minutes and the noise showed no signs of going away. If anything, it was getting louder, as if the first quarter of an hour had just been an overture.

As quietly as he could, he dug a pair of tracksuit bottoms and a hoodie out from the piles of clothes that formed drifts between the floor and his desk. Whatever he was going to be confronting, he'd prefer not to do so in his boxers. Once dressed, he pawed in the dark for his phone on the nightstand, 'nightstand' being something of a grandiose term for a stool he'd taken from the sitting room. The time on the screen read just after five o'clock. The phone's light illuminated the rest of his room and he briefly wondered if he'd been the victim of poltergeist activity before remembering that this was just how he lived.

The sound was even louder in the hallway and allowed Danny to triangulate its source: the living area straight ahead. Cautiously, he made his way towards the far end of the hall and paused at the threshold of the living room. The kitchenette was in view now and he was able to rule it out as the source of the noise. He'd half-wondered this whole time whether it might have just been the contents of the salad-drawer finally gaining sentience, but whatever was there remained in the primordial stages of life. The sound was coming from the sitting room, off to the right and out of view of the hall. If anything, it sounded even less human this close up.

He was about to take a step inside but his breath caught in his throat as he saw the handprint. It was on the frame of the door that led into the sitting room, dark, sticky and glistening a sickly red in the light from Danny's phone torch. He took a breath and stood up to his full height in an attempt to look as intimidating as possible. At five foot nine, this was not terribly effective. Steeling himself, he stepped into the sitting room to confront whatever horrors awaited.

And the sight *was* horrific.

A red-haired man was passed out across his couch. The fact that it was a small leather two-seater and the man was well over six feet tall meant that only his head, shoulders and chest were actually horizontal. The opposite arm of the sofa had forced his legs into a right angle from the rest of his body, the soles of his grubby Converse almost pointing at the ceiling. This awkward position was, Danny supposed, what was causing his drunken snores to emerge as drawn-out groans.

In front of the intruder, the remnants of a Chinese takeaway were leaking onto the cheap laminate coffee table. Danny looked back at the handprint and, after a moment's hesitation, dipped his finger into the dark stain and sniffed at it. Sweet and sour sauce.

He sighed as he wandered over to the sleeping housebreaker and prodded him with one foot. 'Did you at least bring me something this time?' he asked.

The red-haired man didn't even open his eyes. 'Chicken balls are in the bag,' Nudge said and then attempted to curl up in the foetal position to fit as much of himself on the sofa as possible.

Danny dug through the remnants of the takeaway and found the small paper bag, already see-through with grease, as promised. Rent for the night secured, he padded back to his bedroom and left his best friend snoring on the couch.

*

'You told me you lost that key?' Danny asked his friend.

It was three hours later and both Danny and Nudge were enjoying a light breakfast of prawn crackers and leftover fried rice.

'I had,' Nudge said. 'I found the keys in the jacket I wore out, so I figured it was, like, serendipity or something.'

Paul Nugent, known exclusively as Nudge, had hit his height of six foot two towards the end of their second year of school. This, combined with his rail-thin frame and frizzy red hair had made it almost impossible for him to blend in. Sometime around their Leaving Cert, he'd made peace with this and had concluded that, if he was going to stand out anyway, then he might as well lean into it. As such, his outfit of choice for that night started with a pair of ultra-fitted green chinos. These were off-set by a bright blue belt, but the eyes were drawn away from even this towards his shirt. It was yellow, at least, *broadly* yellow. The designer had started with the most eye-catching shade possible but then apparently still felt that it wasn't bold enough and had added an entire menagerie of exotic birds to compensate.

Danny knew that Nudge looked for a reaction more than anything, both in his choice of outfits and in life in general, and the best thing would just be to ignore it.

'You look like a Lidl own-brand Ronald McDonald,' he said.

This prompted a moment of silent chewing from both men as they thought quickly.

'Sid'l McLidl!' Nudge said triumphantly and Danny gave his friend a grudging nod of respect for getting there first. Then he looked around, bemused. 'Where *is* your jacket?'

Nudge stared into space for a moment. 'Shit. I thought the walk from Lok Moon was colder than usual. Glad I took the keys out, so. I could have caught my death walking all the way home.'

'Yeah, and if Ken had been here then you might have caught the business end of a nine iron,' Danny replied.

'Not likely, you're always saying that he's off playing house with his missus.'

Not for the first time, Danny regretted telling Nudge about the golden ticket in the Dublin property market that he'd enjoyed for the past few months. Ken, an old

4

college friend, was ostensibly his flatmate but spent almost all his time at his girlfriend's, who had her own, much nicer place. Ken had, with not untypical male reasoning, figured that by maintaining his room in the dingy two-bed he shared with Danny, he could keep the relationship in a loose, casual state for as long as possible.

While the small flat wasn't much to look at, it had given Danny somewhere close to his own patch in Dublin that he'd had practically to himself for a monthly price that was merely ludicrous instead of extortionate.

'It's partially your own fault that I'm here anyway,' Nudge continued.

Danny allowed a prawn cracker to dissolve on his tongue as he counted to ten in his head. 'Is it now?' he said, finally.

'If you weren't ghosting the lads' group again then I wouldn't have had to come here in person to ask you about Nadine's welcome home party.'

'I wasn't ghosting the lad's grou— Nadine's back?'

Nudge laughed. 'You're useless.'

'Nadine is back?' Danny repeated. His usual thin patience for Nudge's antics had not been helped by the night before. Although he wasn't wrong about the ghosting. He was a member of no fewer than eight different WhatsApp groups but the number of these that were actively muted at any given time provided a fairly accurate barometer of his mental state. Right now, they all were except for the one where people posted pictures of soup. He found that one soothing.

'She got back on Wednesday. If you used your phone for anything other than PornHub you might have picked up on it.'

'I didn't see anything about it on her Instagram,' Danny said, inadvertently revealing how closely he kept track of that particular page.

'She bricked her phone. Made it all the way across South America only to drop it outside Terminal Two. She's having drinks in hers tonight.'

'Okay,' Danny said, slowly, in the flat tone of voice of a submarine captain who has just noticed that his feet are a bit wet.

'So, I wanted to make sure that you were okay, you know, emotionally,' Nudge continued.

'And it had nothing to do with you spending your taxi money on Chinese again?'

'Can you believe it's been a whole year since she left?' Nudge asked, neatly ignoring the accusation.

'No,' Danny replied distractedly. He was very aware of his tendency to overanalyse and worry about things outside of his control. Mostly because he paid a therapist a lot of money to explain it to him repeatedly. So, on the one hand, he was relieved that he hadn't learned about this sooner or else he'd have been a nervous wreck all week. On the other hand, it meant that he now had to try to cram an entire week's worth of obsessive worrying into one day.

'So . . .' Nudge began, as if the thought had just occurred to him. 'That would make it a year since you last got the ride as well, right?'

Chapter 2

Kicking Nudge out onto the street, albeit in a borrowed coat, hadn't cheered Danny up as much as it usually did. His heart hadn't been in it.

After ousting his home invader, Danny was too wired to go back to bed. He showered and dressed quickly before inspecting himself critically in the smudged mirror above his desk. Two watery blue eyes stared back at him from under a sandy brown fringe, although there was a significant expanse of forehead between the two. Danny's head had always looked like it was a size too big for the rest of him. At twenty-four, he'd filled out enough so that it wasn't quite as noticeable but as a teen, he'd had the look of someone troubled by strong winds. He wore a cheap pair of black trousers and a button-up white shirt, his de-facto Eurospar uniform since the branch manager had refused to actually provide a standardised one. A faded, grey hoodie completed that day's ensemble. He also wore a worried expression. Danny was good at worried expressions; he had a lot of face to work with. A worried expression could get a good run-up.

Nadine was back.

This thought had been echoing around his head for most of the morning. She was an old friend who he'd been distantly infatuated with since they were sixteen but, with his usual timing, he'd put off actually doing anything about it until the week before she'd gone travelling in South America. That had been a year ago. Nudge was right that she had been the last person he'd been with. At her going-away party, no less. She'd left on her travels a few days later and they hadn't communicated since, beyond the occasional like of one another's Instagram pictures.

This was a lot to process so early in the morning so Danny decided to deal with it by distracting himself and hoping the anxiety would go away on its own. The strategy had a poor success rate, historically speaking, but it at least had the benefit of not making anything immediately worse.

He wasn't due in work for another few hours but rattling around the flat alone with his thoughts was obviously not an option. Luckily, when Danny finally decided to move out of the nest to spread his wings, he hadn't spread them all that far. The apartment was only a twenty-minute walk from his family home. He hadn't actually been back in a little over two weeks at this point, so decided to make use of his unexpectedly early morning to drop in.

It was a freezing, clear November day. The walk helped warm him somewhat but, by the time he reached the housing estate where he'd grown up, he had pulled his hands inside his sleeves like a small child and was questioning his lifelong aversion to learning how to drive.

Danny hesitated for a moment at the front door. He hadn't quite gotten comfortable with the protocol here yet. Yes, this was his home and he still had a key. Still, he didn't live there any more and was slightly uncomfortable with the idea of just wandering in with no notice, like the wacky neighbour from a sit-com. Or Nudge.

He compromised by knocking as he let himself in and was greeted with a familiar wall of Saturday-morning noise. Danny's parents were adamant that they didn't have any problems with their hearing, but still insisted on listening to the radio at a volume that sound techs working for U2 would consider excessive. Knocking had been mostly a symbolic gesture; he would have had to ram a car into the front room before he made an impression over *Newstalk*.

His mum was standing at the kitchen counter, scrolling through something on an old Android tablet that she insisted on calling her 'iPad'. She looked up as he walked into the kitchen, mild surprise flashing across her round face. 'I hope you're not expecting breakfast,' Tara Hook said in lieu of hello as she moved to give him a hug. 'I have barely enough in to feed the rest of them. I swear that child has gone savage since we started him on solids.'

'I ate before I left,' Danny assured her. 'Just a flying visit before work.'

'Have you run out of clean clothes again?' A voice said from the breakfast table.

Danny turned to look over to where his younger sister was browsing through lecture notes on her laptop while trying to convince a red-faced baby to eat some porridge. Neither enterprise seemed to be going particularly well. Steff had definitely taken after their mum, her strong nose the only feature on a round face that kept their dad from suspecting the local milkman.

'I've had an easier time keeping things clean now that somebody isn't puking on them every other day,' Danny said in a sing-song voice as he wandered over to pick up his nephew. He liked to think that the chubby baby's eyes lit up at the sight of him as he was swept up out of his high chair, but it was more likely he was just excited to be escaping the porridge.

Steff's first year at college had been derailed slightly by her getting pregnant in her second term due to a one-time fling with Connor, a handsome Second Year. Danny had actually been the first person she'd told in the family, so worried was she that her parents were going to go mental. Danny had assured her that she was being silly.

They had gone a *little* bit mental, he had to concede. Nine months later though, Buster had come into their lives and any worries that Steff had had about her parents not being supportive evaporated. They made a show of complaining about how disruptive the new addition to the family was but any attempt to remove him from their house now would need to involve a SWAT team. Even then Danny would only give them 50–50 odds; 30–70 if his mum had any of her garden tools on hand.

Danny would be lying if he said that the whole process had been entirely without challenges, however. If he'd thought that living with his sister had been difficult during her exams then the pregnancy and subsequent newborn had given him an entirely new and sleep-deprived perspective. It quickly became clear that the house was too small for everyone, mostly because Steff repeatedly pointed this out to him. Danny moving out had been the path of least resistance.

'Bloody hell, Steff,' Danny wheezed as he quickly tried to adjust to the new weight. 'What have you been feeding him? Cement?'

Buster overlooked his uncle's fat-shaming and gurgled happily as he was bounced up and down.

Steff threw the spoon back in the bowl. 'Well, he's certainly not going to finish this now. C'mere.' She stood up and undid the bib from around Buster's neck as Danny tilted him dramatically backwards towards her, much to his delight.

'What the hell is he wearing?' Danny asked.

Baby Brian, known as 'Buster', despite Steff's strenuous objections, was decked out in a bright-red jersey. On its crest, a ship sailed between two towers. 'It's a Cork jersey, Dan,' Steff said in a tone that suggested that this wasn't the first time she had had this conversation. 'Connor's parents were up for the week and took him last night. They just dropped him back.'

'And you were waiting until after he's spilled porridge all over it to take it off and burn it?' Danny asked.

Buster's Dad, Connor, had proposed to Steff when he'd found out about the baby, and had been promptly told to cop onto himself. They had worked out an amicable custody arrangement that saw him spend most days after college over with the Hooks, although Steff had had to impose a strict 'No-GAA-discussion' rule on him and their dad. She was also adamant that Buster would not be staying over in the 'slurry pit', which is how she referred to his student accommodation, a two-bed house he shared with five other Ag. Science students, but Buster had been down to stay with him in Cork a number of times.

Steff returned to the kitchen table and continued to scroll through her lecture slides although Danny noticed that there were more tabs open for Asos than PowerPoint.

'He's half-Corkonian, Dan, you're going to have to get used to that.'

Danny pulled his nephew close to his chest and made an exaggerated show of covering the baby's ears. 'Shhh! I thought we decided that we would raise him like a normal child and not tell him until his eighteenth birthday.'

Steff gave Danny the finger without looking up as she switched over from her economics notes to a page of bored-looking, waifish women modelling dresses.

Danny's mum walked over with a packet of baby wipes and a determined expression. 'Go out and say hello to your dad. Breakfast will be ready in a few minutes,' she said as she plucked Buster from Danny's arms. She placed the infant on the stool by the kitchen counter and began to vigorously strip away layers of porridge, drool and, quite possibly, skin.

Danny grabbed one of his nephew's sticky hands. 'We still love you no matter what, Buster,' he said with mock sincerity. 'Even if your existence is a crime against nature.'

Then he quickly made his way to the back door before Steff could get a good line of sight on his head with her bagel.

He walked out into a flurry of russet fur and slobber as Luna, the Hook family dog, bounced up and down around Danny in an increasingly tighter arc, as if trying her best to leave as many muddy paw prints on his trousers as possible. Luna looked as if someone had assembled a dog out of all the parts that had been in the lost-and-found bin. She had the russet fur of a setter combined with the bearded face of a terrier or folk singer. She had lost her tail in some unspecified accident before becoming a member of the family, which made it hard to judge her moods. Mostly it was safe to assume that she was hungry.

'At least you're always guaranteed a warm welcome from one of us when you come home,' his dad said from a few feet away.

There was little doubt where Danny had inherited his difficulty in finding hats to fit. Joe Hook was entirely bald with a prominent, flat nose that gave onlookers the vague impression that one of the Easter Island statues had climbed out of the earth to make a living driving a taxi in Dublin. He was idly swinging a pitching wedge back and forth.

'You know your grandson is wearing a Cork jersey, right?' asked Danny as he managed to catch Luna with all four paws on the ground and tussle her ears.

'I know. Just leave it, would you? I still have to live here.' Joe took a golf ball out of his pocket and bounced it on the concrete once. Luna, the long-awaited reunion with her master instantly forgotten, abandoned Danny and took her place beside the older man, quivering with anticipation.

By some accident of suburban planning, the Hooks' garden stretched back close to a hundred metres. Each side of the garden was lined with large, bricked-off flower beds that were his mum's pride and joy in the spring but now lay bare except for the odd perennial bush. The centre, however, was just unbroken lawn all the way down to the garden shed. One of his mum's flowerpots appeared to be serving as the hole today.

Danny's dad took a few practice swings.

'How's life?' he asked, his tone seemingly innocuous.

Danny tensed involuntarily. Conversations with his dad these days inevitably went one of four ways:

1. The likelihood of Danny getting a 'proper career'
2. Danny learning to drive
3. His love life
4. His mental health.

Danny listed them mentally in the order of how likely his dad would be to bring them up, depending on how comfortable he was with the topic.

'Not bad,' Danny said, picking up another club that was leaning against the side of the house and swinging it aimlessly. 'Still settling into the new place, you know?'

The older man didn't take his eye off the flowerpot. He took another practice swing. Luna didn't even flinch. That sort of amateurism wouldn't fly here in the big leagues.

'Made any progress with the driving?' he asked, as if the thought had just occurred to him in the moment.

Bingo! As a taxi driver, he probably took his son's inability to drive as some sort of personal failing. Both Hook men had tacitly agreed never to speak again about what had occurred the last time he'd tried to teach Danny to drive. It had ended with Danny walking home from where a tricky hill start had provoked a particularly heated argument.

Luckily, he was saved now from having to come up with a lie as his dad struck the ball. The men watched its trajectory as it bounced once in front of the flowerpot before a blur of russet intercepted it mid-air. Unfortunately, even seasoned pros like Luna can sometimes misjudge and the dog's momentum in the air was too great for her to stop. She hit the old flowerpot like a furry torpedo, cracking the terracotta. Luna recovered her feet on the far side and stared back at the destruction she had caused.

Paternal interrogation forgotten, Joe glanced back nervously towards the house. 'How would you feel about taking the rap for this? I really do still have to live here.'

*

One quick father-son trip to the shed to hide the evidence later, both men re-entered the house. Luna bounced in after them with what, Danny felt, seemed like a sociopathic lack of guilt. The dog installed herself under Buster's highchair. She hadn't known what to make of this new addition to the family when he first turned up, but she'd soon learned that, by strategically placing herself under the high chair during meals, she could be guaranteed a feast.

Despite his mum's warnings, there was a plate in front of Danny's chair. Still full from the remnants of Nudge's takeaway, he satisfied himself with a cup of tea and surreptitiously threw black pudding to the dog under the table.

'Oh, don't you start, Dan,' Tara said. 'Between Buster and your father, that dog is going to burst.'

'Can we stop calling my son Buster?' Steff said. 'It sounds like the name of a cartoon bear.'

'We can't help the fact that he looks more like a Buster than he does a "Brian". Isn't that right, Buster?' Danny said, relishing the long-overdue opportunity to wind up his younger sister.

Buster, who now had another bib covering the offending jersey, was too busy trying to stick an entire slice of toast into his mouth to comment.

'Speaking of names,' Tara interjected in an attempt to head off an argument. 'We finally got a date for the christening. It's going to be in two weeks.'

'Yeah, and if you want to stay godfather, you better learn your nephew's bloody name,' Steff warned Danny.

Danny made what he hoped was a conciliatory face and just nodded. He felt partly responsible for the nickname that everyone seemed to agree was better than his nephew's actual name. Mostly because he was *entirely* responsible. It had jeopardised his godfather status for a while but he'd been able to claw things back through ostentatious presents and offers to babysit.

Sensing weakness, Steff leaned forward. 'Can you watch him for an hour or so?' she asked. 'Mum has her walking group and I have to finish this essay before our mother-and-baby class.'

Danny rolled his eyes and begrudgingly agreed, for the look of the thing but, once breakfast wrapped up, he gladly brought his nephew into the front room, Luna trailing after them in case the child managed to shed anything else edible. He used the opportunity to scroll through his phone and sift through a couple of days of unread messages as he bounced Buster on his knee in front of something bright and colourful on the TV. Nadine had indeed returned and she was having a party in her house that night to celebrate.

Had she noticed that he hadn't responded yet to her invite? Did she think he was intentionally ghosting her?

His thoughts buzzed as, on his knee, he bounced Buster up and down with more intensity, to the baby's delight.

It would be rude to turn up without letting her know, surely?

He agonised over this for several more minutes, transferring Buster to his other knee at one point when his leg got tired, as he drafted, deleted and redrafted a post to the group. After much deliberation, he went with: 'Sounds great. See you there.'

Would she even want him to show up?

Danny could count on the fingers of one elbow the number of one-night stands he'd had before this, so he wasn't sure what the protocol was afterwards.

Buster was nearly shot into the ceiling as Danny's phone buzzed with a new message. It was from Nadine. It simply said. 'Great. Can't wait.'

Well, what did she mean by that?

Fortunately, even with Danny's runaway train of thought he couldn't ignore the sound of Buster hiccupping. The jostling had finally become too much even for his robust stomach and Danny barely got him off his knee before he cheerfully spat up that morning's porridge all over his bright new jersey. Danny decided to interpret this as his nephew's Dublin side rejecting his Corkness. 'Good lad,' Danny said, while holding him out at arm's length. 'Steff, I have to go to work.'

Chapter 3

As Nudge's car pulled onto Nadine's road later that evening, Danny felt the overwhelming urge to run away. Fortunately, this wasn't physically possible, as Nudge drove a two-door and Danny had been shoehorned into the back seat. Sven had claimed shotgun because of his injury and the fact that he was physically capable of plucking Danny out of the seat with one arm. Neither of his friends had been willing to move their seats forward, so Danny sat with his knees practically around his ears. Nudge had offered his services as chauffeur and Danny and Sven had grudgingly agreed that being seen in his hideous two-tone, two-door, too-ugly Suzuki Vitara was just about worth the price of not having to pay for a taxi.

Nudge parked a few houses down and Danny was able to birth himself from the back seat with a little bit of midwifery from his two best friends. He took a moment to marvel at the car now that he was free of it. Nudge had bought it from an older cousin for a steal, presumably after the cousin had seen the thing in the full light of day for the first time. There were worse things to inherit from family, Danny would be forced to admit, but the Suzuki had to be somewhere on that list, above male-pattern baldness but below haemophilia.

The reason why Nudge had decided to stay sober and drive was a date with someone from his master's-degree course early the following day. The date had been the subject of discussion for their entire drive. Or, rather, the subject of argument.

'No, you cannot bring a date back to my flat,' Danny said as they walked towards Nadine's house.

'I told you not to give him a key,' Sven said to Danny, carefully placing his crutches down on the loose gravel of her driveway.

Sven had earned his name when a typing error on their school's register had removed the 'te' from his given name of Steven, but nobody could argue that it suited him. At six foot four with blond hair, he looked like he should be crewing the longship of some Viking raiding party or, at the very least, fronting a German electro band. A simple white t-shirt covered a torso that an anatomy professor could have used to point out major muscle groups on. The fact that one leg of his jeans ended in a large black walking cast indicated that his rugby career had taken another hit.

'Grade-three tear of the PCL,' he'd said, unasked, when he and Nudge had showed up to collect Danny. 'Three months maybe before I can train again.'

Danny wasn't completely sure what a PCL was and whether a grade-three was better or worse than a grade-one tear but decided that it was probably not great either way considering Sven's track record with injury. He hadn't so much been the backbone of their school's rugby team as the entire skeletal system and a good portion of the major organs as well.

'C'mon,' Nudge wheedled. 'I can hardly bring her back to mine. My mum will be home all day.' He seemed no worse for wear from his earlier breaking, entering and eviction that morning. However, this evening, he'd gone for a more understated green-and-purple-striped fuzzy jumper that was approximately two sizes too big for him.

'You're awfully confident that she's going to want to come home with you.' Sven opined, ringing the doorbell.

'Well, you know. 'Fail to prepare . . .'

Danny was spared having to continue the argument when the door was opened.

'Gentlemen!' a stocky man in his early fifties announced with faux-seriousness. 'I'm afraid there's no party here. Try next door.'

Danny had been to the house half a dozen times over the years and Nadine's dad, Morris, never seemed to tire of this joke. They waited patiently for a beat before the older man laughed and swung the door wide, giving them each a slap on the shoulder as they squeezed past him. For a brief second Danny panicked that the man of the house might have somehow gotten word about his daughter's last encounter with him, but Morris gave Danny his usual broad smile.

Still, Danny hurried past him, feeling that it was better to be safe than sorry. Nudge followed him into a bright, airy kitchen that led into a sunroom on one side and an open-plan dining room/kitchen on the other, as Sven explained his injury to Morris for what was surely not going to be the only time that night. Around two dozen men and women in their early twenties stood in clusters, talking.

Danny did a quick scan of the room but couldn't see the guest of honour. The crowd seemed like one dense mass but he had been to enough of these things to recognise subtle borders between the milling groups. A large throng of mostly girls gathered around the enormous kitchen island. These were Nadine's oldest friends from school and would have arrived earliest, whereas the sunroom had clearly been claimed in the name of her college mates. Other, miscellaneous friends floated at the peripheries of both but it was early enough that there was little intermingling between them.

Danny and Nudge did a lap of the kitchen island to hugs and air kisses until Sven limped into the room and they both became invisible. Their blond friend reddened at the attention and stuttered out his injury prognosis to his new audience. Even though Sven looked like he'd been hand-carved by Zeus, he was somehow even worse with women than either of his two friends. Danny left him to it, knowing that the only way any of the girls would be able to get his full attention was if they dressed up as a sexy IRFU contract. He didn't bother to see if there was any room in the fridge and, instead, went straight out the back with his box of beers where the night air would keep them cool.

It was here that he ran into the guest of honour. As he walked out the back door, she stepped out of a group of smokers to his left. The collision caused Danny to lose his grip on the box of beers he had been clutching and it tumbled to the ground, via his foot. 'Mother-fuck!' he wheezed, hopping up and down in a way that he hoped was more charmingly awkward Hugh Grant than Elmer Fudd.

'Oh my God!' Nadine said, suppressing laughter. 'Danny, I'm so sorry! Are you okay?'

It didn't help that she was just as beautiful as Danny remembered. Logic dictated that the mental picture he'd been sustaining from the past year had been some idealised version that no actual woman could live up to: Nadine insisted on being as gorgeous in real life.

Travel had definitely suited her. South America had given her a tan that complemented her blonde hair, which had now almost reached her elbow after a year away from Peter Mark. Huge blue eyes dominating a heart-shaped face were currently filled with equal parts concern and concealed laughter.

'I'm fine,' Danny managed, as he gingerly put his weight back on his injured foot. It screamed in pain but right now he would have stood casually in a bear trap if it meant recapturing some momentum.

'Nadine was just admiring my jumper,' Nudge said, wandering up beside them. Danny couldn't tell if his friend was giving him a chance to recuperate or if he just wanted to be the centre of attention again.

'I actually said that it took a confident man to wear something like that,' Nadine corrected him.

Nudge shrugged as if it meant the same thing and took a swig from a cocktail he'd scavenged from somewhere. Danny realised that he now owed Sven a fiver. He'd bet that Nudge would make it at least a half an hour before breaking his vow of sobriety for the night, but they'd only been there fifteen minutes.

'Morris was making Old Fashioneds,' Nudge said, answering Danny's unasked question.

'What about your big date tomorrow?' Danny asked.

'I'll get the bus out this way beforehand and pick up the car,' Nudge said.

'A Sunday-morning date?' Nadine said. 'What are you doing? Bringing her to Mass?'

'Bit of "Eucharist and chill"?' Danny chimed in.

'You're just jealous because women agree to go out with me when they're sober and you still have to settle for whoever's left when the lights come on in Coppers,' Nudge replied, before adding, 'She works in a bar on the weekends so we're gonna go for brunch and a walk before her shift tomorrow.'

Nadine and Danny managed a synchronised, pantomime 'Oooh' in response.

'Who is this young lady?' asked Nadine in mock-scandalised tones. 'Does she come from a good family? Will your mother approve?'

Danny didn't think that there was any way he could find her more attractive, but her playful taunting of Nudge had proved him wrong.

'I never missed you, you know,' Nudge said petulantly. 'Not even for a moment.'

'I, on the other hand, am thrilled to have the back-up,' Danny said.

'Thanks,' she replied. 'It's good to be back. How are you?' she turned to Danny as Nudge took another swig of his cocktail. 'What are you doing with yourself now?'

Danny's heart sank. He'd hoped that they would be able to just chat about her travels while he subtly steered the conversation away from his career, dating prospects and life in general. 'Oh, I'm actually still in the Spar,' he said in a way that, he hoped, indicated that he expected this to be a temporary thing before his inevitable rise to fame and fortune. 'Assistant manager now though, so . . . that's good,' he finished lamely.

Nudge came to his rescue. 'Danny's sister had her kid; a little boy.'

'Oh my God! That's right. You're an uncle now!' Nadine said. 'You'll have to show me a picture.'

Danny gratefully fished his phone out of his pocket and scrolled through his photos. Luckily, Buster made up a large part of his social circle these days so there was no shortage. He selected one from a few weeks back, where his sister had dressed the unfortunate child up as Michael D Higgins for Hallowe'en, and held it out to her. Danny had actually spent the entire time making fun of Steff for putting so much effort into the costume, threatening to call Childline in the process. He made a mental note to text her to apologise for this as Nadine leaned in closer and grabbed his arm, while making a noise so high-pitched that only dogs and military satellites could hear it.

'Oh my God, Danny. That's so cute!' she said, managing to fit three syllables into the word 'cute'.

Danny felt hope surge. Was the nephew card something that he could play to endear himself to women? The question of whether it was morally right to leverage his only nephew in a cheap attempt to pick up girls briefly raised its head and was just as quickly dismissed as he tried to think of another picture he could show Nadine, so she'd keep holding his arm like that.

'Babe, c'mere, you have to see this. Remember that photo I showed you of Michael D?' she called across the garden.

Danny had already pulled up another picture, of Buster chewing the ear off a toy lamb like an infant Mike Tyson, when his brain caught up with her words. *Babe?* The word seemed to form into ice in his skull and sink through his throat as the most attractive man Danny had ever seen separated from a tight knot of people near the door and sauntered over. Danny hadn't actually ever seen anyone saunter in real life before, but it was the only way to describe how the tall, coal-haired man walked confidently towards them.

'The leprechaun-looking guy?' he asked.

Danny was momentarily worried that he'd suffered some sort of brain-bleed from the shock, as the words that came out of the guy's mouth seemed strange, but he realised that he just had some sort of accent. American or Canadian maybe.

Nadine playfully slapped him on the shoulder. 'That is our president. Show some respect.' She offered him the phone and its arguably-less-respectful representation of the man in the Áras.

'Oh, that's hilarious!' he said. *American, definitely.*

Nadine suddenly remembered herself. 'Sorry, I'm all over the place tonight. Danny, Nudge, this is Clark: we met while I was travelling. Clark, this is Danny and Nudge.'

Danny accepted a firm handshake and stuttered a hello. Any hopes that he might have briefly harboured about Clark being just a friend were sunk by the comfortable way he slipped his arm around Nadine's waist.

Danny took a second to regroup by digging a bottle out of the box (his foot had provided something of a cushion during the collision earlier, so they had all survived). Nadine excused herself as another group of young women entered and was quickly swept into a chorus of 'Oh my God!'s

There was an awkward moment of silence between Danny, Nudge, and the new arrival.

'Where did you two meet?' Danny asked. It had come out a little louder and more manic than he had intended, but if Clark noticed he gave nothing away.

'We were staying at the same hostel in Lima. I kind of crashed her group, to be honest.'

'And are you going to be in Ireland long?' asked Nudge.

Clark smiled shyly and Danny marvelled at how someone's teeth could be that straight and white in real life. 'I don't know yet, really. I'm not a big planner. I just like to take each day as it comes, you know?'

Both Danny and Nudge smiled back and nodded as if they, too, routinely followed women half way across the world with no plan.

'That's how I travelled,' he continued. 'You can't plan out every single day. Sometimes you've got to just pick a country at the airport and see how it goes. No guidebook. No TripAdvisor. Just see what happens.'

'I'm always saying that, aren't I, Danny?' Nudge said. A sly grin had spread across his face.

Nudge had never even gone to a restaurant without checking the menu first but Danny recognised that smile. Winding up Americans was one of his life's great passions. 'That sounds fascinating,' he continued. 'You should have documented it somehow.'

'Oh, man, did Nadine not tell you about my podcast? I should send you the link.'

'Clark,' Nudge said sincerely, putting his arm around the American. 'Nothing would make me happier.'

Danny excused himself as Nudge got the details of his entertainment for the next week. *Perhaps one of Morris' Old Fashioneds would help soothe the sting of disappointment.*

Chapter 4

The night didn't get any better from there. As the hours moved on, Danny did a lap of the conversational groups, catching up with old friends, being introduced to new significant others and listening to people talk about their jobs or their master's degrees or their PhDs. Eurospar, formerly Spar, formerly Clark's Newsagents (est. 1987) had been responsible for most of his income since Danny had turned sixteen. It didn't seem like that long ago that they'd all been laughing about being lost and aimless after getting off the reassuring conveyor belt that was the Irish education system. Danny's tendency to take the path of least resistance, college course-wise, had somehow led him to graduate with a degree in Environmental Science. Thus far he had failed to convince several potential employers that his knowledge of botany would be an asset to their business.

As he opened another beer, Danny tried not to think about how everyone seemed to have their life together except him. He was going through them at a steady clip. Self-pity was thirsty work.

There had been half-hearted suggestions about where in town they should move on to, but Danny could recognise a house session when he saw one. It was after one o'clock by the time he got the opportunity to speak to the hostess again one-on-one. He had stepped out of the now-thinning crowd in the main room, into the hall when he met her coming down the stairs.

'Oh, hey,' she said as she descended. 'Having a good time?'

'Yeah, it's good to catch up with everyone,' he lied.

'I know. Listen, I hope I didn't catch you off guard earlier? With Clark, I mean.' She stood opposite him now, huge eyes filled with drunken concern.

'What!? No! Don't worry about it!' he said, again a lot louder and more urgently than he had intended. 'He seems great. Very adventurous.'

Nadine winced. 'He didn't mention the podcast, did he?'

Danny was rescued from having to answer when the door to the hall opened, revealing the limping form of Sven. The bigger man faltered slightly at the sight of the two of them standing so close together.

'Hey,' he said. He looked embarrassed for a second before a frown of worry crossed his face. 'Have either of you seen Nudge? He said he was going to the jacks but one of the lads said he saw him leaving.'

Seeing an opportunity to extricate himself from an uncomfortable situation, Danny held his hand out to Sven. 'You stay where you are. I'll go have a look. I'm sure even he's not stupid enough to drive in his state.' He hoped he sounded more confident than he felt. Nudge had actually been known to drink and drive on a number of occasions. It was a miracle he hadn't been caught by the guards yet.

Nadine called after him. 'Tell him he can stay here tonight if he doesn't want to have to come back tomorrow.'

Danny waved a hand at her in response on his way out the door while internally cursing. He jogged down the driveway to the road, a little unsteadily due to drink and the gravel, and glanced to where they had left the Shitara a number of hours earlier.

The good news was that Nudge hadn't driven away in it. The bad news was that this was because he was currently struggling with a fifteen-point turn so that he could get the Suzuki pointing in the correct direction to drive away in it. He had finally managed to succeed at this as Danny ran up to the car. He saw his friend hesitate and consider pulling away before sighing and putting the handbrake on.

The key thing to remember was not to lose his temper, Danny thought. 'What do you think you're doing, you fucking idiot?'

'I think it's called an "Irish goodbye",' answered Nudge, unfazed by his friend's tone. 'Which I've always thought was weird because, if anything, Irish—'

'—It's called "Operating Under the Influence", you daft prick,' Danny interrupted. He was shivering due to a combination of the cold, the drink and anger at Nudge and climbed into the passenger seat of the car, partly so he couldn't just drive off and partly to get out of the wind.

'Would you stop being so dramatic! I had my last drink hours ago.'

'You're still over the limit,' Danny countered, on the back foot now. He tried to grab at the keys from where they hung in the ignition, but Nudge just slapped his hand away.

'Barely, if even,' replied Nudge, still unflappable. 'A few beers and that Old Fashioned is all I had tonight.'

One of Nudge's many irritating qualities was the fact that he was very good at arguing, no matter how poor his position might be. 'Look,' he said, 'Why don't you come along to keep an eye on me? Or would you prefer to stay in there watching Nadine score her new boyfriend with everyone knowing she gave you the elbow?'

'She didn't give me the el—'

'—This isn't my first rodeo,' he continued over Danny's protests. 'I'm going to go well below the speed limit and, if at any time, you feel uncomfortable, you can say so and we'll pull over.'

'I don't know,' Danny said, all his earlier rage and certainty draining away in a drunken fog.

'Well, I do. Look, we can shoot Sven a text when we get back and ask him to bring your coat home.'

Danny had completely forgotten about his coat. Nudge *did* seem a lot more sober, but Danny's drunkenness was hardly a good comparison.

Taking his silence for assent, the lanky redhead undid the handbrake and eased them out of Nadine's estate. He was driving slowly, Danny had to admit: any accident that they had at this speed wouldn't even trouble the Suzuki's paintwork. He relaxed slightly. He relaxed further once they'd edged onto the main road and made their way down the deserted streets. Nudge was being true to his word and keeping it at a sensible thirty.

They drove in silence for a while before Danny spoke. 'Do you ever feel like everyone else has moved on but us?'

'What do you mean?' Nudge asked.

Danny stared out the window rather than look his friend in the eye. 'I don't know, it just feels that everyone else has their shit together and I'm still stocking shelves for a living.'

'Is that why you've been moping all night?'

'I wasn't moping,' Danny protested.

'You had a face on you like a dog in one of those vet's cones the whole time.' Nudge continued, ignoring him. 'You have your own place and two intact legs. That's more than me or Sven can say.'

'That's your advice?' Danny sneered. 'Look on the bright side?'

'Of the two of us, which one spent the night sulking like a stroppy teenager and who spent it dancing, winding up an American and drinking free cocktails?'

'I wasn't sulking,' Danny insisted again. 'Hang on, "cocktails"? Plural? I thought you said you just had the one?'

*

The accident was a marvel. Later on, Danny would wonder at not only how quickly it had all gone down, but also the number of unlikely things that had to go wrong in a row for it to happen.

They were approaching the junction where the main road met the city's Grand Canal. The traffic light had changed from green to amber and Nudge sped up, out of pure instinct, increasing their speed from a sensible thirty to a more unwieldy forty-five. The light changed to red just as they reached the junction but Nudge turned left regardless. Unbeknownst to them, a car was heading up the canal road at speed and took advantage of the fact that the light had gone green at just the right moment.

It careened through the junction without slowing down. As the headlights flashed suddenly across the windscreen, Nudge frantically pulled on the steering wheel and gunned the engine to try and avoid the oncoming car. It hit the Suzuki diagonally, between the driver's door and the bonnet and this, combined with Nudge's earlier acceleration, sent them hurtling towards the canal.

There were any number of reasons why what occurred next shouldn't have been possible. The canal has a low wall that runs more or less along its entire length for this precise reason. Unfortunately, there had been a similar incident three days before and a van had crashed into it, completely destroying a section about seven feet wide. The emergency services had towed away the wrecked van but, not having fifty kilos of cement handy, had marked the hole with fluorescent cones until the council could sort it out.

The Suzuki's momentum carried them towards the break in the wall as if they'd been fired from a sniper rifle, its high suspension dealing with the kerb as if it wasn't even there. The sides of the car didn't even brush the cement as it sailed through.

The Grand Canal wasn't that deep for most of its stretch through Dublin, except they'd managed to intersect it just where it met a lock, the water pooling deep against the barrier, swollen by recent heavy rains, so that it was almost spilling onto the bank.

Neither Danny nor Nudge had time to even swear as the car plunged into the icy waters.

Chapter 5

Consciousness crept back to Danny slowly, like honey poured over the back of a spoon. His head throbbed. There was a blissful moment of delusion where he wondered if he'd just woken up in his bed hungover, like on any other Sunday morning, but this notion evaporated under the blowtorch of his self-preservation instinct.

It was freezing. He sucked air into his lungs and gasped at the pain in his chest. He felt like he'd spent an afternoon helping Sven with his tackling drills. Danny coughed and winced at the pain as he tried to get his eyes to focus.

He was momentarily relieved when the spreading dampness in his jeans turned out to just be canal water and not the result of the shock of the last few moments until he realised the implication.

The pressure on his chest was where their collision had thrown him hard against the seat belt. It had locked on impact and the car's current 45-degree angle was causing him to fall forward against it, keeping it tight. Even as his vision began to clear, he struggled to make sense of the scene through the windscreen. Amber light shimmered and bounced across a narrow strip at the top while the rest was almost completely black. Danny realised that he was looking on as water crawled up the glass, the halogen light from the nearest streetlamp contrasting against the inky blackness of the water underneath. They were sinking. His eyes had adjusted to see that water was streaming in and filling the front of the car, the level already as high as his knees.

If at any time, you feel uncomfortable, you can say so, he thought to himself. That's what Nudge had said. Out loud he said: 'Nudge, I'm starting to feel uncomfortable.'

The sarcastic response he was expecting didn't come.

'Nudge!' he repeated with more urgency.

With difficulty, he turned his head. The rapidly disappearing light did enough to reflect the blood dripping from his friend's temple as he hung limply from his own seat belt. The window on his side looked like static on an old-fashioned television from where it had shattered. Danny thought he saw enough movement to suggest breathing but he couldn't be sure.

There was a terrible moment as the car shook suddenly and Danny cried out as the momentum forced him against the seat belt even further. The water began to rise up the windshield as the front of the car submerged completely. It was around his waist now and rising, which was lucky in a way because he couldn't be sure that this time, he really hadn't had a little accident. He slapped ineffectually at the buckle of his seat belt to no avail. The button refused to depress all the way.

We're putting too much pressure on the seat belt, pitched the small, rational synapse that was all that was left of Danny's logical mind. *That's why it won't release.*

He struggled to push himself back in his seat to take some of the weight off the restraint, but the sharp tilt of the car wouldn't let him. *Well, it's either that or the collision broke the mechanism*, his mind added unhelpfully.

Danny grunted a curse, took another agonising breath, and then tried to lift his legs. The freezing water seemed to be trying to suck them back in, draining every last bit of strength they had. His chest screamed as the pressure returned tenfold, but he managed to raise his feet enough so that he could press them against the footwell and ease some of the strain against the seat belt.

The buckle was now fully submerged in the dark canal water, but Danny was still convinced that he'd heard an audible click as his seat belt was released. He was granted a split second of relief until gravity threw him forward against the dashboard. Danny put his hands out to steady himself and came into contact with something alien. He recoiled as a white shape rose in front of him, a brief moment of insanity making him question when they'd introduced jellyfish to the Grand Canal.

The rational synapse pointed out that it was just the deflated airbag. He flopped on his side and pushed himself into an awkward position, one leg in the tilted footwell, one knee against the glovebox, and surveyed his friend. Nudge hadn't moved since their dive and didn't respond to Danny's frantic tugs on his arm.

'You have to wake up, Nudge. Come on!' Danny begged as he continued to shake him.

The creeping, cold sensation of the water moving up to his navel made Danny struggle not to panic. All traces of alcohol felt like they had been burned out of his bloodstream by the adrenaline and fear. He pushed himself across to the driver's seat and tried to grab at the buckle of Nudge's seat belt.

Bracing his legs against the centre console, stabbing himself in the shin with what would turn out later to be a ninja-star-shaped air freshener, Danny pressed his shoulder into his friend's frame. This elicited a groan from the driver and Danny almost whooped with relief at the sign of life and redoubled his attempts. With tortuous effort, he managed to press Nudge back far enough into his seat that he was able to disengage the seat belt. Danny was gifted another nanosecond of consolation until Nudge's full weight, no longer restrained, threatened to push both of them down under the water. Danny pulled away and tried to reassess their surroundings. The water, which had previously been creeping up the length of their bodies, was now only half a foot below the headrests of the front seats.

Now that they were both loose, they would actually have to get out, Danny realised, rapidly assessing his disappearing options. He pushed himself back across to the passenger side of the car and flailed for the door handle.

How long had it been since they had hit the water? Ninety seconds? Two minutes? Ten years?

He wrapped his fingers around the handle and threw his shoulder against the door. Nothing. He tried again, a sustained push this time, with his legs braced against the tilted floor. Still nothing.

You're shoving against the weight of about a million cubic feet of water, you moron, the rational synapse chided.

The water was splashing around his throat now. His air pocket was shrinking with every heartbeat. His grasping fingers found the button for the window, and he pressed it down, more out of exasperation than any expectation that it would still work. He was equal parts surprised and delighted when the window began to move down. This was almost instantly washed away by regret as water flooded through the gap. Danny didn't even have time to grab a breath before it engulfed him completely. He thrashed about in the sudden darkness, letting go of the button in his panic. His head pounded as his ears popped at the sudden change in pressure. His arm bounced off the floating form of Nudge and Danny grabbed a handful of his jumper and felt blindly back towards the window with his other hand. To his dismay he could feel that the window had opened barely an inch. He reluctantly let go of Nudge and stabbed at the button again with one hand while using his other to gauge the size of the opening.

It seemed to take an age for the glass to recede and Danny's lungs burned with exertion and the time taken. The window had widened to slightly more than half open when whatever miracle that kept the electronics working this long gave up and it refused to move any further.

He made sure that Nudge was close by and then threw himself through the narrow gap. The pitch-blackness around him had gained a purple halo. If Danny had thought he'd been panicking before, he now moved to a new, higher plane of hysteria. The blade of the half-open window scraped against his chest as he slid himself free of the car. This, combined with the exertion, was the last straw: he could not hold his breath any longer and his mouth gasped involuntarily open.

He inhaled the terrible, jet-black liquid and his hands went to his throat, as if to remove some invisible attacker's fingers. He was still only two-thirds of the way through the window and by a lonely stroke of good fortune his convulsions tipped him the rest of the way out of the car until he splashed free beside it. He wouldn't be able to pull Nudge through, he knew as his vision started to tunnel, he would need to go up for air. *He could come back down once he had and pull him out*, he told himself. *There might even be someone there to help by the time he breached the surface. He could call for help.*

He tried to raise his head out of the water, to kick upwards, but he felt like all the energy had been forced out of his body when the water had entered his lungs. He was so tired. *He couldn't be that far from the surface*, he thought, perhaps he could just float up? Danny's vision, dark and purple as it was, began to tunnel away from him, as if his eyes were a television set from which his brain was being dragged farther and farther away. The darkness of the water was a sunlit day compared to what was streaming into his mind now.

His last, irrational thought before it engulfed him completely was: *I never texted Sven about my coat.*

And his world ended.

Chapter 6

If the last time consciousness had returned had felt like honey over a spoon, this time it was like a pickaxe to the forehead.

He was lying on his back. He could feel the grass. He could feel his sodden clothes sticking to limbs that felt like they were made of concrete. He could feel the cold November air trying to sap whatever leftover warmth the water hadn't managed to steal from him. Mostly, though, he could feel a pair of strange lips over his.

Danny sat bolt upright, or at least tried to. In fact, he managed to raise his head maybe three inches from the ground before fireworks sparked across his vision and the pain that had been waiting politely for him to wake up completely rampaged across every nerve. The lips pulled away and he heard a distant voice shout, 'He's breathing!' It sounded as surprised as Danny felt.

What Danny was actually doing was coughing; heaving hacks that threatened to catapult his lungs through his teeth. He tried to turn on to his side and felt hands helping him. He managed to point his face downwards as he retched twice and then vomited a stream of water and bile onto the grass.

His vision was returning in fits and starts, like a jigsaw being put together over the course of a long weekend.

He could make out the glittering, dark body of the canal to his right. There were a number of people at its edge, shouting and running up and down.

'Nudge,' he managed to wheeze, through lungs that felt like deflated footballs. 'Nudge, the driver. Is he okay? Did he . . .?' His question was interrupted by another coughing fit that resulted in a further eruption of water.

'Just stay still,' the voice said. 'Help is coming.'

This seemed entirely reasonable and Danny let his head fall back to the grass. He felt something being draped over him, a blanket, or more likely a coat, and fought the urge to pass out again.

In Danny's eyes, what occurred next did so in a series of still images: an ambulance arriving. New, strange hands patting him up and down with professional urgency. A plastic mask being pulled over his mouth and a tinfoil blanket being wrapped around him. He asked about Nudge several more times and was told each time to just lie still and keep breathing. The former he could do quite easily. He would be lying still for the next year if he had his way. The latter was proving a little bit more difficult, as his lungs felt as if they were lined with sandpaper.

He was jostled gently as practised hands moved him to a stretcher and felt another surge of concern as he was moved away from the canal. He still hadn't seen Nudge yet. *Were they still treating him?*

'Wait. My friend, the driver. Where is he?' Danny croaked through the clear mask covering his mouth. He tried to sit up again but felt a firm hand on his shoulder. The paramedic, a lean, heron-faced man with close-cropped, salt-and-pepper hair, patted him on the arm.

'Don't worry, son. We're bringing your friend in the other ambulance.'

Danny relaxed and let out a sigh that stuttered into another series of coughs. The rational synapse, which had somehow managed to make it through the whole ordeal intact, tried to raise some questions about the paramedic's story but the rest of his body overruled it and Danny let himself drift away.

It wasn't sleep. It was more like recovery mode, as his brain refused to process any further upsetting information.

*

When Danny drifted back to consciousness for the third time in as many hours it was due to the aggravating and unrelenting beep in his ear. He flailed around with his eyes closed to silence whatever alarm it was and the movement triggered a domino effect of pain across his entire body. His eyes snapped open as the events of the night rushed back to him.

He was in bed. This was a good start. He would take a bed over a coffin. It clearly wasn't his own though, as the sheets, while feeling cheap and worn, were undeniably clean. He couldn't remember when he'd last changed his duvet cover. His bed also wasn't usually surrounded by this many scary machines. He felt like someone had smashed his entire body apart with a hammer and then put it back together again with an even bigger hammer. It was too much of an effort to raise his head, but he could see from the glow of the monitors around him that he was on some sort of hospital ward.

Danny had no idea how much time had passed but it didn't seem to be morning just yet.

'Oh, thank God!' said a voice from his right. He recognised it immediately and for a giddy second, he teetered between the decision to cry with relief or get out of bed and throttle its owner. He was much too tired to get up, so he grudgingly allowed tears to stream down his face as he responded.

'Nudge. Thank fuck!' he said, his voice cracking with emotion and the strain of the last few hours.

'Danny. Can you hear me?' His friend stepped into the corner of Danny's vision, next to the bed. Danny's head still swam and he could only make out Nudge's vague shape. Nudge moved closer, near the head of his bed, still just out of his eyeline, and Danny felt a pang of anger through his relief. It was bloody typical that Nudge seemed practically unhurt while he felt like he'd been passed through a combine harvester.

'Danny, can you hear me?' Nudge repeated.

This time, Danny could make out the notes of panic and insistence in his voice. The anger faded. Nudge had been really worried about him by the sounds of things. He must have the healing powers of Wolverine to be up and about so quickly.

'Yeah, I can hear you,' his voice cracked again. 'Could I get some water?'

The blurry form of Nudge moved closer and Danny felt strangely cold.

'Danny, I'm so sorry. I didn't mean to . . . I should never have . . .' He heard his friend take a deep breath to steady himself. 'I'm glad you're okay.'

42

Danny reached a hand out to pat Nudge's arm reassuringly but misjudged where he was standing and missed. 'It's okay, mate. I'm just glad that you're back on your feet. I thought you were a goner.'

'Yeah. About that,' Nudge said in a strangely quiet voice.

Danny was about to ask him what he meant by that when they were interrupted by the squeaking of sensible orthopaedic runners approaching down the ward. The curtain to his right was twitched aside and a woman in blue scrubs looked him up and down with professional concern before walking up and placing a hand gently on his shoulder. 'It's good to see that you're awake,' she said. 'But you should really get some rest.'

He tried to give a reassuring smile back but found that he didn't have the energy. Instead, he muttered, 'That sounds like a good idea. Nudge, would you just let my parents know that I'm okay? Do you still have Steff's number?'

There was no answer from his left and the nurse's look increased a couple of notches in intensity. 'Who are you talking to, love?' she asked.

Nudge didn't respond. He'd slipped out of the corner of Danny's eye once the nurse had turned up. With a herculean effort, Danny managed to turn his head to look over at his friend but found his bedside empty except for all the scary machines. He sighed. The fucking idiot had probably sneaked down from his own bed on the ward and fled when he heard the nurse coming. Knowing him, he'd already been disciplined for talking too much while the other patients were sleeping.

'Just the other idiot they fished out of the river,' Danny said. You may want to go check on him by the way. He's gone walkabout.'

The nurse's eyes filled with unease and she pulled a tiny torch from her pocket and shone it in his face. She moved her finger over and back across his field of vision and asked him to follow it with his eyes. Doing so felt as taxing as a fifty-mile run but Danny just about managed it.

'Seriously, he shouldn't be out of bed this early, the stupid bastard.'

'Who are we talking about here?' the nurse asked.

'Nudge. I mean, Paul Nugent. He was the driver of the car,' Danny explained.

The nurse nodded. 'I'm very sorry,' she said with sincerity. 'Nobody else was brought here from the crash. Your friend. He didn't make it.'

Danny almost laughed out loud. He was about to explain the nurse's mistake and tell her that Nudge had been to see him, when he fully appreciated the look she was giving him. It did not look like that of someone who was unsure.

'No, he was right here! A minute ago.'

The nurse nodded and smiled sadly as she moved towards the machines by his bed.

Danny wanted to argue again, to tell her she was wrong, but as she fiddled with the touchscreen on one of the monitors there was an unsettling whir of machinery and Danny's brain filled with a pleasant fog.

Chapter 7

They'd made the papers.

Not the front page obviously. This was taken up by a story about a container full of cocaine that had been seized at Dublin Port and some Twitter gaffe the minister of housing had made the evening before. No, they had made page four. 'Dublin man (24) dies in car accident on Grand Canal'.

Nudge smiled out from one of the pictures underneath the headline, in stark contrast to the accompanying photo of his car being dredged from the canal. The article detailed the night's terrors in a disturbingly sterile way, although Danny was at least pleased to learn that the driver of the other vehicle had survived with few injuries. He was able to watch, over the three days he was kept in St James' Hospital for observation, as it went from a half-page story on page four, to a shorter article on page nine, to a single short update from Dublin City Council buried on page fourteen.

The papers had described his own condition as 'serious but stable', which had given him a laugh. He couldn't remember a time when he'd felt less stable. 'Serious but stable', in his case, translated to a mild concussion, whiplash and three cracked ribs. He had been put through a series of scans and tests to monitor his heart, lung capacity and brain function but he was in remarkably good shape for someone who'd gone through what he had.

They had been initially hesitant to tell him what exactly they'd meant by that, and it had been down to the paper again to give him the full details. He had read the interview with Steven Prescott (27), an Australian backpacker who had been walking home from his own night out when he witnessed the collision. The Aussie had been on the wrong side of the canal initially, but, once he had sprinted across the nearby bridge, he'd been able to fish the passenger out of the canal and perform CPR on him. Steven Prescott had continued to perform CPR for eight minutes. He'd had to. Danny's own heart and lungs had stopped at the time.

Eight minutes. It didn't seem terribly long, but the doctors had been pretty adamant that, as a general rule, you didn't want your heart and lungs to stop for any length of time and that it was a borderline miracle that he hadn't suffered any symptoms of brain damage. Danny had neglected to mention the hallucination of Nudge at his bedside on the night of the crash. They'd just seemed so happy that it would be a shame to ruin it.

He'd had enough visitors to keep him occupied. An earnest young guard had taken his statement of the events on the canal, managing to keep his ruddy face remarkably impassive as Danny described how he'd completely failed to stop Nudge from driving drunk. He offered his condolences as he'd left and muttered something about there being an investigation into how the gap in the wall had been left unprotected.

His mum and dad had to be politely but firmly asked to adhere to the ward's visiting hours as they set up camp beside his bed. Steff had come in with Buster the first day, but Danny had asked her not to bring him next time, partly out of concern he might catch some horrible disease and partly out of worry that he might try and chew through some important medical equipment. Sven even dropped by, risking the wrath of the nurses and their family-only policy; although the two of them mostly just sat, stone-faced, in shared misery until Sven made his excuses and left.

Each one had told him that it wasn't his fault and he had thanked them, despite not believing a word.

After he was discharged, he'd made a vain attempt to convince his mum and dad to take him back to the flat but had been overruled. Buster's cot was moved back into Steff's room and Danny's old mattress was pulled down from the attic to his nephew's bedroom. This was why, on the day of Nudge's funeral, Danny found himself examining his reflection in a mirror covered in space-themed stickers. A pale, tired young man in a charcoal-grey suit stared back at him, at odds with the cartoon dog in a spacesuit declaring him, OUT OF THIS WORLD!

He looked . . . well, he looked like someone who had been fished out of a canal recently. Each strand of his sandy brown hair refused to agree on a communal direction, his skin was the shade of curdled milk, and his eyes didn't so much have bags under them as a full Louis Vuitton luggage set. His appearance was in stark contrast to the rest of Buster's room, which was decked out in bright blue and yellow with more space stuff covering each wall. He looked like a suspect in a gritty ITV drama who had mistakenly wandered onto a CBeebies set.

His hands went through a pattern buried deep in muscle memory that resulted in a passable schoolboy knot in the black tie he had dug out for the occasion, but as he went to fasten it around his collar, he hesitated. For a split second he was back in the car, the seat belt biting into his throat, the oppressive wall of water surging towards him. The last of his breath leaving him in the darkness of the canal. Danny breathed heavily as he felt the familiar, rising waves of a panic attack crash over him.

A knock at the door caused him to turn. His mum stuck her head around the bedroom door. 'Are you okay?' she asked.

Another flashing mental picture, of his mum identifying his dead body in the morgue following the accident, came and went as he answered. 'I'm fine,' he said, with a lightness that was at odds with the crushing weight that seemed to be trying to press him into the floor. He undid his tie and threw it in the corner. His mum raised an eyebrow at this but didn't comment. 'I'll be down in a minute,' he assured her.

After he was sure she had padded downstairs, he sank, boneless, against the mirror and hyperventilated as the panic attack took him.

*

Hiding the after-effects of a panic attack was a skill that Danny was happy to learn he hadn't lost. He'd joined the rest of the family downstairs less than ten minutes after his mum and dad, managed to pass off his unsteadiness as general nerves and they all went out to the car. Oblivious to the solemnity of the situation, Buster sat in his car seat and made several determined attempts to grab at Danny's suit lapels as they drove to the church. Danny batted his hands away intermittently and stared out the window in silence.

They reached the church after too short a drive. Hundreds of people milled about in front of the doors. Danny wished that he could find some place to lie low before the family arrived; he couldn't bring himself to think the word 'coffin' yet.

He tried to tell himself that he was imagining it, but he could sense people shifting away from him as he walked through the press of mourners. He imagined that, from above, the scene must have looked like a drop of ink falling into a bowl of water: a sea of black spreading away from the centre.

Sven had managed to fit his torso into a white shirt and suit jacket that made him look like an Eastern European hitman and, as they hugged, Danny idly thought that it was a good thing that Sven's walking boot was already black or else it could have clashed with the mood.

He felt a hand on his shoulder and was surprised to see someone who looked even worse than him. Sven's dad looked closer to seventy-five than fifty-five. He'd once been of a height with his son, but the years had given him a stoop that put him closer to Danny's. His hair, which had been lost completely during chemotherapy, had grown back in wispy, almost colourless tufts. If Danny's eyes had the full Louis Vuitton luggage set under them, then Ian Kelly had the entire contents of a medium-sized baggage carousel at Terminal 2 under his.

The older man gripped Danny's arm with a hand that felt like twigs wrapped in an old pair of tights. 'You've no idea how sorry we are about Paul, Dan.' His voice was thick with emotion and the ordeals of the last few years. 'We're just so glad that you're okay.'

Danny allowed himself to be drawn into a delicate hug as his mum asked the question that he'd been too shocked to ask himself.

'Ian. Should you be out and about like this?'

'No, he shouldn't!' answered his wife, Denise, who wasn't so much on his arm as supporting most of his body weight. The last few years had robbed Sven's mum of a lot as well. She was still blessed with whatever genes had resulted in Sven, but the solemnity of the surroundings looked comfortable on her face.

'I couldn't not be here,' Ian started, gripping his son on the forearm, as if afraid to let him go. 'Paul spent too many afternoons in our house for us not to pay our . . .' He faltered for a moment and then sighed and continued. 'I can't imagine what Linda and Craig must be going through.'

Sven's mum looked as if she could offer some ideas but didn't say anything.

For the second time in as many minutes, Danny felt a hand grab him by the arm. For a split second he thought that it was some friend or family member finally building up the courage to take out their anger on him but instead he was faced with Nadine throwing her arms around him, causing him to make a noise like a boiling tea kettle.

'Nads, broken ribs! Broken ribs!' he gasped.

The blonde girl reluctantly pulled away, her eyes red-rimmed. 'Jesus, Dan! When I heard. I thought we'd lost both of you.'

A small, dirty part of him acknowledged that she managed to look incredible even when devastated. Tears brought out the blue of her eyes. Behind her, Clark had managed to cobble together a funeral outfit from the contents of his rucksack. A black cardigan over a dark grey shirt and black trousers combined with a tie he'd presumably robbed from Nadine's dad. He looked like he was modelling for River Island.

Danny wanted to say something back but, 'I'm sorry I ruined your party' didn't seem to cut it. Before he could think of something else, however, a distinct change in the demeanour of the crowd revealed that the funeral procession had arrived. The mass of people compacted to make room for the dark Mercedes that pulled up in front of the church, from which the family emerged.

Nudge had gotten his lanky frame from his dad, although the elder Nugent had acquired a noticeable potbelly of late, giving him the look of an anaconda that was digesting a basketball. His face was set with the look of someone who had decided he was going to stay strong for as long it took to get through the public part of today before crumbling later in private.

Nudge's mum, in contrast, was a shorter woman, her red hair colour being the only thing she'd shared with her son. She wore a lost, confused expression along with her black dress and Danny wondered whether she'd been sedated. She looked around the crowd as if surprised to see them there. As she glanced across to where he was standing, Danny fought the desire to hide but her eyes slid past him without really seeing him. A woman who he recognised as an aunt gently took her by the elbow and led her over to where the coffin was being unloaded and Danny forced himself to look at it as it was hoisted onto the shoulders of the pallbearers.

It didn't look big enough.

Sure, it was long enough, wide enough and deep enough for Nudge to fit in but it still looked too small to contain everything he'd been.

Too small to contain a life.

The pall-bearers moved forward in lockstep towards the church. The noise of suppressed sobbing came from Danny's left and he placed his hand on Sven's arm as his shoulders shook softly. Behind them he could hear Nadine sniffling as well. No tears came for Danny though. Intellectually, he knew they were coming, but right now he was in a place beyond them, although no less miserable for the lack.

Danny wasn't much of a judge when it came to funerals but Nudge's seemed pretty standard. He found himself unable to take any of it in though, as if it were a Monday-morning lecture after a particularly heavy weekend. He was too busy convincing himself that everyone at the Mass was turning to give him surreptitious looks and whispering.

His rational synapse, apparently the only part of his brain that had absorbed his year or so of therapy, chided him that, in this particular circumstance, nobody was paying attention to him and to get over himself. It went largely unregarded. The grief at losing his friend was only matched by his shame at being the one to leave him at the bottom of the canal. He faced nightly intrusions where he pictured Nudge in the driver's seat under the water. He would be known as the guy who let Nudge drive drunk and left him to die. He was sure of it.

Even the eulogy, which was delivered by Nudge's dad in the tones of someone who was just barely holding himself together, washed over him without much effect. In fact, so immersed was he in his own misery, Danny almost didn't notice when he found himself being pressed towards the top of the church. With a start, he realised that the queue he was in was to file past the coffin and the family itself. He wanted to flee, to slip out of the procession of people and slink back to his seat, but he felt that this would draw even more notice. Plus, he needed to do this; as a penance if nothing else.

The long queue of mourners took simultaneously several ice ages and not enough time at all before Danny and Sven were standing over the coffin. He took in the details one at a time, not trusting himself to do it all at once. They'd dressed Nudge in a bright blue suit that Danny recognised from his twenty-first. A red and yellow tie stood out on a white shirt. He was glad that they'd decided to dress him in what he would actually wear. He would have been unrecognisable in monochrome colours.

Not that he was very recognisable as it was. The funeral home had done a decent job, Danny supposed, his hair had been styled into some semblance of order and whatever make-up they'd applied gave his skin-tone a healthier glow than the one Danny was currently sporting. Still, lying there, he looked nothing like the man Danny knew, as if, without his usual manic, irritating energy to power it, his face had become a blank.

Looking down at him, the ghost of a memory floated back to Danny. The morning after the accident, at the hospital, the dream he'd had before he'd woken up properly. That his friend had been okay. That Nudge had spoken to him, before he'd gone back to sleep and woken up in his awful new reality.

Both Danny and Sven awkwardly blessed themselves and shuffled sideways to the part that Danny was truly dreading. Ahead of them, the line of people was filing past the front pew of the church and offering their condolences to the family. Some went past quickly, a pat on the shoulder, a hug or handshake for each and then onwards. Others took the time to have quiet, sobbing conversations.

Danny shook hands with nameless aunts, uncles and cousins as he moved inexorably towards Nudge's parents in the middle of the row. He wanted to run away, he wanted the ground to open up and swallow him. Mostly, he wanted to throw himself at their feet and beg for forgiveness through heaving sobs. Too quickly, he found himself in front of them, face to face with Nudge's dad.

'I'm so sorry,' he said. He wished he could cry. He wished he weren't some emotionless robot. 'I should have stopped him.'

The mask of determined grief on Nudge's father's face slipped for a second to one of despair and Danny cursed himself. This wasn't about him. He could seek absolution another time. He tried to move past, but Nudge's mother, through whatever pharmaceutical haze she was currently viewing the world, recognised him. She reached out and grabbed him by the arm and Danny was convinced that this was it. She was going to finally declare to God and the congregation that it was all his fault.

He almost welcomed it.

Instead, she buried her head in his shoulder and wept, pulling him closer. 'What are we going to do? I don't know what to do!' he heard her whisper. Danny wasn't even sure she was directing this at him or to the universe in general. The iceberg of self-absorption and self-loathing was vaporised by the anguish in her voice and Danny felt the sorrow hit him like a harpoon. He wasn't sure who led him away, but he was weeping all the while.

*

His eyes were still red-rimmed as he sat at a corner table of the pub after the funeral Mass. A half-eaten ham sandwich sat in front of him next to a fully drunk pint of Guinness. His parents had been hesitant about him attending the afters and had made a number of increasingly strenuous 'suggestions' about him returning home to rest instead. He'd been adamant though and had been dropped off in front of the pub with his friends. There were a number of reasons that he'd wanted to come. Partly as a mark of respect for his fallen friend. Partly because, if anybody did want to angrily confront him and blame him for the whole ordeal with some Dutch courage in them, he wanted to give them the opportunity.

Mostly though, he'd come because he really, really did not want to be sober anymore.

He surveyed the rest of the glasses on the table. Technically he wasn't drinking faster than anyone else but, considering that the table contained Sven, this wasn't necessarily a good sign. Usually, he could put away maybe two-thirds of what his larger friend drank, but now, he was way ahead of him. Nadine looked concerned: she'd only managed a few mouthfuls of her vodka and Coke in the time it had taken him to finish his last pint.

'My round, I think,' Danny said, ignoring her worried expression. He suppressed a groan as his broken ribs protested at him standing up.

It was actually Sven's round, but he seemed to be deep in conversation with Clark about how certain Central American tribes viewed death as just a beginning. Sven held one of his crutches in front of him as if he were considering bludgeoning Clark, or himself, into unconsciousness with it.

'I'll give you a hand,' Nadine said, grabbing her phone from the table and going to stand up, but Danny waved her away. 'I've got to visit the little boys' room first,' he said, realising that this actually wasn't a lie. A week ago, he would have leapt at the chance of any one-on-one time with Nadine but now she was just one more hovering, concerned person whose sympathy he couldn't stomach.

She nodded reluctantly and he weaved through the crowd in the packed lounge bar, trying his best not to noticeably stagger. He knew that he was being childish and short-sighted and that five pints of Guinness wasn't going to have a positive impact on his mental state. Still, the forces of self-loathing and self-absorption had rallied impressively after the incident at the funeral and had brought their friend, self-destructiveness, along.

Danny made it into the gents and entered his usual state of semi-zen in front of the urinal. He was trying to avoid making eye contact with himself in the long mirror that ran along the wall above the urinal when he saw him: a lanky, red-haired man in a lurid, purple and green jumper standing by the sink.

Danny spun around and immediately wished that he'd taken the time to finish as his stream went rogue and splashed the floor and wall to his left. There was no one by the sink.

The door opened suddenly, and an older man walked in. Danny realised that he was now standing with his back to the urinal and hurriedly made himself decent. The other man had the tact not to draw any attention to his predicamant and Danny washed his hands and exited before anyone could attribute the mess on the wall to him.

He made a beeline for the bar as soon as he got back outside and ordered the round for the table, adding a glass of whiskey to the request. Danny watched, half-hypnotised, as the glasses were filled with black liquid and left to settle. He started a bit in fright as the whiskey was placed in front of him and handed over his bank card in response. He wasn't usually a big whiskey drinker. The lads would occasionally have a glass towards the end of the night if they'd been on a session in the pub, more out of machismo than any fondness for the stuff, but Danny was still shaken from the phantom redhead in the bathroom and needed a nerve-settler.

It's just guilt, he told himself. It didn't help that a few of Nudge's cousins bore a striking resemblance to him. There had been a number of times throughout the night when Danny had been startled for a moment by a flash of ginger hair on a tall frame. Still, seeing things that weren't actually there was an unsettling step up. He gripped the tumbler and downed the whiskey in one gulp, instantly regretting the decision as the fiery liquid scorched his throat. His eyes watered as the topped-up pints were placed in front of him, along with Nadine's vodka. He gave the barman a nod of thanks as he turned away to head back to the table.

And almost walked right into someone who had been standing directly behind him. Danny pulled back sharply, drunkenly marvelling at how the surface tension of Guinness allowed it to be tilted to almost twenty degrees without spilling and looked up to apologise to the person in question. 'Sorry, pal,' he said, his eyes clearing enough to get a look at the guy.

'Don't worry about it,' Nudge replied.

Chapter 8

Danny recoiled so quickly that the small of his back slammed into the bar before the glasses even hit the floor. The crash made the whole bar turn and stare at him. Stare at *him*, a distant part of Danny's brain couldn't help but notice, and not at the recently resurrected friend/family member standing in front of him.

Someone from the corner of the bar shouted, 'Wahey!' and was quickly shushed.

Nudge stood in front of Danny and took a step forward as he saw his reaction. 'Dan,' he said. 'Danny, you can see me, can't you? I fucking knew it!' Danny only managed a noise somewhere between a squeak and a low scream in response. Most of the conversation in the pub had restarted but a lot of people were still staring at him.

Nadine made her way over from their table, stepping carefully around the broken glass and rapidly expanding pool of Guinness. She walked obliviously past Nudge and placed a hand on his shoulder. 'Danny, are you all right?'

Nudge stepped through the spillage as if it wasn't even there and thrust his face inches from Danny's. 'Hello!' he shouted, waving his hands in front of Danny's face. 'Answer me, you bollocks.'

Danny looked across to Nadine, who was still staring at him, radiating extreme concern, apparently oblivious to the fact that the friend whose funeral they'd just attended was standing less than a foot away from her.

'How the hell are you here?' Danny asked, managing to find his voice at last.

Confusion crossed Nadine's face as she glanced, unseeing, in the direction of Danny's question.

Nudge was doing some sort of celebration dance as he answered. 'I've no fucking clue but you have no idea how happy I am to be able to talk to someone.'

'Danny, we came here together,' Nadine answered simultaneously. 'I think maybe you should get a drink of water and then we'll get a taxi home, yeah?'

Danny turned back to Nadine and grabbed her by the shoulder and pointed at Nudge. 'Nadine, please tell me that you're able to . . .' he trailed off at her look of incomprehension.

'She can't see me, man,' Nudge said, redundantly. 'Nobody can, except you.' By way of demonstration, he waved his arms an inch from her face as she resolutely ignored him.

'Dan, come on. Let's sit down,' she said, pulling him towards their table.

'Danny, don't you fucking dare!' Nudge said at the same time. 'We need to figure this out.'

Danny tugged himself out of Nadine's grasp, glanced frantically between her and Nudge for a moment, and then fled to the gents again.

Danny ensured that the door closed firmly after him and rushed over to the sink as he tried not to hyper-ventilate. He smacked his palm against the cold tap and splashed his face in the short burst of water. What the hell was in that whiskey? He triggered the tap again, cupped his hands underneath the flow and slurped the water in greedy gulps.

'Alone at last,' an all-too-familiar voice said from behind him.

He hadn't heard the door open.

He looked up into the mirror and let out a whimper as Nudge stood behind him. He slowly turned around to confront the apparition.

'What the fuck is going on?' Danny whispered hoarsely, more to the universe in general than to Nudge.

Through the familiar opening salvos of a panic attack, Danny forced himself to examine Nudge critically. He appeared as he had the night of the party, like someone who'd gotten dressed in a Build-A-Bear Workshop, but Danny noticed now that there was something off. He wasn't exactly transparent as *fuzzy* around the edges. Staring at him in the harsh light of the toilet's fluorescents, he couldn't quite tell where the door behind him ended and Nudge's shoulder began. His voice sounded the same as it always had, but Danny had to concentrate to hear him properly, as if he were being drowned out by ambient noise, even though all he could hear was just the dull chatter from the pub outside.

'Danny, please!' Nudge said, taking a step towards him and causing Danny to jerk back once again, painfully, against the chipped ceramic of the sinks. 'I have no fucking clue what's going on, but I've been like this since the canal.'

'Been like what? Dead?' asked Danny, as he fought the urge to climb up on to the sink.

The excitement that had been in Nudge's face since their encounter at the bar drained away, to be replaced with stoney-faced sadness. 'Yeah, I guess?' he said. 'The last thing I remember is that fucking car hitting us and then . . .' he trailed off with a dark look on his face and then shook his head, as if to clear the thoughts away. 'The next thing I know, I'm on the bank of the canal and everyone is ignoring me. At first, I figured it was because they were busy saving your life, which, you know, fair enough. Eventually, I figured it out. I have to admit that watching my corpse being dragged out of the canal was a pretty big clue,' he finished, a little embarrassed.

Danny had heard enough. He put his palms to his face and squeezed them against his eyelids. 'I've gone mad,' he said. 'None of this is happening. It's the booze, or the brain damage or—'

'—You're not mental!' Nudge hissed angrily. Danny opened his mouth to retort out of pure habit, but Nudge talked over him before he could start. 'Or at least no more mental than you were before,' he amended. 'You're a nervous wreck and a borderline social cripple but you don't see shit that's not there.'

Danny had to admit that, for a hallucination thrown up from his rapidly deteriorating brain, it was doing a good job with the impression of Nudge. Everything, from how his face moved when he spoke, to the way he held his hands when he was insulting Danny, was precise.

'Right, then,' Danny started, figuring that, if he was going to argue with his own psychosis, then he might as well do a better job. 'Why haunt *me*? Why not try contacting your parents or Sven or *literally anyone else*?'

Nudge passed his hands through his ginger hair in frustration. 'Don't you think I've tried? I jumped in the ambulance that night and followed you to the hospital because I wanted to make sure that you were okay. It's bad enough I caused my own death: I didn't want to be responsible for yours as well.' He said this with a look of profound sadness, which made Danny want to reach out and pull him into a hug. Although not enough to actually risk it.

'But then,' he continued. 'That night in the hospital. You could see me. I was sure of it. You spoke to me.'

Danny recalled his dream. The figure by his bed-side, strangely out of focus and unable to be touched. 'I thought it was the drugs, or brain damage, or just wishful thinking,' Danny admitted reluctantly.

'Exactly,' Nudge said, excitement flooding back into his voice. 'But then the next day, you were as oblivious as everyone else. I tried to go see my family then. I figured it would only take me an hour or so to walk back to my house from the hospital but . . .'

'But what?'

'I couldn't,' he said as if both words had to be prised out of him with some difficulty. 'It's hard to explain. There's a . . . pull,' he finished lamely.

'A "pull"?' Danny repeated mockingly. 'Oh, well, that explains it then. Say no more.' He figured that if he couldn't be harsh to his own manifested psychosis, then who could?

'Ever since I . . . ever since the canal,' Nudge started, stumbling over the euphemism, 'it's like I'm being tugged at, pulled at, by some invisible force. It's hard to explain but it's there constantly, as if I've a rope around my waist and Sven is on the other end of it, heaving away. It feels like, if I lose concentration for even a second, I'll be carried away by it. Except . . .' he faltered again. 'Except when I'm near you. It's like you're an anchor or something.'

'Wow,' Danny said, a little embarrassed. 'I mean, I know we've always been close—'

'—I'm not making some philosophical point about the strength of our friendship, you tit,' Nudge interrupted indignantly. 'I mean it literally. There's some sort of physical connection that's preventing me from being carried off. If I try to move too far away from you, then that connection weakens, and I feel the pull growing stronger. Believe me, if I could pick someone else for my immortal soul to be linked to, I would.'

Danny marvelled at how awkward silences could overcome the bounds of death. Then a dark thought occurred to him. 'Have you considered that this pull might be whatever comes next trying to get you to move on?'

'Do you think that hasn't crossed my mind?' Nudge said, exasperated. 'I've spent the past few days doing nothing except wondering that same thing but, I can't explain it, this doesn't feel like that. It feels *wrong*!' He sighed and turned to stand beside Danny, almost but not quite leaning against the sink. 'I thought, *I'd hoped*, that the funeral would be the thing. To put my spirit to rest. But it was just another big room of people who couldn't see or hear me. Nice service though,' he added after a pause. 'Not as many beautiful women tearing at their clothes and throwing themselves on my coffin as I would have liked but, still, good turnout, I thought. All things considered.'

Danny finally built up the courage to reach out and gingerly try and pat his friend on the shoulder. His hand passed through it; he had expected some kind of shock, as if he'd stuck his fingers in a plug socket or a bucket of iced water, but instead there was just a strange sense of coolness on his skin. Nudge appeared not to notice.

Danny decided that he'd had enough. If he was going to have a mental breakdown, he was probably better off having it in the comfort of his own home. He stood up in preparation to stagger towards the door, towards home and more than likely some sort of mental ward, but Nudge stood bolt upright and put himself in Danny's path. 'Woah! Where are you going?'

Danny tried to walk around him, but his late friend sidestepped, and he couldn't bring himself to walk through him.

'It's been nice catching up, Nudge. But I reckon I'm going to go home, get some rest and then probably institutionalise myself.'

Nudge looked as if he was about to claw his hair out. 'I'm not a hallucination, you utter bollocks,' he said through gritted teeth.

'That's exactly what a hallucination would say,' Danny countered, once again trying to dance around him.

'Wait! Wait! If I were a hallucination, then I couldn't possibly tell you anything you didn't already know, right?' Nudge said desperately.

'Right,' Danny conceded after he'd thought about it for a second.

'Exactly. So, I just need to tell you something that you couldn't possibly know.'

'I guess?' said Danny. He'd stopped trying to dance around Nudge.

'Great so . . . Hang on.' Nudge suddenly looked panicked.

Danny grimaced and made to barge past the apparition on his way to the door, wondering whether a course of lithium would be expensive. 'Great. Enjoy the afterlife. Say hello to Tupac if you see him.'

'Hey, it's like when someone asks you to name your favourite film and suddenly your mind goes blank,' Nudge shouted defensively at Danny's retreating back.

His hand was on the door handle when Nudge suddenly exploded. 'Electric Picnic!' he shouted triumphantly.

Danny turned around, out of surprise more than anything. 'What?'

'Electric Picnic, last year. Someone took a shit in your tent, and you never found out who it was.'

Danny briefly forgot about hallucinations and ghosts in a moment of pure outrage. 'That was *you*?'

'Of course not.'

Danny calmed down slightly.

'It was Sven.'

'What?'

'In his defence he was very drunk and very stoned, and we thought it would be funny,' said Nudge, who had the decency to look embarrassed. 'We assumed you'd see it before you got into the tent.'

'Well I didn't, you bastard!' Danny said, his skin crawling at the memory.

'Mistakes were made,' said Nudge quickly, delighted that Danny was so enraged that he'd stopped moving towards the door. 'But I like your energy. Let's channel it into something productive. I think I've figured out what my unfinished business is.'

Danny tried, with some difficulty, to drag his mind away from the extreme betrayal he had just learned about. 'Your what?'

Nudge was back to his usual animated self. So much so that Danny almost forgot they were at his funeral.

'Come on. You've seen a ghost movie before. Unfinished business. The thing that's stopping my soul from moving onto the next plane of existence.'

'And you think you know what it is that's keeping you stuck here?' Danny asked sceptically. Dead or alive, Nudge had never struck him as someone who did a lot of self-reflection.

'Yes,' said Nudge. 'Just listen. I've had a lot of time to think about this, but it didn't occur to me until the funeral today.' He looked suddenly more morose than ever. 'When I saw my mum,' he said, his voice cracking. 'I never got to say goodbye. They went to bed and I went and did something so stupid, and it must have been . . . God, to wake up and get that news.'

He looked so lost and bereft now that Danny almost went to give him a hug before he remembered himself. He settled for platitudes instead. 'It wasn't your fault.'

Nudge's head snapped up. 'How the fuck wasn't it my fault? I'm the one who drove drunk. I'm the one who convinced you to get into the car. I'm the one who nearly got you killed as well. No, it's my fault but I know my parents won't see it that way. They'll be blaming themselves.'

'But there's nothing they could have done!'

'I know that but that's how they'll feel, and they'll carry that around for the rest of their lives, he said in a low, sad voice. 'Unless . . .'

'Unless what?' Danny asked.

'Unless you tell them that I'm at peace and that there's nothing they could have done,' Nudge said urgently, moving his face close to Danny's. 'You can put their minds at ease.'

Danny recoiled. 'Are *you* fucking mental?' he asked. 'I'm not going up to your grieving parents and saying, "Hey, how's it going? Having a good night? Your dead son popped by to say not to feel bad and that he's with the angels now. I know! Weird, right? Anyway, safe home."'

Nudge made a face. 'Well, sure, when you say it like *that*.' When Danny didn't crack a smile, he redoubled his pleading. 'Man, I wouldn't ask if I wasn't desperate. I can't just hang out here for the rest of my . . . for ever.'

Nudge's pleading was interrupted by the door slamming open, causing both of them to flinch in shock. Sven's massive frame filled the doorway, his face radiating concern and Guinness fumes. 'There you are,' he said to Danny with some relief. 'Nadine has been looking all over for you. Are you okay?'

Danny noted with disappointment, but no real surprise, that he, too, was oblivious to Nudge's presence. He glanced at Nudge, who gave him a shrug. 'I hope you're not expecting me to answer for you.'

Danny ignored him and focused on his living friend. 'I'm fine, yeah. Just got a bit overwhelmed out there and needed a minute. That's all.'

Sven nodded and let out a deep breath. 'Look, let's just head home? I want to make sure my dad is okay after being out this morning anyway.'

Danny nodded and the bigger man grinned and clapped him on the shoulder. 'Let me just strain the spuds then we'll go grab a taxi.'

'Ask him!' Danny started as Nudge whispered in his ear. He hadn't heard him move closer, although he guessed he wouldn't these days. He also had no idea why Nudge was whispering but he guessed that some habits were hard to break.

'Sven?' Danny mumbled as his friend turned to the urinal.

'Hmm?' Sven grunted back over his shoulder.

'This might be a weird question, but do you remember Electric Picnic last year?'

It might just have been his imagination, but he thought that he saw his friend involuntarily flinch in mid-stream at the mention of the festival. Sven finished and after making himself presentable and turned around a little warily. 'Yeah. What about it?' he asked cautiously.

'Well, I was just wondering. I had heard . . .' Danny wasn't sure exactly how to phrase this particular accusation. He caught Nudge's eye; the ginger ghost had returned to hover by the sink. Although not literally, Danny noticed with some relief.

'Oh, just ask him!' Nudge said.

Danny took another deep breath. 'Was it you who took a shit in my tent?'

Shock and confusion warred with one another in Sven's expression and for a moment, Danny was convinced that he had indeed gone completely mental.

However, a split-second later, guilt won out over both and settled on his face. 'Who told you?' he asked, sheepishly. 'I'm sorry, man. It was a stupid fucking thing to do but I was out of my mind.'

Danny would have liked to be angrier about this but a) it seemed a little trivial in light of recent events and b) it's hard to be mad when the ghost of your dead best friend, who only you can see, is doing a dance of victory.

'Ha! I fucking told you,' Nudge crowed.

Sven went to put a hand on Danny's shoulder in a conciliatory manner but then stopped, remembered himself, and shuffled over to the sink to wash his hands first. 'I know it's no excuse but I was bananas-drunk at the time.' He cracked a small smile in the mirror. 'Not to speak ill of the dead or anything, but it was Nudge's idea.'

Nudge's look of triumph quickly turned to one of embarrassment, as Danny shot him a poisonous look.

Sven finished at the sink and turned to face him. 'I really am sorry. I was so fucking embarrassed the next morning and I wanted to come clean. So to speak. But you were so angry, and Nudge convinced me that it was best to say nothing.'

Over his shoulder, Nudge looked like someone who was really regretting which hidden truth he'd chosen to reveal.

Danny let out a breath of stale air, a reminder that perhaps he'd been in this bathroom too long. 'It's okay, man. Any other day I might have taken a hammer to your other leg but, now?

Sven looked relieved. 'Thanks, man. Life's too short, yeah?'

'You're fucking telling me,' Nudge muttered to himself, in an aggrieved tone.

Sven moved towards the door and pulled it open. 'C'mon. Let's head out.'

Danny nodded and followed him out to the noise and heat of the pub outside.

Nudge followed quickly on his heels. 'You can't leave now. It's not as if you're going to get a better chance to talk to them and put their minds at ease.'

Nudge sounded even fainter in the bustle of the pub proper and the presence of other people reinforced for Danny how ridiculous he felt about humouring the whole stupid concept.

As they approached their table, they ran into Nadine returning from the smoking area. 'There you are,' she said with a look that made it seem like she was in two minds whether to hug or strangle him.

Sven seemed to sense this as well and strategically moved himself between the two. 'We were just going to grab a taxi home.'

She relaxed visibly at this. 'Clark is already outside . . .' She paused as the words, '. . . looking for you,' passed unsaid between them. 'Looking for a taxi,' she finished, unconvincingly.

The three of them made their way back to their table in the corner of the busy pub, Nudge dogging Danny's steps the whole way, pleading with him. Although perhaps 'pleading' was the wrong word. 'Abusing' might be closer to the mark. 'Danny. Stop acting like you can't hear me, you prick. I know you can,' he urged over the murmur of the rest of the patrons.

'We're going to head, lads!' Sven announced to the other occupants of their table. Danny noticed that everyone's eyes darted to him as Sven said this.

Nadine was glancing across the pub to where Nudge's immediate family were huddled in a tight group in the snug. His mum had been taken home shortly after the food had been served but Nudge's dad was still sitting at one of the tables in a knot of older men. 'We should probably say goodnight, right?' she asked.

Sven had shrugged on his jacket and was attempting to pull his crutches from out under the table without knocking anything over. 'I suppose so,' he said, without much enthusiasm.

'I swear to God, Danny, if you don't do this, you're going to spend the rest of your life with the knowledge that, every time you go to have a wank, I'll be there, watching,' Nudge warned, not sounding happy with the plan but looking terrifyingly resolved.

Now that he was surrounded by the living and breathing, the idea that this wasn't a hallucination and that Nudge was really there in front of him felt so stupid. Danny resolved to ignore it until he could get himself set up with some nice antipsychotics. This thought cheered him up somewhat as he allowed himself to be shepherded behind Nadine up to the family table.

At his side, Sven looked like something had just occurred to him. 'Hey! Who told you about EP anyway?' he asked. 'Nudge swore me to secrecy.'

'Surely you told someone else?' Danny asked. Had he known already? Deep down? It wasn't the sort of thing you forgot but maybe he'd just always suspected.

'It's not exactly something we wanted to brag about, believe me,' Sven replied.

Nadine had reached the table and managed to catch Nudge's father's eye. Sven seemed happy to allow her to act as their envoy in this particular circumstance. Craig Nugent stared at them glassily for a moment before recognition dawned.

'So sorry Craig. We are going to head off now. Again, we're really sorry for your loss and if there's ever anything . . .' she trailed off lamely and Danny couldn't blame her. It was the thing you said at funerals but it still felt trite.

'Thanks . . .' Nudge's dad had obviously forgotten Nadine's name but manfully stumbled on. 'Thanks very much. Safe home!' He reached across to grab Sven tightly by the hand and then, after a split second of hesitation, he reached out and touched Danny on the shoulder. 'Thanks for coming, lads. Paul would have . . . Thanks.'

Danny would later not be able to explain what changed his mind. The confirmation that Sven and Nudge had been the only two to know about the Electric Picnic incident. The presence of Nudge in his peripheral vision, promising to spend the rest of his afterlife watching Danny's sister get undressed. Probably, it had been the look on Craig's face: the sadness, regret and guilt that were carved into his features. Danny recognised it from every mirror he'd looked into lately. If there was a half a chance that he could take some of that away, then he had to try.

Danny stepped out from where he'd been half-hiding behind Sven. The older man turned to face him, and Danny was struck by how similar he looked to Nudge.

'Look, Craig. I just wanted to say that, I mean, I'm sure Nudg— Paul would have wanted you to know ...' Danny faltered as he realised that the rest of Craig's table, Nudge's close relatives and family friends, had stopped their conversation and were now focusing on them. Sven looked as if he were considering whether just rugby-tackling Danny would cause less of a scene than allowing him to keep talking.

Danny struggled on in the face of this unexpected audience. He cleared his throat and continued. 'He told me that he loved you both so much, even if he maybe didn't say it often enough.'

Sven and Nadine relaxed a bit. This was unconventional but harmless.

Craig nodded slowly, clearly wishing this could be over so he could return to his own private misery.

Danny was about to quit while he was ahead, but he saw Nudge, out of the corner of his eye, giving him a 'go on' gesture. 'I ... I also think that he wouldn't want you to blame yourselves.'

As soon as he'd said it, he regretted it. The entire pub seemed to have the air sucked out of it with the collective intake of breath and Danny watched Craig stiffen. He desperately tried to correct himself. 'Not that you have anything to blame yourself for,' he said hurriedly. 'But Nudge just wanted you to know that this was his fault and his fault alone.'

Another mass inhalation at this. It was a nightmare that Danny couldn't stop. 'Not that I'm blaming him for it. He just said that you might blame yourselves.'

Nudge's dad was now giving him his unwavering attention. 'I see,' he said icily. 'And when did he tell you this?'

Danny opened his mouth to answer but Craig kept going. 'Did you two talk often about how we'd feel if he drowned?' he asked. 'Son, if this is your attempt to lie and make me feel better, or get rid of your own guilt then—'

'—No!' Danny responded, belatedly realising that he was shouting. The entire pub was watching them now. He could feel it. 'He just told me . . .'

'When did he tell you?' snarled Nudge's father, no longer able to hold back the emotion that he'd buried for the day. 'When you let him drive you home drunk? Or was it when you left him at the bottom of the canal?'

Danny was caught off guard by the venom, so much so that, for a half second, he forgot to lie. 'No, of course not. He told me tonight.'

The resulting silence was so palpable, you could have cut it into bricks and constructed a soundproof bunker out of it. Danny wished that he could do so and throw away the key. Nudge's father was bristling with barely contained anger. Another man, one of Nudge's uncles possibly, stood up and put his hand on Craig's shoulder in a move that was half-support, half-restraint. Nadine and Sven were staring at him with open mouths, the latter looking as if he regretted not having taken the option to rugby-tackle him earlier.

Danny suddenly felt very sober, as if the alcohol in his bloodstream had evaporated through sheer mortification.

'I'm sorry?' Nudge's father said slowly and carefully. 'He told you tonight? Dan, I think you've had too much to drink.' He looked at Sven. 'Steven, would you mind?'

Danny felt Sven's massive hand wrap itself around his upper arm, and he almost allowed himself to be towed in the larger man's wake towards the door. Something inside him couldn't let it end this way though.

'Electric Picnic!' he said in a voice of dawning realisation.

'What?' said Craig and Sven, almost in stereo.

'No, I mean. I just need something that only Nudge would know, right?'

The assembled masses just stared at him blankly again, but Danny couldn't figure out how he hadn't thought of this earlier. He whirled around looking for the ghost. 'Nudge! Nudge, what's something only you'd know?' But the spirit wasn't where he'd been standing a few moments before. With rising panic, Danny frantically scanned the rest of the bar. He couldn't see Nudge anywhere. He took one last 360-degree view of his surroundings, which continued to fail to present the ghost of his late best friend. He could only see an audience looking at him with pity and regret.

This time, when Sven dragged him towards the door, he didn't resist.

Chapter 9

The psychiatrist's waiting room had changed, and it was annoying Danny that he couldn't figure out how. Admittedly, this was pretty low down on his list of worries but one of the rarely mentioned benefits of an anxiety disorder was an ability to multitask on such things. He was sure it wasn't the wallpaper, which was the same bamboo reed print that had been there the last time, and the couch was certainly the same vinyl abomination that was about as comfortable as a bus-shelter seat. Something had changed in the year or so since Danny had last been, though. He was sure of it.

The clinic was based in a converted Georgian house off Camden Street, above a chiropodist's practice and below a physiotherapist's. One day, Danny dreamed of meeting a depressive with a bad back and flat feet so he could recommend a one-stop shop.

He wondered if it was the carpet that was different. It didn't look new exactly, but he supposed his fellow patients could have anxiously paced some character into it in the last year.

The receptionist poked her head out the door of her office. 'You can go on up now.'

Danny nodded his thanks and stood up, taking a moment to work the kinks out of his back after twenty minutes on the awful excuse for a couch. The doctor's office itself was located up a back staircase leading to a narrow corridor above the waiting area. Danny wondered what the Georgians who originally owned the house would think of its current use: their living room being used to crack backs while a doctor dealt with the mentally unwell in what probably used to be their bedroom. He realised that he wasn't actually sure when the Georgian period was. He was picturing people in frilly collars and bustles but was almost positive that that was wrong.

He reached the top of the steps and was confronted by a narrow landing with one open door to his left leading into Dr Choi's large office. Opposite was a closed door, and Danny didn't actually know what was in there. He liked to think it's where the doctor kept his most deranged patients, drugged to the gills lest they wake up and wreak their dark desires on a helpless city.

Either that, or it was a cupboard.

He paused on the threshold of the office itself and knocked twice to announce his presence. The room took up most of this floor of the house. It was divided into one side that contained a large wooden desk, a computer and some filing cabinets and another, which consisted of two comfortable armchairs and side tables.

'Danny, come in. It's nice to see you again. Although, I wish it were under better circumstances,' Dr Choi said, as he stood up to greet Danny. He looked out of place in the old room. Barely out of his forties, he still had the trim figure of someone who made time at the gym. His accent was American but fifteen years plying his trade on this side of the Atlantic had caused a Dublin brogue to creep in on the odd word. A pair of designer glasses were a new addition to a tanned face topped by close-cropped, salt-and-pepper hair.

He gestured to the armchair opposite him. Danny had long since gotten over his disappointment that there was no couch for him to lie down on during his sessions. If nothing else, it would have given him an excuse not to make eye contact.

'Yeah, we have to stop meeting like this,' Danny replied tiredly, sinking into the chair.

Choi gave a small half smile that Danny had come to recognise as his 'patient deflecting a serious question with humour' face.

'Quite,' he said, sitting down himself. 'How are you, Danny?'

'Oh, you know? Can't complain. How are you?'

This earned Danny another half smile. The doctor didn't reply but merely continued to stare at him with the look of infinite patience that only someone who has been paid €110 in advance for their time can achieve. There were two types of therapy sessions, from what Danny could recall. The ones where he made flippant jokes and talked about easy, surface-level anxieties for most of the appointment before having to cram anything real into the last ten minutes, and the ones where he bit the bullet and stopped fucking about. He thought this probably warranted option B.

'I'm having a tough time,' he said slowly, as if having to drag each word from somewhere far away. He was out of practice. Danny knew that he probably wasn't the only Irish man who struggled to speak about his emotions, but he was always caught off guard by how much *effort* it took not to filter his responses through the usual layers of irony and self-deprecation.

He felt like a crab without its shell.

'Why don't we start with the accident that you mentioned?'

Danny wouldn't have normally been able to get an appointment so quickly but, luckily, when he'd explained his recent circumstances to Dr Choi over the phone, it must have seemed suitably urgent and he'd been able to set up a last-minute cancellation. He had already given the psychiatrist the CliffsNotes version of his mental breakdown but dutifully repeated the abridged overview of the weekend before. When he got to the part about the events of the canal, he found himself at a loss for euphemisms. 'Nudge is dead,' he said hoarsely, realising that this was the first time that he'd said it out loud. The weight of the words seemed to press him down further into the armchair.

'And you feel responsible?'

Danny took a deep breath, pushing back the wave of emotion that managed to keep surprising him with its intensity. 'I was sent out to stop him from driving off while drunk and instead, I ended up letting him give me a lift. What do you think?'

The last question was spat out with more venom than Danny had intended, and he opened his mouth to apologise but Dr Choi held up a hand. The psychiatrist took off his reading glasses and began to clean them with a cloth from the table beside him. Danny was fairly sure that this was for dramatic effect more than any actual need, but let it go.

'Danny, when you first came to these sessions, we discussed that one common thinking error you exhibited was the overestimation of your own sense of responsibility for things that are out of your control.'

'This is hardly the same thing—' Danny started but the older man held up a hand in acknowledgement once more, silencing him again. Danny was really beginning to think he might be a Jedi.

'Your friend, as tragic as the circumstances were, made the decision to drive drunk. From the conversation you've relayed to me, he lied to you about his sobriety and convinced you to get into the car.

'You didn't force him to drive drunk. You didn't crash into his car. You didn't knock down the barrier to the canal. I'm not denying that you made some bad decisions that night, but I do not think it's realistic for you to take responsibility for your friend's passing. Why don't we talk about what happened at the funeral?'

Danny had thought long and hard about what happened that night. Looking back, admittedly without the haze of alcohol, it seemed even more ridiculous than it had at the time. The further away he got from it, the surer he was that it had been some trick of his brain.

He was also hesitant to mention it here. Even though it was essentially the main reason he'd decided to come. He figured that 'carrying on conversations with people who aren't there' was on the big list of psychological no-nos, one that would cause Dr Choi to slam a hidden button, dropping him through a trapdoor into the waiting arms of people with straightjackets. It occurred to Danny that he might have to add 'paranoia' to his list of symptoms. He was being ridiculous.

If he was dropped through a trapdoor, he would just end up surprising the chiropodist anyway.

'I had a lot to drink that night and I thought that I could see Nudge. That he was talking to me.'

Nurse Ratched failed to abseil in through the window at this bombshell, so Danny continued. 'It was like he was right there.'

The doctor scribbled another quick note. 'What did he have to say?'

'He wanted . . .' Danny coughed to clear the unexpected welling in his throat. 'He wanted his parents to know that he was okay. He wanted to move on.' He sank his face into his hands. 'Christ, it all sounds so mental now. I'm totally fucked in the head, aren't I?'

Choi let out another sigh and tapped his pen on his notebook. 'Danny, can I ask whether you've been sleeping?'

This question caught him off guard. 'Not really,' he said, after some thought. 'Not since the night of the accident anyway. Although, I'm not sure if that counts as "sleep" *per se*. More "sedation" and, you know, "death" for a little bit.'

The psychologist smiled sadly. 'Your body went through an incredibly traumatic experience. This, combined with the lack of sleep, the heightened emotion of the last few days and, not to put too fine a point on it, the alcohol consumed on the night itself put your brain under a tremendous amount of stress.

'It's not uncommon for patients with PTSD to experience auditory and visual hallucinations. These symptoms can be exacerbated by lack of sleep, increased stress and consumption of drugs or alcohol,' he continued.

'Hang on,' Danny interrupted. 'PTSD? Where did PTSD come from? We've only been here for five minutes. I was in a car accident, not Afghanistan.'

The older man remained irritatingly calm. 'I'm aware that most people associate PTSD with soldiers returning from combat but it's actually a very common reaction to any sort of trauma. People suffer from it after muggings, illness and, as in your case, accidents. And I actually diagnosed you with PTSD about thirty seconds after you walked in the door.'

Danny felt like that last bit had been unnecessarily smug.

'The upshot is that I don't, at this point, think you suffer from schizophrenia or any other condition that might otherwise cause hallucinations. I think that this sounds like an isolated psychosis caused by the trauma and the emotion of the funeral itself.'

'So, I'm not mental?'

This resulted in a disapproving look. 'You are certainly experiencing symptoms of a mental illness but there are steps we can take to start addressing it and I'm reasonably confident that we can work towards allowing you to move past it.'

'Steps, such as?'

'Well, there are some additional questions that I'm going to get to but, for a start, we should resume our sessions, on a weekly basis. At least at first.'

Danny nodded. He'd expected this. Although he'd hoped for bi-weekly.

'Right now, I'm concerned about the insomnia, as that's only going to aggravate your other symptoms. I'm going to write you a script for something that will help you sleep. I'm also going to suggest returning to a course of SSRIs.'

'So, some antidepressants and a few sleeping pills and I'll be fixed?'

This only received another reproachful look. 'The medications will be one part of our therapy strategy, along with cognitive behavioural therapy and lifestyle changes to help address your condition.'

'Lifestyle changes?' Danny asked.

'I'm concerned with your alcohol intake. While I can't force my patients to do anything they don't want to, I must strongly advise that mixing alcohol with your current mindset is just going to amplify all these negative symptoms. I strenuously recommend that you take a break from drinking. At least for the next few weeks.'

'I completely agree,' Danny said.

Chapter 10

Reynard's was a cosy little pub around the corner from Dr Choi's office. Danny sipped his second whiskey and thought about how good he'd feel when he gave up drinking the following day.

He hadn't exactly lied. He'd had every intention of taking the advice but when he'd got out of their session the bus hadn't been due for another thirty minutes, so he'd stepped into Reynard's to get out of the cold. Granted, that had been about forty-five minutes ago, but Danny rationalised that he was owed one before he went cold turkey completely. He'd even opted for some rather fancy whiskey since this was going to be his last hurrah.

He was also purposely not looking at his phone as this would mean acknowledging the sheer number of unanswered messages and calls that were building up. So far, the only one he'd returned was to his boss asking for a few days' leave. The shop manager agreed, saying that he could take all the time he needed, as Danny's psychological health was extremely important to him as an employer. As long as he didn't expect anything ridiculous like paid time off.

A large portion of them were from Nadine too, who seemed to feel some responsibility for things since they'd occurred at her party. Danny would normally never have ghosted her but she'd made the mistake of suggesting that he and Clark go out for a drink together to talk about things. Apparently, he was a great listener.

The bartender, a bald man in his early forties, wandered past and Danny ordered another round. The barman wordlessly refilled Danny's glass and accepted the twenty that was passed over the bar. Danny looked at the change, or lack thereof, and winced. Hurrah or no hurrah, he would need to wrap things up if he wanted to have enough left for a bus fare. He glanced up at the mirror behind the bar, making a concerted effort not to catch his own eye in the reflection and ended up spraying a fourteen-euro glass of whiskey across the taps. Behind him, in the mirror, a tall red-haired man in a vibrant green and purple jumper stood with a look of desperate triumph on his face.

'It's about fucking time!'

It said a lot about Danny that his sheer embarrassment about spitting the drink out in public almost trumped his shock at seeing his dead friend again. He waved an apologetic hand towards the barman. 'Sorry,' he coughed, as he tried to breathe through the surprise and lingering, aerosolised Yellow Spot. 'It went down the wrong pipe.'

The bartender merely grumbled under his breath as he wiped down the taps with a cloth.

Danny had bigger things to worry about immediately, though, as Nudge was shouting in his ear. 'Hello! Don't pretend you can't hear me. I saw the way you reacted.'

Danny squeezed his eyes closed tightly and tried to remember what Dr Choi had said about stress and lack of sleep. It was a little difficult to maintain a sense of calm when there was an angry ghost screaming in your ear, however.

He reluctantly opened his eyes and turned to face Nudge. Like at the funeral there was something off about how he looked, like a magic-eye painting, where the dolphin would fade into the background if you didn't concentrate properly. *A magic-eye poster may have actually been the inspiration for that jumper,* Danny thought, as his sanity crumbled again.

Nudge clapped his hands together. 'I knew it! Fuck, it's good to be able to talk to you again.'

Danny glanced at the third of whiskey that he hadn't distributed over the opposing wall and sank it in one quick gulp. Then he carefully placed his hands on the bar and whispered to himself. 'I'm recovering from brain death and eighty-some hours without proper sleep. This is just my mind's way of coping with loss and trauma.'

'Not that again. I thought we'd resolved this?'

'Yeah, and then you left me high and dry in front of your dad and half your family.' Danny couldn't help himself. It was one thing to have hallucinations, but it was another thing to let them win an argument.

'Yeah, sorry about that,' Nudge said. He had the decency to look embarrassed. 'I think I might have misjudged the reason why I'm still here.'

'No shit,' Danny replied bitterly. The barman was looking at him strangely. Danny grabbed his headphones off the bar and stuck them in his ears. He nodded in understanding and wandered off.

Better he thinks that I'm an ignorant arsehole having a phone conversation in a pub than mental, thought Danny.

'Good idea,' Nudge said, encouragingly.

'Don't you start, I'm paying through the nose to get rid of you. What the hell happened at the funeral? One minute you were all over me and the next minute, you'd bailed.'

Nudge sat down on the stool next to him. Or, at least, he made some approximation of sitting down. Danny couldn't help but notice that he wasn't making full contact with the seat.

'That's the thing,' he said. 'I didn't go anywhere. It was like the hospital all over again. I was still there but you couldn't hear me.' A note of frustration cut through his voice. 'And I still can't go too far from you, or else I feel like I'm being pulled away.'

An unnerving thought occurred to Danny. 'How close are we talking? Like when I'm on the toilet or . . .'

Nudge made a face. 'Get a grip. I'm not in hell yet.'

Danny shook his head to clear it, both from the alcohol and the recurring mental breakdown.

'This is ridiculous. I'm going back to Dr Choi.' Then a terrible thought occurred to him. 'Did you eavesdrop on my session?' he asked, outraged.

'I thought I was a figment of your imagination?' Nudge replied sarcastically. Seeing the look on Danny's face he continued. 'No, of course not. I waited outside. I wasn't dragged up.'

Danny was embarrassed at how relieved he felt. He shook himself. 'No, this is crazy.'

Nudge looked as if, were he physically capable of doing so, he would be banging his head off the bar. 'What about Electric Picnic?'

Danny scoffed. 'Deep down, I always suspected.'

'Oh, bollocks!' Nudge retorted. 'If you'd known, or even suspected, I would have woken up to a welly full of piss and you know it.'

'That's absolutely not true,' responded Danny, knowing full well that it was a little true. 'Either way. It proves fuck all, except that Sven needs more fibre in his diet.'

Nudge took another deep breath, Danny assumed out of habit more than anything else. 'Okay, I've been thinking about this. Something that you definitely didn't know about.'

Danny, despite his misgivings, was intrigued. 'What could you possibly say at this point that would surprise me?'

His friend looked quite uneasy and Danny couldn't help himself. He laughed.

'C'mon, what could be so bad that you wouldn't tell me even after you died?'

'I kissed Steff.'

Danny could feel his expression struggle to remain neutral. 'We better be talking about some other Steff. Some not-my-younger-sister Steff.'

Nudge looked suddenly very glad that he was incorporeal. 'Let me explain.'

'Don't bother. I know I must be mental now. There's no way—'

'—Call her,' Nudge interrupted. 'Call her now and ask. If she says it didn't happen, then, well, she's a liar, but I'll leave you alone. I'll walk away and let whatever force is coming for me have me. But if she says it did . . .' he left it hanging and looked towards Danny's phone on the bar in front of them.

Danny motioned to the barman for another round and then, reluctantly, reached for his mobile. Steff was in his mobile under 'Devil Spawn' and, as the phone rang, he tried to recall what had prompted that name change. It might have been the time, during her first trimester, that she'd thrown a dessert spoon at his head, but he couldn't be sure.

She answered on the third ring, saving him from having to leave the most awkward voicemail in the history of telecommunications. 'All right, Dan. What's up?' She sounded different but he reckoned it was because she was making an effort to be nice to him with everything that was going on.

'Not much. Just waiting on the bus home here. Wanted to see how Buster is doing.'

He'd been up most of the night with some sort of head cold and by extension, so had the rest of the house. Danny would have been more annoyed at his nephew but, as he'd told the psychiatrist, he wasn't sleeping much at all himself these days anyway.

'I think he might have picked up a bug in nursery. I'm worried they don't sanitise the play area enough.'

Danny had witnessed Buster try to eat a snail more than once and so doubted the play area was the real issue. 'He's a tough little guy. He'll be fine,' he said vaguely, wondering how he was going to transition to his actual topic.

'How was your appointment?'

Danny was caught off guard by the question. 'It was okay. A lot of work to do still, he reckons, but a good start.'

Suddenly, his actual line of questioning felt like a relief. 'Listen, Steff, this might sound weird, and you can blame this on the brain damage if you like, but did you and Nudge . . .' he trailed off.

'Just ask her!' Nudge said irritably. Danny had almost forgotten about him.

'Did you and Nudge ever kiss?' He said it quickly: if he got it out fast enough, she wouldn't hear it.

There was silence on the other end of the line. Danny wasn't sure if she was surprised, disgusted or, more likely, that Buster had gotten hold of the phone and was trying to eat it. After what seemed like twenty minutes but was probably only as many seconds, she replied.

'Who told you?'

'You're kidding me?' Danny said, giving Nudge a look that said he was planning on killing him all over again.

'We weren't carrying on behind your back or any-thing,' Steff said hurriedly. 'It was just the once. A quick, drunken thing. We never said anything because it was really nothing. Both of us wanted to forget about it.'

'When was this?' Danny said, through clenched teeth.

'Nearly two years ago now. At that house party you threw when Mum and Dad went to Portugal.'

Danny was now glaring at Nudge, as if trying to figure out if it were possible to punch a ghost.

'How did you find out?' Steff asked. 'He swore me to secrecy. I didn't think he'd be telling anyone.'

'Huh?' Danny said, as realisation surfaced through the sea of vengeful anger in his head. 'Oh. Nudge kept a diary. Sven was helping his mum clean out his room and found it.'

'That's a bit intrusive, Sven telling you.'

'I guess he thought I already knew,' Danny said, not without a little resentment.

'Listen, it was nothing. You should have seen how bad he felt afterwards. I think he was more worried that you'd never talk to him again than anything else.'

When she was met with nothing but furious silence on the other end of the phone, Steff clearly decided to cut her losses. 'Look, Buster needs a nappy change. I gotta go. Bye.'

She hung up before Danny could respond. He very carefully put the mobile back on the bar and gripped his glass of whiskey tightly.

'Look, mate,' Nudge started. 'I didn't want you to find out like this.'

'Like what? Posthumously?'

'Well, actually. That would have been ideal,' Nudge replied honestly. 'I was really hoping I'd be able to take that secret to the grave. I just didn't expect that wouldn't be long enough. Look, let's just move past this and work on—'

'—Nope. You can absolutely get fucked!' Danny hissed in poorly concealed rage.

'C'mon, man. Don't be like that. Are you going to leave me stuck like this because of something so silly?'

'Yeah, it's good enough for you. Maybe this is your punishment for being a fucking paedo in life.'

'Hey!' Nudge said. 'She was eighteen, so let's not throw around words we can't take back.'

Danny didn't respond and continued to stare into his drink.

'Oh. You're just going to ignore me? Is that it?'

'You're just a figment of my fractured psyche anyway,' Danny replied petulantly.

'Oh, please! I expect you're going to say that you secretly knew about me and Steff all along? As if you wouldn't have skinned me alive if you had even a suspicion.'

Danny considered this. A friend coming back from beyond the veil of death did trump him kissing his sister. Just.

Nudge seemed to sense the anger drain away and moved in closer. 'I need your help, man!' The sheer desperation in his tone was enough to shift the self-righteousness that was currently coating Danny like ash from Pompeii. He turned to look at his friend and noticed that he seemed a little more in focus than he had initially.

'Okay. If only because I'm sick of the sight of you already.'

Nudge rubbed his hands together in satisfaction. 'Yes! Barman, the drinks are on me. Champagne for everyone!'

The rest of the bar utterly failed to react.

'Well, it was worth a go. If that didn't get through to them then I don't know what will.'

A thought that had been nagging at Danny but had been derailed by recent revelations came to the forefront. 'How come I can see you again?' he asked. 'You've been around since the funeral? Right?'

Nudge nodded. 'Yeah, but you were like everyone else. I couldn't get through.'

'So, what changed?'

Both men were silent, deep in thought. Danny went to take another sip of his drink and paused with it half-way to his lips. He held out the glass in front of him and watched the light play through the amber liquid.

'No fucking way,' Nudge whispered, as he caught up.

'It's the only thing that links the night of the funeral and now.'

'You weren't able to see me then until you were fairly well gone,' Nudge said.

'I wasn't able to see you here until my third drink,' Danny said. Realisation dawned. 'That night at the funeral. The mortification of talking to your dad. All those people looking at me.'

Nudge winced. 'Yeah, again, sorry about that.'

'No.' Danny waved a hand dismissively. 'I mean. The whole experience, the adrenaline. It sobered me up.'

'And you were suddenly not able to see me anymore,' said Nudge. 'It can't be that simple, can it?'

Danny was about to respond when the barman came up behind him. 'Sorry, pal. I'm going to have to ask you to leave. I think you've had too much and you're disturbing the other patrons.'

Danny looked up in surprise. He still had his earphones in but realised that he must have been wildly gesticulating at thin air for the past five minutes. Looking around, he could see everyone else in the pub staring at him. The barman had one of his colleagues behind him for backup and didn't look like he was in any mood for explanations. Not that Danny would be able to provide one.

'No worries,' he said, as placatingly as he could. 'You're right. I should head home.' He got up off the stool and gathered up his belongings. As he stood up, he swayed slightly and realised that he was more drunk than he thought. Which, for once, he guessed was a good thing.

The barman visibly relaxed at his compliance. He reached down and gently handed Danny his coat, which had fallen to the floor.

'Good lad. Get yourself a cup of coffee on the way. Yeah?'

Danny paused as he pulled on his coat. 'That,' he said in a thoughtful voice, 'is an *excellent* idea.'

Chapter 11

'I still don't think this is a good idea,' Nudge moaned, invisibly, as they waited in the queue at Starbucks on Dame Street. Outside the fogged windows, early Christmas shoppers bustled about on their own errands as buses inched their way around Trinity College. It seemed like far too normal a scene to Danny, who was holding his mobile to his ear so he could talk openly to the ghost of his best friend. 'Look, you said it yourself,' he said. 'It's the only thing that lines up. We need to see if we're right.'

'What if I'm not able to get back through to you?'

Danny was currently entertaining the same worry but resolved to keep things positive. 'Then I'll try something else, but this will work. I can feel it.'

He glanced up at the board behind the counter. He wasn't a big coffee drinker, nature having seen fit to gift him with an endless supply of anxious energy. 'What's the strongest coffee they have?' he asked his phone/ unseen companion.

Nudge had been an unrepentant caffeine addict, back when he still had a digestive system he could destroy. 'I think the blonde roast? But honestly, this stuff is muck. We should really go to Bean There, Done

That on Camden Street. They have this mix of beans that's . . .'

Danny stopped listening as he moved to the front of the queue and ordered a triple espresso with an extra shot for luck. Nudge was still monologuing about the virtues of different Java blends. Danny guessed he was just glad to have someone who could hear him.

He tuned back in at a question, as they waited for his order.

'What else do you think is real?' Nudge asked.

Danny looked over at his friend and then hurriedly acted as if he were transferring his phone from one hand to the other when he received a strange look from the lady behind him in the queue. 'What do you mean?'

'Well, if ghosts are real then what else could be. Magic? Zombies? Vampires?'

'Pretty sure vampires still aren't real,' Danny replied as he moved to collect this coffee. The young lad behind the counter gave him an odd look at this but he ignored it. Danny looked down at the dark, bitter liquid scepti-cally. He emptied three packets of sugar into it but— was still less than optimistic about the impact that was going to have on the taste. Even the smell was making his heart beat faster.

He slipped into an empty seat by the window as he waited for the drink to cool. He was okay with taking a massive caffeine overdose for the purposes of science but drew the line at burning the roof of his mouth. Once again, Nudge managed a passable impression of sitting down in the chair opposite.

In the unflattering lighting of the coffee shop, sur-rounded by tourists, shoppers and people typing over-enthusiastically on MacBooks, Danny felt a surge of doubt cut through the euphoria he'd been experiencing since Reynard's. Seeing Nudge again had eased some of the iron bands of guilt that had encircled his chest since the accident, but what if Dr Choi was right? What if this was all just some coping mechanism cooked up by his PTSD-riddled brain? Maybe he should run, screaming, back to the psychiatrist for help?

This grim train of thought was interrupted by another question from the (possibly hallucinatory) Nudge. 'So, what's the plan if this works?' he asked, nodding at Danny's coffee.

Danny noticed that, behind all his usual bluster, his friend was looking genuinely worried. If this was real, then Nudge needed help. The alternative was that Danny would never see his best friend again. It really wasn't much of a decision. 'I'll give it half an hour and then drop into another pub to confirm that drinking alcohol brings you back.'

'And then?'

'Then we figure out why you're still here.'

'How do we do that?'

Danny took a first, cautious sip of his coffee. It was still too hot but at least the scalding pain took his mind off the bitter taste.

'Never mind ghosts. You'll see through time after a few more of those,' Nudge said. He waved his arms in front of Danny's face. 'Still with me?'

Gingerly, Danny probed the burnt ruins of the top of his mouth with his tongue. 'Yeah. Look, it stands to reason that, if you're real, then at least some other ghost stuff is. There must be someone else out there who can see them. We track one down and they might know more about you moving on!'

Nudge looked surprised. 'That's not a bad idea. At the very least I'll get to talk to someone else for a change. So, we track down, what? A psychic? A ghostbuster?'

Danny took another sip of coffee. This time it was merely eye-wateringly hot instead of actually scalding. 'I think they are called "mediums". My aunt used to visit one after her husband died.'

'Okay,' Nudge said, with more enthusiasm than Danny had seen him express to date post-mortem. 'We find ourselves a Mystic Meg, they tell me how to shuffle off this mortal coil and we're laughing.'

'It's probably not going to be that simple,' Danny replied after another mouthful of bitter coffee. 'The real deal has to be pretty rare.'

'Medium rare?' Nudge offered, looking entirely too pleased with himself.

Danny winced at the combination of coffee and terrible pun. 'Quite. It might take a while. Which brings me to my next problem.'

'You've so many. Enlighten me.'

'If I can only see you when I'm shit-faced, then it's going to be pretty hard for me to get anything done. I need to be drunk enough to pierce whatever veil is keeping you from the land of the living but not so pissed that I'm getting sick on myself.'

Danny was sure that Nudge was harder to see now. The coffee was working.

'That's a fine line to walk all right. How are we going to manage it?'

'Like anything else worthwhile in life,' Danny said. He took a big swig of the last quarter of his coffee and slammed it back on the table. 'Practice!' he said dramatically.

But he was sitting alone.

Chapter 12

Danny managed to re-establish contact after a quick stopover in another bar, much to their relief. This time, it had only taken a drink and a half for Nudge to become visible again, as the coffee had only masked what he'd drunk in Reynard's.

Danny was a man of science at heart and the next phase of action was to establish a baseline from complete sobriety, after an espresso-fuelled night where Danny worried he might never sleep again. It had taken much trial and error but, after meticulous experimentation, which had all but drained his parents' drinks cabinet, they managed to figure out that it took about four standard drinks for Nudge to become visible. Danny had decided on whiskey as the tool of choice for these experiments. Beer and wine took too long and trying to keep the balance between just drunk enough and too drunk with cans and bottles was a hassle. No, spirits were clearly the only way to go and since mixers complicated Danny's already-pretty-slapdash booze maths, it had to be something that he could drink straight. This left whiskey as the only real option, as a teenage incident with a naggin before a disco had left Danny with the inability to even smell vodka without gagging.

Thankfully, the visit to Dr Choi and Danny's more upbeat attitude, partly thanks to all the experimentation, helped convince his mum and dad to let him return to his apartment, although with strict instructions that he needed to check in every day. They were all for him proactively taking charge of his own mental-health journey, as long as that journey involved him calling one of them every day. They had read somewhere that this could reduce feelings of isolation and anxiety. Danny appreciated their concern but made sure to mostly ring his dad, so that the conversations were less about his mental health and more about the scourge of pedestrianisation in Dublin city centre and the government's disregard for its impact on hard-working taxi drivers.

He felt bad about deceiving his parents but it wasn't the first time he'd hidden deep emotional problems from them and, as he'd said to Nudge in the coffee shop, practice made perfect.

Danny was finally able to make use of two presents left over from his twenty-first: a litre bottle of Jameson that he had never got around to opening and a small steel hip flask. Granted, the latter had been a present from Nudge and so had the words YASS QUEEN! engraved on it but it held a surprising amount of liquid and fit comfortably inside his jacket pocket.

The days of experimentation had also given them time to come up with a more complete game plan.

'Right,' Danny said, the day after he'd moved back into the flat, a full week after the funeral. He cleared some space on his bedside stool to prop up his laptop. 'Here's what I have so far.'

It was eleven in the morning and Danny had consumed his starter drinks over the last hour until Nudge had become available again. The certainty that Nudge was real and that all this was actually happening seemed to drain away from Danny each night and, despite all their 'research', he was desperately relieved each time his friend appeared every morning. Still, he tried to avoid actually drinking spirits with breakfast. That was the domain of alcoholics and music festivals.

Nudge was standing at the end of the bed looking critically around the room. 'I still can't believe you live like this. No wonder it's been a year.' He turned back to Danny after a pillow sailed through his head and clattered into the wardrobe behind him.

'Pay attention!' Danny chided. 'This is for your benefit.'

Nudge focused on the screen. 'You didn't exactly go on a quest here. You just googled "psychics",' he muttered.

'Hey! it was more than that,' Danny replied, a little more hotly than intended. 'There's more of these guys than I thought, and they all do different stuff. It took me ages to narrow it down to these two.'

Nudge looked at him sceptically. 'So, you didn't just pick ones that are close to the number twenty-seven bus then?'

Danny took a swig from his hip flask to avoid the question and pointed to the screen again. 'I reckon these are probably our best bet to start off with. If they don't pan out, then we can start looking further afield.'

His late friend stepped closer to the laptop and squinted at the open tabs. He didn't look too impressed by the supernatural experts that Dublin had to offer. 'Christ, they don't look like they can work Zoom, let alone contact the other side.'

Danny closed the laptop screen in frustration. 'Then we'll look further afield. Maybe even England? I can't be the only one who's able to see you.'

Nudge's face softened a little and he reached out to pat his friend's arm. Or at least, the space just above his arm. 'Sorry. I'm being an ungrateful prick. I'm just nervous,' he admitted.

Danny nodded in sympathy. 'Let's just get going,' he said, standing up and pocketing his keys and wallet.

'How are we getting out to them?'

'Well, we are getting the number twenty—'

'—I fucking knew it!'

*

The first of Danny's psychics lived on the far side of Tallaght. There were relatively few people on the bus at this hour of the day, so Nudge was spared the ignominy of someone trying to sit on top of him. They continued to use a pair of headphones as a cover, so the other passengers on the top deck didn't think he was a raving lunatic. Not that this would have been uncommon on Dublin Bus, although Danny did receive some dirty looks for swigging from his flask at eleven in the morning.

They found the spiritualist's place of business after some trial and error. The bus left them on the main road, but her office was a ten-minute walk through a warren of identical-looking housing estates. Google Maps eventually led them to a small retail strip that consisted of a Centra, a hairdresser's and a chipper. They'd walked past the building twice before they realised the address was located on the floor above the salon.

'Here we are,' Nudge said, reading a small sign on a door around the side of the building. 'Joyce Shelton: Spiritualist. Psychic. Clairvoyant.' He looked up at Danny. 'What does "clairvoyant" mean?'

'It means she has a thesaurus,' said Danny, grumpy from the walk. As he passed Nudge, he noticed that the sign had originally said CLOTHING ALTERATIONS, but somebody had roughly sellotaped Joyce's over the top of it.

Joyce Shelton had covered the door to her office with a large poster of her name and the services she offered. It was quite impressive, a lurid purple background with blue font, further decorated with stars, dreamcatchers and other supernatural paraphernalia.

Unfortunately, someone had also decorated it with a crude drawing of a penis.

Danny stepped forward and knocked. They waited in silence for a few seconds and, just as he was about to knock again, they heard a commotion on the other side of the door, before it was opened by a blonde woman who Danny guessed to be in her mid-fifties. Although he hadn't really been expecting somebody dressed like a stereotypical fairground fortune teller, he was still a little bit disappointed at how normal she looked. She was wearing a worn red fleece over a white blouse and jeans. He'd at least hoped for a little bit of occult jewellery, maybe a pentagram necklace or moon-and-star earrings, but the only accessory that Joyce wore was an outdated Fitbit.

'Welcome!' Her voice, at least, sounded the part. It was a hushed whisper with an unusual lilt that suggested the Welsh valleys. 'Come inside and we can explore the mysteries of—' she seemed to notice her poster for the first time, '—the little prick!' she finished, in an accent that suddenly became more Coolock than Caerphilly. Joyce caught herself and shot Danny an apologetic look. 'Sorry. This is the fourth time I've had to replace that bloody poster. Forget talking to his mam, I'm going to give him such a kick up the hole.' She noticed Danny's blank look. 'Brendan. His mam works in the hairdresser's downstairs, and he keeps sneaking up here with that marker of his,' she explained.

'How'd you know it was him? ESP?' Danny asked hopefully.

'No, the Centra has CCTV outside and the manager showed me the video after the last time,' she said, still angrily examining the poster. Then she seemed to remember that she had a customer. 'Sorry. I'm rambling. That happens when I haven't had my coffee yet. Come in. Would you like one? It's just the instant stuff but it's nice.'

Danny stayed where he was and pointedly looked over to where Nudge was standing but the blonde medium seemed just as unaware of his presence as everyone else. 'None for me. Thank you, though,' he said, after a moment. He hurried past her as she held the door open, and his hopes were further dashed when she closed it in Nudge's disappointed face. Not that it slowed him down.

The interior of Joyce's office looked, well, it looked like a former alterations shop that someone had decorated with a load of dreamcatchers. Danny was slightly mollified to see that at least the circular table that dominated the room was covered with a black velvet tablecloth decorated with stars.

She indicated the nearest seat and walked across to a door on the opposite side of the room. 'Just sit down, love, while I sort myself out.' She slipped into what Danny could see was a cramped kitchenette.

Nudge walked around to the other side of the table. 'What are you doing? She clearly can't see me. Save your money and let's just go.' One benefit Nudge had discovered about his new condition is that he no longer had to bother with an inside voice. He boomed in Danny's ear.

'Just hang on,' Danny whispered in response. 'Maybe she has to, like, *get in the zone* to be able to see you.' He held up his hip flask, and after taking a quick sip, shook it as evidence. 'That might be an Irish coffee she's making for herself.'

Nudge huffed slightly but stood aside as Joyce re-entered the room with a steaming mug of coffee in one hand and a deck of cards in the other. She placed both down on the table in front of her, although she had the presence of mind to grab a coaster from one of the side tables before putting her coffee on the velvet.

'Right, love,' she said, riffling the deck like a poker shark. 'What are we doing for you today? Problems with your career? Love life? The Arcana have helped many a lost soul to find meaning again.'

'No,' Danny said, his expectations sinking even further. 'I emailed about the medium services. I recently lost a friend.'

Joyce, to her credit, looked instantly abashed. 'Oh, I am sorry. Of course. We can try to reach your friend. Before we get started though, there is the matter of the fee. I'm sorry to bring it up now but, often, people can become quite emotionally overwhelmed by the experience itself and it can be awkward to talk about the money.'

Danny nodded, reaching for his wallet and ignoring the huge raspberry Nudge had just blown. 'Right, "cross your palm with silver", eh?'

Joyce smiled. 'Cash is usually preferred. My daughter keeps telling me to get one of those debit-card readers but I'm not very technical.'

Danny counted the notes out into her hand and the older woman smiled and disappeared them somewhere about her person in the most impressive feat of magic that Danny had seen thus far. She leaned forward in her chair and pulled up the sleeves on her fleece. 'All right. It's important to know, going in, that your friend might not be able to speak to us today. You shouldn't be discouraged. There are times when the link to the spirit world is stronger than others and sometimes, especially for the recently passed, they might not have found their way to us yet.'

Danny avoided making eye contact with Nudge over her shoulder. 'I understand. I just feel that he's with me all the time lately.'

Joyce went to reach across the table to Danny, hesitated a moment, and then bent down to grab something from underneath the table. She re-emerged with a small bottle of supermarket-brand hand sanitiser, which she proffered to Danny. 'Sorry, love. Would you mind? Can't be too careful.'

Danny dutifully covered his palms with the alcoholic gel and rubbed it in. Joyce took the opportunity to squirt a small amount on her own hands before once again reaching across to him. Her grip was surprisingly strong as she took his hands in hers. Danny was forced to lean forward slightly in order to meet her halfway. His ribs protested at this, but he ignored them.

'What was your friend's name?' she asked, in a voice that was suddenly all business. She hadn't gone back to the Welsh accent, but she was still speaking in hushed tones.

'Nudge. Paul Nugent,' Danny said.

'I need you to focus on him for me. His face, his voice, the last time you spoke. Hold these things in your mind.'

'That should be easy,' Nudge chimed in.

Danny looked up to give him a warning glance, but Joyce interrupted suddenly. 'Close your eyes. Think about Paul. Do not think about his death. Focus on his life. Your friendship. The things he cared about.'

Danny obediently squeezed his eyes shut.

'Paul,' she called out softly. 'Paul, if you're here, then please join us and make your presence known.'

Nudge wandered up to her chair. 'I'm here, you mad old hippie!' he yelled in her ear.

Joyce gasped and looked around. Danny felt her squeeze his hands suddenly. Even Nudge looked a little surprised and regretful about his comments.

Danny's heart was in his mouth. Could she hear him? Maybe it worked differently for different people.

'Paul, is that you?' Joyce called out. She had her eyes squeezed closed now, as if in tremendous concentration.

'Yes. It's me. I'm right here!' Nudge shouted excitedly, his earlier scepticism instantly forgotten.

Danny was about to ask why she could only hear him and thought about offering her a nip of his flask to help grease the spiritual wheels a bit, but she interrupted him. 'I've made contact,' Joyce whispered.

'He wants you to know that he's at peace,' she continued soothingly, 'And that he's in a better place.'

Danny was simultaneously crushed and thankful that she couldn't hear the tirade of abuse that Nudge was directing at her. 'I'm in some fucking charlatan's office in the arse end of Tallaght. I couldn't be further from a better place,' he raged.

Danny struggled but ultimately failed to keep his dismay from showing on his face and pulled his hands away from hers but luckily, Joyce was about as good at reading expressions as she was at talking to the dead.

'It can be overwhelming,' she said kindly, reaching into the pocket of her fleece and offering him a packet of tissues. 'Especially at first. Take all the time you need. Speaking to the dead can be a very intense experience.'

Danny nodded. This was probably the only thing that she'd said so far that had been true.

'I think I'm going to go,' he said, pushing his chair back.

'Are you sure, love? You've still got twenty-five minutes left. I could do you a tarot reading.' She picked up the deck of cards from the table again. 'It can provide much-needed answers about what's bothering you. Professionally? Romantically?'

Right now, what was bothering Danny was trying not to react to Nudge's tirade, which had moved on from Joyce's skills as a medium and progressed to the nature of her parentage via some hurtful comments about her appearance.

'No, I'd really better be going.'

'Well, if you're sure,' she said in the voice of someone who'd just remembered they'd been paid in advance. 'Go safely.'

Danny offered an anaemic thanks and moved towards the door. Outside, he was confronted by a very surprised-looking child in school uniform, holding a permanent marker. They looked at each other in shocked silence for a moment before Danny remembered himself and pulled the door to an angle that shielded them from Joyce's view.

'Thanks for everything,' he said out loud to her as he exited. Whispering, he said, 'There's two ls in "bellend",' as he walked past the boy and down the stairs.

Chapter 13

Their next stop, at least, started more promisingly. Diana O'Hare worked out of a small shop in the city centre, which had been rather more impressively mystified than Joyce's. Like Joyce, sessions as a medium were just one service she provided along with tarot, aura cleansings and past-life readings. She also offered missing-person searches and police consultation.

Danny asked whether the police had ever actually consulted her, but she'd just given a wry smile and cited client confidentiality.

She was a tall, thin woman in her forties who looked rather more the part than Joyce had. Which just meant that she wore a lot of silver jewellery and her long black dress looked like it had been picked out from Morticia Addams' collection.

Unfortunately, like Joyce, she initially seemed to be completely unaware of Nudge. What intrigued Danny, however, was that, shortly after they'd sat down, she'd suppressed a gasp, as if in surprise, and then looked around the shop in confusion. 'Sorry,' she said. 'I just had the strangest sensation; like being underwater.' She shook her head and smiled. 'It must be a senior moment. What can I do for you then?'

Danny was about to launch into his request when she held up a hand, a look of confusion crossing her face again. 'You lost your friend. Recently. Traumatically.'

It wasn't a question.

Danny nodded. 'Yeah, just last week—'

Diana spoke over him. '—You were close?'

'Well, yeah. He was my best friend.' Danny felt embarrassed saying that out loud with Nudge still in the room. He made a mental note to be mean to him later, so it didn't go to his head.

'No,' Diana said, 'I mean physically. You were with him when he died?' She put her hands to her mouth in shock. 'I'm so sorry.'

Danny was stunned and very confused. On the one hand, she still didn't seem to be acknowledging Nudge's presence but, on the other, she certainly had knowledge of things she shouldn't.

Seeing his shocked reaction, Diana put her hand out to steady him. 'I'm sorry. Usually, it doesn't come through this strongly. Normally, we have to wait until I start the reading properly but it's just really powerful today.'

Danny glanced over at Nudge, who shrugged.

'Do you mind if we get the awkward bit over and actually start?' she asked.

Danny looked blank for a moment before he realised that she meant the payment and pulled out his wallet. Diana did, in fact, have a card reader and he tried not to think about how much he'd spent in psychic services that afternoon as he entered his PIN.

'Right,' she said after she'd confirmed that the transaction had been approved, 'Let's give this a go, shall we?'

113

She reached across the table and took both of Danny's hands in hers.

'His name was—' Danny started.

'—Paul' she interrupted, to his shock. 'Although, no. That's not right.'

'No, that's it.'

'No, I mean nobody called him "Paul", his actual name was . . .' she wrinkled her forehead in confusion. "Push"? No, wait, "Nudge".'

'That's right,' Danny said, utterly riveted.

She smiled. 'He was quite a colourful character, wasn't he? Not a blend-into-the-background kind of guy, I'm guessing?'

Danny looked up to marvel at this with Nudge and discovered that he wasn't there. He silently cursed himself. He hadn't topped up his own psychic abilities since the last appointment. The walk from the Luas stop must have put him under the limit.

Diana's smile faded. 'He drowned. God! That's why I felt like I was under . . . sorry. I didn't mean to bring anything back.'

Danny swallowed back emotion, still surprised by how intensely he felt it. Rather than trust himself to speak, he shook his head.

'It wasn't just him. You passed over as well, didn't you? Not for long but for a moment?'

Danny nodded.

'That must be why I'm feeling this so strongly,' Diana said in awed tones.

'Do you think you could contact him?' Danny asked.

She smiled back sadly. 'With a connection like this, I think so. It might take us a few more sessions though.

There can be a lot of background noise to something like this. It can be hard for the spirit to make its voice heard.'

'Never mind. She's a fucking fraud,' Nudge said loudly, coming into the room.

Danny nearly jumped a foot out of his chair in surprise. The ghost of his friend hadn't disappeared after all but had just wandered into the back of the shop for a nose about.

'What?' Danny said out loud.

Diana gripped his hands and gave him another sympathetic smile. 'Don't get me wrong. Your connection to Nudge is really strong. I'll just have to work to build that connection myself. It can take a while for the spirit to build up trust.'

'Don't trust her,' Nudge said with a look of righteous indignation on his face. 'It's all on her laptop back there. My obituary, the story in *The Irish Times*. She even has my Instagram page. She just mined them for details to con us.'

Diana interpreted Danny's rising confusion and outrage as due to him being emotionally overwhelmed. 'I'm willing to do whatever it takes to help you contact him. However many sessions you need.'

Danny pulled his hands out of hers and pushed his chair back. The psychic was caught off guard and flinched at his sudden movement. He wanted to shout at her, to confront her for being such a charlatan but didn't trust himself to open his mouth.

Nudge, on the other hand, felt no such restriction. If anything, this latest betrayal after the day of disappointment had finally caused him to lose it. 'I mean, the other one was bad enough,' he shouted at the oblivious woman. 'But at least she kept it vague.'

Diana, like Joyce earlier, interpreted Danny's sudden reticence as shock. 'Danny, it's okay. A lot of people get overwhelmed in these situations. Especially when they have as strong a connection to the deceased as you.'

Danny found himself choking back anger on top of all the emotion that she'd wrought out of him but managed to croak in response, 'I'd better go.'

'Oh, okay. I really felt like we were getting somewhere though. Would you like to book in for another session later this week?'

'Fucking vulture!' Nudge shouted. 'Actually, no. At least vultures have the decency to only feed on the dead and not their loved ones, too.' Nudge was angrier than Danny had ever seen him, as if all the frustration with his circumstances had come bubbling out.

'I don't think so,' Danny said, moving towards the door, hoping to exit the shop before Nudge blew whatever the ghost version of a blood vessel was.

'Well, look,' Diana said, and suddenly he was aware that her calm, engaging tone had shifted to that of a car salesman who can feel a deal slipping away. 'Take my card. It has my direct line for regular clients and you can call me if you want to try again.' She gestured to a narrow counter behind her where a stack of business cards sat next to different flyers and specialist magazines. As she went to reach for the card, Nudge snapped and slapped his hand at the counter in a fit of rage. He was more surprised than anyone when its entire contents flew into the air.

Well, maybe not as surprised as Diana. 'What the fuck?' the psychic screamed, her voice going from a soothing hush to a terrified scream. She turned to look at

Danny who, luckily from an alibi standpoint, was standing on the other side of the shop in the unexpected blizzard of paper. He decided that a hasty exit might be the best bet and moved for the door.

'Wait!' Diana shouted as he moved to leave. 'What the hell was that?'

'Must have been that strong connection,' said Danny, pulling a paper handbill out of his hair and exiting as quickly as he could. He didn't stop until he was safely down the road and around the corner before ducking into the doorway of a closed vape shop. He took a swig from his flask, more to steady his nerves than to strengthen his second sight. A few moments later, Nudge followed, looking dazed and staring at his hands like they might shoot lasers.

'What the hell was that?' Danny asked, hoarse from the emotion of the last few minutes and also because some of the whiskey had gone down the wrong way.

'I have no idea,' Nudge said in an awed tone. 'I was just so angry. I don't know what came over me.' He reached out towards Danny and, delicately, tried to pluck the piece of paper out of his hands. Danny had forgotten he was still holding it. Nudge's fingers passed right through.

'Maybe it's something you need practice at?' Danny suggested. 'Or, it's only when you get really worked up? I don't think I've ever seen you like that.'

'I know,' Nudge said weakly. 'The other one, Joyce, she was disappointing, but *her*.' He spat the word out with venom. 'It's all well and good when she's talking to you, but I just pictured her doing that to my mum and saw red.'

'Well, just don't go throwing shit around my room,' Danny said, relieved that his friend seemed to be feeling better now, all things considered.

'As if you'd notice, with the state of that place. What are we going to do now?'

Danny wasn't listening. He'd finally taken time to glance at the piece of paper he'd pulled off his head in the shop. It was a black-and-white flyer that looked as if it had been done on a photocopier from the early nineties. Black spots and streaks speckled an advert that appeared to have been written, very neatly, in black marker. '"Adella Price. Clairvoyant, Seer and Medium,"' Danny read aloud. '"Speak to your lost loved ones."'

'How come she wasn't on your list?' Nudge asked.

'She must not have a website.' Danny scrutinised the smaller text at the bottom of the flyer. '"We accept no responsibility for offence taken at what the departed have to say."' Underneath there was a phone number, a landline, in the same careful handwriting.

Nudge turned his head to have a proper look at the flyer. 'Give her a bell,' he said after he'd chuckled at her disclaimer.

'Look at this. It has to be over twenty years old. There's no way she's still going.'

'Only one way to find out.'

Danny had to admit that he didn't have any better ideas and so pulled out his mobile. Much to his surprise, the number was still in use. He pressed the loudspeaker button so that they both could hear and waited impatiently as Nudge stared intently at a coffee cup someone had left by the wall and, posing like a martial artist, swung his hand in a karate-chop motion that utterly failed to connect with it.

Danny was about to hang up when someone answered. 'Hello?'

He was caught off guard. 'Hello! Hi. My name is Danny Hook. Is this Adella Price?'

'Hello, Danny, is this about the Tesco order? I'm terribly sorry. I found the sausages under the table. They must have fallen out. Please apologise to your delivery driver for me.'

Nudge decided that this would be more entertaining than honing his ghost-fu and wandered over to Danny. 'No, I'm calling because I have one of your flyers. For the seance sessions, I was wondering if I could book an appointment?'

There was silence on the other end of the line for another moment. 'A flyer? Where did you find one of those? I haven't done a reading in years.'

Danny felt a familiar sinking in his spirits. 'That's okay. It was a long shot anyway. I just thought I'd ring on the off-chance. Sorry to bother—'

'—Who were you looking to contact?' She interrupted him.

Danny was wrong-footed again. 'I recently lost a friend. Very recently, really, and . . .' he looked at Nudge. 'I just feel that he's been with me ever since.'

There was another lull on the other end of the phone. 'Can you make it out to Harold's Cross this evening?' she said finally.

'Yes,' Danny said. 'Are you sure? I feel bad calling out of the blue like this.'

'Yes, I think it might be fun,' she said, clearly warming to the idea. 'It's just a seance you're looking for, right? Because I'm not sure where my tarot deck is. I think my grandchildren mistook them for those Pokémon cards back in the nineties.'

'A seance is fine,' Danny said hurriedly.

She gave him her address and Danny agreed to meet her there later that afternoon. 'But make sure you're here before six,' she cautioned. 'I like to watch *The Chase* with my dinner. It's supposed to help prevent Alzheimer's. I used to watch *Pointless*, but I prefer *The Chase* because it gives you a choice of three—'

'—I can be there in an hour if that's okay?' Danny interrupted.

'That would be fine. It will give me a chance to clean up.'

Danny thanked her and then hung up before the conversation could go off on any more tangents.

Nudge wasn't bothering to try and hide his laughter. 'You're not actually thinking of going to see her, are you? She sounds older than my granny.'

'I don't see any other options right now,' Danny said. Secretly, he agreed with Nudge but if they went home empty-handed, he would be faced with another night of drunken research on the paranormal. He typed the address into Google Maps. It was only about half an hour's bus journey away. That was lucky: Danny was working through his flask faster than he'd anticipated.

'C'mon!' he said. 'I need to commune with the spirits.'

Chapter 14

Adella Price lived in an old part of Harold's Cross, a narrow street of single-storey cottages which looked as if some absent-minded town planner had accidentally dropped them just off a busy street in Dublin instead of in the rural fishing village where they belonged.

Danny was intensely aware of how close he was to where they had crashed just over a week before. In fact, he walked out of his way to avoid having to cross the canal at the bridge where it had happened. If Nudge noticed, he seemed happy enough not to bring it up.

The journey had been as short as promised, so they killed time in a pub around the corner from their destination.

Danny was feeling sufficiently in touch with the spirit realm after two more Jamesons when they decamped from the bar. He was just about to turn off the main road when Nudge stopped short. 'I don't believe it!' he said.

Danny turned to look but couldn't see what had got him so riled up.

'It's Lisa,' Nudge said, pointing at a woman with short blonde hair across the road. Danny thought that he recognised her from the funeral but couldn't be sure.

'Who's Lisa?' he asked.

'She's who I was supposed to meet the day after . . . after Nadine's party. Remember?'

'Oh, yeah,' Danny said, looking at her with renewed interest. He could guess what had made his friend so irate. She had walked up to a stocky guy outside a café and embraced him before the two of them went inside.

'She's going out with *him*?' Nudge said incredulously.

'Who's "him"?'

'Niall. He's a prick from our course. He's been sniffing around her for months.'

'Well,' Danny started, trying to be as diplomatic as possible. 'It's not like she's cheating on you. You never actually did go on that date and, well . . .' Diplomacy failed. 'You're dead.'

'I know,' Nudge said, petulantly. 'But I'm not even in the ground a week. Whatever happened to a mourning period?' Nudge began to walk across the street.

'Where are you going?' Danny hissed, trying not to draw attention to himself.

'I just want to see if it's actually a date,' he said, stopping to allow a car to pass, presumably out of habit.

Danny looked at his watch. They were nearly late, their stopover in the pub having delayed them more than expected. He was also reluctant to stalk a possibly semi-grieving woman, given that he didn't have Nudge's advantage of being invisible.

'We're going to be late.'

Nudge had reached the other side of the road and was trying to look in through the window of the café. 'Just start without me. I'll catch up.'

'What about the tether thing?' Danny asked, feeling foolish that they hadn't come up with a better name yet.

'The house is practically on the corner. I'll be fine.'

Danny sighed and watched his friend disappear through the front of the coffee shop. It would be typical of Nudge to get dragged off to an unspecified afterlife just because his ego was bruised over a woman.

He had been right though. The address that they'd been given was barely off the main road, which just made the cottages' quaint, old-school styling more incongruous. Danny rapped on the door of Adella's house, disturbing a few flakes of ancient red paint, and then stepped back. There wasn't much in the way of a front porch, and he didn't want to loom over the woman when she answered.

The door opened unexpectedly quickly. Either Adella had been waiting eagerly for him or there just wasn't that much house to navigate.

'Hi, Mrs Price,' Danny said in the slightly-too-loud voice he reserved for the elderly and young children, having little experience with either. 'My name is Danny; we spoke on the phone earlier?'

'Of course, dear. I haven't lost my memory yet.'

Adella had either been a very short woman all her life, or else age had shrunk her. She barely came up as far as Danny's shoulder. Her hair had been shorn almost shorter than his own in what he was half-confident was called a pageboy cut. Either she was meticulous about maintaining the auburn colour or else L'Oréal should be requesting her body for medical research. A pair of sharp brown eyes surrounded by an ordnance-survey map's worth of lines stared out from underneath her fringe. Danny fought the urge to shield her from the gentle-but-persistent November breeze in case it blew her away.

'Great,' Danny said. 'Do you still feel up for doing a seance?' He wouldn't have blamed her for changing her mind. An hour probably made a lot of difference when there weren't all that many left in you.

'Yes,' replied the old woman. Although she didn't move from the door, Adella looked to be in two minds about something.

'Is everything okay?' he asked.

'How do I know you're not some sort of criminal?'

Danny had faced a lot of unusual things in the last week, but this still managed to catch him off guard. 'Excuse me?' he reacted, instinctively taking another step back.

'Only, they warn us about this, in our social club. About strange men asking to be let in and then stealing all our valuables.'

Danny looked about for support and, finding none, cleared his throat and did his best to appear as non-threatening as possible. 'If you're not comfortable with letting me in, then that's . . . I'm not a . . .' He stopped, at a loss. At the very least, he was glad Nudge wasn't around to see this. 'Should we maybe leave it, so?'

Adella looked him up and down. 'I think you're probably okay.' She slowly stood aside and ushered him in.

Danny was half-tempted to cut his losses and run but, after a heartbeat of indecision, he squeezed past her.

'Just know that I've arranged for my friend Joan to call in half an hour and if I don't answer, she's going to call the guards.'

At this, Danny paused in the doorway for a moment.

'Would you like a cup of tea? Tesco didn't have any Club Milks, but I have some Viscounts left if you'd like?'

'That would be lovely, thanks.' Danny said, deciding that he was going to be as agreeable as possible during this whole experience in the hope that he could get out of here without being charged with elder abuse.

He followed the old woman into the house. The front door led directly into a small living room and Danny had to step carefully to avoid knocking things over. A beige reclining chair took pride of place in front of a surprisingly modern-looking flat-screen TV where *Tipping Point* was playing on mute. The rest of the floor space was taken up by an overstuffed couch and an enormous collection of end tables, cabinets and shelves teeming with pictures and ornaments. The photos featured a collection of toddlers gurning at the camera, infants staring, wide-eyed, at the too-close lens and teenagers posing awkwardly with certificates or prizes. They ranged from ultra-HD to grainy, sepia-toned photos to Polaroids. Adella clearly had an extensive family.

She motioned for Danny to walk through the maze of obstacles to a small but nicely appointed kitchenslash-dining area. There were fewer pictures in here, although the ones that did adorn the walls were noticeably older. Danny's eyes were drawn to a black-and-white photo of two young women smiling awkwardly in bright white uniforms.

Adella caught him staring. 'That's my sister and me after I qualified as a nurse. Two in the family. Daddy was very proud, although, I still think he would have preferred at least one boy.'

Danny sat down, as directed, at an ancient Formica-topped dining table as the medium busied herself with the kettle and produced some chocolate biscuits, as promised.

'How long has it been since you've done a seance?' Danny asked.

'Oh, I haven't done it regularly in nearly twenty years,' Adella said, staring critically at the inside of a cup until she finally decided that it would be fit for guests.

'How did you get into it?' Danny asked.

She paused, as the kettle boiled, as if she'd never thought about the question before. 'I've always had the gift, of course, but I didn't start to use it properly until I transferred into hospice nursing. I would occasionally help some of the troubled souls transition and, I suppose, word got around.'

'You could actually see and hear them? These souls?' Danny asked. Her story sounded good, but he'd been soured by his other experiences so far that day.

'Oh yes,' she said solemnly, as she picked up two steaming cups and carefully started to carry them the short distance between the kitchen and dining table. 'The ones that hang around are usually lost and in need of some help. You just have to treat them with kindness and compassion.'

Nudge chose this moment to walk through her front door. 'The fucking neck on that prick. You should have heard him,' he announced, not bothering to lower his voice. "Oh, Lisa," he said in a nasally whine, "this must be so hard on you. If you ever need a shoulder to cry on . . ."'

'Jesus fucking Christ!' screamed Adella and promptly keeled over.

Chapter 15

Danny had done a first-aid course back in school, mostly because signing up qualified you for a day off actual classwork. The very serious man leading the lesson had spent a great deal of time explaining the steps to take after someone has a heart attack. The first few minutes of care, he had told them, could make the difference between the victim's life and death.

Regrettably, all this information had fled Danny's mind in panic as he surveyed the broken crockery, spilled tea and the octogenarian lying face down in the middle of it all. He tore his gaze away towards Nudge, who was staring down at the prone old woman in horror. They made terrified eye contact.

'She could see me!'

'What the fuck do I do?'

'You have to save her.'

'Save her how?' Danny asked, even as he moved gingerly to check for a pulse. That was definitely one of the steps, although he wasn't sure whether it was supposed to come before or after establishing an airway. He couldn't even really remember what 'establishing an airway' meant. So, the first thing Danny did was to try and roll her onto her side. She was surprisingly heavy for someone so slight. Her slack face pretty much told

Danny all he needed to know but, to be sure, he pressed two trembling fingers to the side of her throat. He probed around the area where he figured the pulse was supposed to be but found nothing. 'I don't think she's breathing,' he said.

'Well, don't just sit there. Do the thing. What's it called? CPR!'

Danny nodded and rolled the older woman fully onto her back and then hesitated. It was ironic that he'd had a first-hand refresher session on the process just the week before, but he'd been otherwise engaged at the time, being dead and all. He knew that it was supposed to start with the chest compressions though and there was something to do with a Bee Gees' song. He clasped both his hands over where he guessed the old woman's breastbone was and was about to start pushing when an unexpected voice interrupted him.

'What the hell do you think you're doing?' Adella asked. She stood, confusingly, a few feet from her own rapidly cooling body.

Nudge and Danny gawped at the standing Adella and then slowly, almost in unison, panned back down to the collapsed woman on the floor.

'Who is that?' she shrieked, pointing at the body. She then turned to Nudge. 'And who are you? How did you get in?'

A lightbulb switched on in the recesses of Danny's brain. 'You're a ghost,' he said and felt immediately stupid for doing so.

'A ghost!?' Adella scoffed. 'What are you talking about? That doesn't make . . .' She trailed off as she took in the body on the floor.

Now that Danny was looking at her properly, he could see similarities to Nudge's condition. Her outline was hard to define from the cabinets behind her and her voice had the same strange quality as Nudge's, not quiet but like dialogue that had been badly sound-mixed in a movie. You had to concentrate to hear them.

'Oh no,' she said, as realisation dawned. She looked again at Nudge and anger seemed to replace confusion. 'What the hell were you doing, storming in here like that? Were you dragged up?' she shouted.

'I'm so sorry,' he replied sincerely. 'I've gotten so used to people not being able to see me.'

'That's no excuse to act like a . . .' she struggled for a harsh enough word '. . . barbarian!' Then she seemed to remember something with a start. Her head whipped around to Danny. 'Well, what are you doing just sitting there? Save me!'

Danny snapped back to reality, or what approached it these days. 'Yes! Sorry. How?'

Adella stepped up to Danny's shoulder. 'Well, first move me away from all of this broken china, unless you want to drive shards of the stuff into my spine while you're doing the compressions.'

Danny moved to comply as her nursing training seemed to come back to her. 'I suppose there's no need to check for breathing, considering, so I need you to find the breastbone and firmly . . .' Adella trailed off and blinked, as if to clear her head. 'Firmly press down with the palms . . .' Again, she stopped as if interrupted and looked around in confusion.

Danny looked up from where he'd been pulling her body to a more suitable patch of floor. There was serious fear rising in her face now. Even more so than earlier.

'Adella, are you all right?' Danny really felt he was due some sort of award for asking stupid questions.

Nudge stepped towards her and then stopped, as if he wasn't sure what the protocol for ghost-on-ghost contact was. 'What's wrong?'

Adella was looking around her with increasing panic. 'No. No,' she muttered. 'This isn't right. This isn't how it's supposed to—'

It happened so quickly that both Nudge and Danny jumped back in fright, Nudge stepping entirely through a cabinet and Danny hopping backwards, still half-crouched, into the dining table.

As if someone had tied a bungee cord around her middle and then attached the other end to a speeding lorry, Adella was suddenly pulled completely off her feet and through the back wall of the house. Danny jumped up and got a split-second view through the back window of her flailing form as it was hauled, two feet off the ground, through the garden fence, before disappearing.

For a moment there was complete silence in the tiny cottage until the sound of a phone ringing made both men flinch in fright. It was an old landline, attached to the wall, between the kitchen and the living room.

'Who the hell could that be?' Nudge asked.

'I think it's Joan,' Danny said, still in shock.

'Who the fuck is Joan?'

*

Danny sat solemnly on the kerb a few doors down from Adella's house. The small street had been too narrow for the ambulance, so it had been parked further back on the main road as the paramedics shuttled their trolley over the short distance.

Once the initial panic about watching a disembodied spirit be yanked away against her will had passed, it had been replaced with an entirely new feeling of panic about being alone in a house with the corpse of a stranger. There didn't seem to be much call for continuing with the CPR, so Danny had done the only other thing he could think of and dialled 999. The ambulance had responded twenty minutes later and the paramedics only took a few moments to declare the obvious. The police had arrived shortly afterwards and were very curious to know how Danny had found himself in a house with a dead pensioner.

Danny had told the truth. Well, *obviously*, he hadn't told the truth, but he'd told a version that was close enough to the truth without getting himself sectioned. He'd explained his recent accident and showed the guards the flyer he'd obtained earlier. He recounted how they'd met as arranged and that the old lady hadn't closed the door properly after he'd come in. The door had blown open suddenly and the slam had given her such a shock that she'd keeled over.

Luckily, Adella's friend Joan had kept ringing and eventually, one of the guards had answered. She was able to confirm, once her initial shock had passed, that Adella had indeed planned a seance session. A few more minutes of questioning revealed that she'd also had a weak heart, and that this had not been her first heart attack.

A cursory search of her room had revealed a prescription that hadn't been refilled in over a month and so they were begrudgingly prepared to accept his explanation, although the older guard had told Danny that he would have to stay in the city for the next while until they completed their investigation.

Danny was just about to ask if he would be allowed to leave when he'd heard a commotion.

'The next of kin's arrived,' one of the younger guards had muttered to a paramedic.

Danny had craned his head to see a pale young woman push her way to the front door of the cottage. There was a brief moment of argument before the guard had let her in. It was almost a full half an hour before she'd re-emerged, while Danny waited on the kerb.

Nudge had been urging him to get out of there ever since they'd rung for the ambulance. The incident with Adella's spirit had terrified him and he looked like he wanted to get as far away from where it had happened as possible. But even though Danny couldn't explain why, he felt like he owed Adella's family an explanation. Although, God only knew what he was going to say to them.

At last the young woman came back out of the cottage, in conversation with the more senior of the guards. They talked quietly for a moment before he nodded in Danny's direction. The woman turned and fixed him with a gaze that made his mouth go dry. She said a few more inaudible words to the guard before walking purposefully towards Danny. 'I need to talk to you,' she said brusquely.

Then, to his surprise, she turned and stared Nudge dead in the eye.

'*Both* of you.'

Chapter 16

The three of them left the circus of high-vis jackets behind and made the short walk to a small park nearby. It was too late and cold for families to be wandering through it and too early for any teenagers to be surreptitiously smoking there, so they didn't have to worry about being overheard.

Well, they'd *eventually* made the short walk. The woman, who had introduced herself as Lucy, had to reiterate several times that she could see Nudge and then impatiently wait for both of them to pick their jaws up off the floor. After she'd explained that this was a conversation that should probably not be taking place within earshot of the police, they followed her into the rapidly darkening evening.

Lucy was bundled up against the cold in an oversized camelhair coat over a green woolly jumper and maroon cords. To Danny's eye it looked like each article of clothing had been taken from someone with a vastly different body shape, age and personal style, but he assumed it must be some sort of vintage, thrift-shop chic.

In the park, the steam that condensed in front of her face from the cold was joined by wisps of smoke as she lit a John Player Blue and, after checking that it wasn't too damp, sat down on a bench and examined them critically. She took a particularly deep drag on her cigarette before speaking for the first time since they'd met outside the house. 'So, what in the blazes actually happened?'

Danny looked to Nudge for support but his friend's delight in finding someone else who could see and hear him had apparently departed.

'Well,' Danny started, taking a nip from his flask to ward off the cold and the awkwardness of this conversation. 'We arranged to do a reading with Adella. Actually, we found her flyer at another medium's office. We went to a few today, you see? But they couldn't see Nudge. This is Nudge, by the way. I'm Danny—'

Lucy held up a hand to stop him and then pointed at Nudge. 'How about we start with how he ended up like this?'

Danny nodded and gave an abridged overview of their recent ordeals. Lucy didn't interrupt much except to make a face when he mentioned the other psychics they'd been to see. It was a nice face, Danny couldn't help but notice (and immediately felt guilty for doing so). It was also familiar. She must have been one of the many grandchildren in the photos that adorned Adella's house, Danny assumed.

He didn't quite get the reaction he'd expected when he finally explained how Nudge's abrupt appearance had caused Adella's demise. She let out a snort of laughter that descended to a fit of hysterical giggles. Seeing the alarmed expressions on both their faces Lucy held up her hands in an attempt to explain. 'Sorry, it's not what it looks like.' She took a deep shuddering breath and seemed to get a grip on herself. 'It's just, Adella spent her entire life helping send spirits to the other side and one ended up sending her.'

Her shoulders continued to shake slightly but Danny could see that there were tears in her eyes now as the shock wore off. He looked at Nudge, but he seemed equally as lost and uncomfortable about the situation. Luckily for everyone concerned, Lucy took a series of deep breaths and steadied herself before either of them had to try and console her. 'I told her that she shouldn't be living alone at her age,' she said, more to herself than anyone else.

'Were you two close?' Nudge asked.

Lucy looked up. 'We were. Once, at least.'

Danny was a bit out of his depth. His grandparents had all passed away before he'd hit his teens, so he'd never had to deal with that kind of loss as an adult. In fact, the only loss he'd really had to face was currently standing five feet from him.

'I'm sorry. I really am,' Nudge said. 'I didn't mean to scare her like that.'

Lucy leaned back on the bench, glanced down at her smoke, which had gone out, and flicked it in the general direction of the bin next to her. 'You weren't to know. You were probably the first ghost she'd seen in close to twenty years. It fades, you see? With age.'

'What fades?' Nudge asked.

Lucy stared at them with a dawning realisation. 'You boys really don't have a clue, do you?'

'No!' they both said. Danny tried to ignore the fact that this statement could pretty much sum up his life in general and not specifically his knowledge of the supernatural.

'Bloody hell.' She paused while she tried to gather her thoughts. 'It's not something you can exactly sum up in a sentence, you know?' she said defensively, seeing their eager faces.

'Just take your time,' Danny urged.

'Okay.' She took off her woolly hat and ran her hands through her long black hair in a way that resulted in Danny suppressing more guilty thoughts. 'Most people die and that's just it. Right? Their spirits or souls or what-have-yous just move straight on to whatever is next.' She studied them again as if she were making sure they were paying attention before continuing. 'Sometimes, though, people's spirits get stuck here, on this plane, instead of moving on. It's rare and usually only happens when a death is particularly violent, or the deceased has some powerful reason not to cross over.'

'Unfinished business,' Nudge said.

Lucy nodded. 'That's the line these days, yeah.'

'So, what happens to them?' Danny asked. 'The stuck ones?' He tried not to make eye contact with Nudge as he did so.

'Some eventually pass on of their own accord,' Lucy replied. 'Others? Well, imagine a lifetime of not being able to speak to or interact with anyone. Several lifetimes.' Now *she* was the one trying to avoid Nudge's gaze. 'The ones that stick around can become detached from reality over time. Not a person any more really. Just an echo that can't move on.'

Nudge did not look delighted at this information.

'But Adella, she mentioned that she could help souls pass on,' Danny urged.

Lucy nodded, although her expression told them that she didn't share Danny's optimism. 'Yes, she could help them. A lot of the time they were just confused as to what had happened and needed someone to help them make sense of it.'

'So could she always see them?' he asked. It was something that had really been bothering him.

'As long as she could remember, anyway. Some people are born with the ability.' She pointed at herself. 'It's hereditary, obviously.'

'Then how come I can see them?' Danny asked. As far as he knew, nobody in his family could talk to the dead. His dad had mentioned occasionally that his grandad had been too fond of the spirits in life, but Danny didn't think he'd meant it literally.

Lucy lit another cigarette. Danny got the feeling this was more out of nervousness than any desire to smoke it. She looked at him. 'You died, didn't you? For a short time at least? In that accident you mentioned.'

He nodded.

She looked thoughtful as she exhaled another stream of smoke. 'There are stories about people who've died and come back. That, with training, they could see the other side again. I once read about a sect of monks. They would slow their hearts to a standstill with a special tea and then, once it had gotten to the point that it stopped completely, they'd be revived. The story goes that they would then spend years meditating, praying and training their minds until they were finally able to reach a state of consciousness that let them see the other side again.'

Danny and Nudge looked at each other.

'What's that got to do with me? I couldn't even get through my first session of the Headspace app,' Danny said.

'Well, later research into the area has suggested that the state of mind that they were working to achieve was . . .' She looked embarrassed.

'Was what?' Nudge asked, curiosity overtaking his obvious dread at spending an eternity as an undying echo.

'Was remarkably similar to how it feels to be a little drunk,' she finished.

There was a moment of shocked silence as the two men took this in.

'You're kidding me?' Danny said finally.

'I bet the monks who spent years meditating felt pretty stupid when they heard that,' Nudge added.

'That makes no sense,' Danny complained but, even as he said it, he knew it wasn't quite true. Alcohol did seem to suppress that part of his brain that couldn't help obsessing over the past or worrying about the future. Wasn't that just what meditation was all about? Being completely present?

'It does explain why you can only see me when you're pissed, *and* why you've only been able to see ghosts since the accident,' Nudge said.

Lucy stood up from the bench and stretched her back. 'Yeah. It's like a car radio, you know?'

'What?' Nudge asked when she didn't immediately elaborate.

'Well, it has pre-set stations and it's able to go between them automatically. People like me and Adella have both

138

the living and the dead stations pre set. We can switch between them at will.'

'Okay?' Danny said in a voice that he hoped gave the impression that he was absolutely following but also to please continue.

'Whereas you had to manually navigate to the dead station.'

'By dying,' Nudge chimed in helpfully.

'Yes, but now your "radio" has saved it as a pre-set and you can switch back at will.' She glanced down at his flask. 'Well. *Almost* at will.'

Danny nodded. He'd broadly understood the analogy, despite not having a car or having listened to the radio in ten years. 'Okay, well that clarifies the "how", I guess, but not the "why"? Why is Nudge still here and how come he's tethered to me?'

Lucy raised an eyebrow. '"Tethered"?'

'Ever since that night on the canal I've felt this pull,' Nudge explained. 'Like something's trying to drag me away. Staying next to Dan is the only thing that stops it. Like he's an anchor and if I get too far away . . .' Nudge trailed off.

'Could this "pull" be whatever comes next trying to get him to move on?' Danny asked, hoping that it might be that simple.

'This pulling force. Is it coming from a consistent direction?' she asked.

Nudge thought about it, then nodded and pointed off to his left, back the way they'd come, towards the canal. It occurred to Danny that this was the same direction that Adella had been pulled in after she'd passed away. He was about to comment on this, but Lucy spoke over him.

'And your accident. It happened near here?' she asked. There was a level of concern, of urgency in her voice, that hadn't been there before.

Nudge nodded again. 'Yeah, literally five minutes up the road.'

'What is it?' Danny asked, forgetting about Adella for a moment.

Lucy shook her head, as if to clear a troublesome thought. 'I'm not sure. I'll need to look into it. As for why you're linked to him, that's more straightforward.'

'It is?' asked Danny. The last few days had really warped the definition of 'straightforward'.

'Isn't it? You both died, only one of you came back. Nudge must have felt this pulling sensation and instinctively reached out and latched onto your spirit as it came back into this world. Like a drowning person grabbing onto someone else in the water. What was the last thing you remember before you blacked out?'

Danny avoided making eye contact with Nudge. 'I was trying to get us both out of the car. Trying to pull him out.'

'You were trying to save him. In a way, you may have,' she said.

'So, what? We're just stuck together now for the rest of our, well, *his* life?' asked Nudge.

'Can't you help?' Danny added, hoping it didn't come across too much like begging.

Lucy clawed her hair with her hands in frustration. 'Look, this was never my thing, Okay? This doesn't make any sense.'

Once again, Lucy was met with a pair of blank, uncomprehending stares. 'I mean, it's not a standard ghost MO. Spirits usually hang around because of particularly violent deaths or unfinished business. As tragic as your accident was, that doesn't sound like what's happening here.'

Danny nodded slowly. 'Okay, so we figure out what's causing this pulling force and then maybe he'll be able to pass on.'

'Maybe.' She didn't sound confident. 'Yes?'

This last comment was addressed to Nudge, who had raised his hand. His oversized jumper made him look like a small child, albeit one with a wild school uniform. 'Are vampires real?' he asked.

Lucy looked at him and, realising he wasn't joking, turned to Danny for support. 'Did he suffer brain damage in this crash?' she asked.

'No, he's always just been sort of like this.'

'Well, excuse me!' Nudge said sulkily.

Lucy stood up from the bench. 'Look, I have to go. Give me your number and I'll ring if I figure anything out.' She pulled a mobile from the pocket of her overcoat. At least, Danny assumed it was a mobile. It was enormous: like she'd accidentally brought her TV's remote control with her. It still had buttons; Danny couldn't remember the last time he'd seen a phone without a touchscreen.

'I dropped my smartphone last week,' she explained, seeing their reaction to the artefact. This is all I have while I get it replaced.' She seemed not to be used to it yet, as it took her almost two minutes of muttered swearing to get the contacts section open before she handed it over to Danny to type his number in.

He did so and then hit 'call' immediately afterwards so that her number popped up on his own. She was currently their only hope at figuring this out, so he wasn't comfortable with a 'we'll call you' deal in this instance.

'I'd better go,' she said, trying to disappear further into her coat so that there was as little face exposed to the cold air between her collar and hat as possible. 'I have family to call.'

Danny and Nudge were loath to let her walk away after providing so few answers but said nothing and just trudged alongside her back to where she'd parked her car.

Between the mobile and the car, they were beginning to identify a pattern. The off-white 1996 Ford Fiesta made Nudge's late Vitara look elegant. As Danny stepped aside to allow Lucy to open the door he could see where rust was beginning to eat into the door panel and wheel arch.

'It's an old family heirloom, okay?' Lucy replied tersely to their unasked question.

Danny and Nudge kept their opinions to themselves, not wanting to alienate the only person they'd met so far who could possibly help them.

Lucy paused as she sat into the driver's seat before closing the door. Danny was willing to bet it was because the window didn't wind down any more.

'I'm sorry about this,' she said, looking at Nudge.

This seemed strange coming from the granddaughter of someone who, less than two hours ago, they'd literally scared to death.

'Sorry for killing your granny,' Nudge replied, as circumspect as ever.

'I'll figure this out,' was all she said in reply. She closed the door and started the engine. After only two false starts, it puttered away into the evening.

'Well,' Danny said, grasping for a sentence that could possibly sum up their afternoon.

'Yeah,' Nudge replied, watching the car disappear around the corner. 'She's a fucking ride.'

'Jesus, Nudge!' Danny exclaimed in exasperation. 'She's our only hope of sorting this out. Could you not?'

'I was just saying,' Nudge retorted defensively.

'Anyway, I don't think the best way to introduce yourself to a woman is by killing her granny,' Danny added.

'I suppose,' Nudge agreed as they started in the direction of the bus stop. He stopped. 'We didn't tell her about Adella getting yanked through the wall.'

Danny realised he was right. 'I was going to,' he protested. 'But then she started talking about meditation and monks and I got distracted. Hopefully she'll be in contact soon and we can tell her then.'

'Yeah, can't wait,' Nudge said, suddenly gloomy.

'What's up with you?'

'I thought once we found someone else who could see me that we'd have some answers. But all I have is more questions.'

'Look, at the very least, we know that there are other people out there who can see you.' Danny didn't add that it had taken a considerable weight off his mind. 'If Lucy can't help us then she might know someone else who can. Or we'll find them ourselves.'

Danny was acting more confident than he actually felt and Nudge knew it, but he seemed to at least appreciate the effort. 'Yeah, we just need to get the contact details of some of those drunk monks,' he said with false cheer.

Danny leaned against the bus stop and tried his best to retreat inside his coat as much as possible.

'Danny?' Nudge said after a moment of silence. He sounded like he'd been deep in thought.

'Yeah?'

'Do you think those monks needing to get shitfaced is why they ended up inventing Buckfast?'

Chapter 17

The oddest thing about discovering that everything you know about the concept of life and death is totally wrong is how quickly normal life bleeds back in.

Danny was considering this with some self-pity as he waited for his second session with Dr Choi. He might have just learned that there was a hitherto unknown plane of existence where the unquiet dead roamed, but if he didn't show up to today's session, he'd have to pay a cancellation fee.

The only change to the waiting room between now and his last visit was the addition of Nudge, who was pacing in front of the couch. 'I still don't see why you're bothering with this,' he said.

Danny didn't reply. They had been over it enough times at this stage. Also, he was trying to convince the therapist that he was doing better and talking to himself in the waiting room felt like falling at the first hurdle.

He hadn't originally intended on bringing Nudge with him. While he knew he didn't actually have a choice about him tagging along, Danny had been fully intent on not performing the necessary 'meditations' to make him visible. The incident with Adella had shaken his friend considerably though and he had become more and more agitated during the periods where they weren't able to talk to one another. It had led to a big argument the night before. Nudge didn't see why Danny still had to go to therapy, if they knew what he was seeing was real. Danny figured that Nudge was worried that Dr Choi would somehow convince him that he was still hallucinating.

If he did have to go, then Nudge had begged him to still drink enough so that they could see and hear one another. He had fully convinced himself that, if they didn't check in properly each day, their tether would weaken and he would be abducted, like Adella had been.

Danny had wanted to refuse: the sane choice would have been to refuse.

But Nudge had been so afraid.

So, he'd gone as close to the margin as he dared, stopping immediately after Nudge had faded into the foreground.

It had seemed like the right thing to do at the time but now, sitting in the psychiatrist's waiting room, he was more than a little concerned that the doctor would be able to tell he'd been drinking. Turning up to your therapy appointment drunk didn't really sell the fragile-but-trying image he was trying to put across.

Dr Choi's receptionist informed him that he could go up. Danny used the loud tramping of his Converse on the wooden staircase as an opportunity to give Nudge one last warning. 'I swear. If you take one step inside that door, I'll go teetotal.'

'Don't worry. I'll wait out here and stare at the wall. It's more interesting than you are anyway.'

They reached the top of the stairs and with a final glare at Nudge, Danny knocked on the door to the office. It was answered mid-knock and both Danny and

Dr Choi looked slightly surprised to see the other there so soon.

'Danny. Sorry, I didn't mean to jump out on you there,' the therapist said, stepping past him out into the hall. 'Go on in and sit down. I just need to use the toilet and I'll be back to you.'

Danny nodded and walked into the office as the doctor made his way down the stairs. He had only taken two steps into the room when he was forced to stop short in surprise. He was not alone. A young blonde woman was sitting, cross-legged, on one of the small wooden chairs that lined the wall beside where the doctor normally sat.

Danny's first thought was that Dr Choi had an intern working with him today. However, by her wan expression and the threadbare blue dress she wore under a white apron, she looked like someone more familiar with receiving psychiatric help than giving it. Perhaps Dr Choi thought that Danny would benefit from a group session? Or maybe he'd just double-booked? Either way, Danny mused, it was a bit unprofessional for him not to mention it before letting him walk in here. He must have been really bursting to use the bathroom.

'I'm so sorry,' Danny said, trying not to spook the young woman. 'I didn't know anybody else was in here.'

She didn't respond immediately. In fact, she looked about the room as if trying to find who he could be talking to.

'Are you seeing Dr Choi as well?'

Whatever he was prescribing her, it clearly wasn't working. She seemed very alarmed at being addressed. 'You can see me?' she whispered, as realisation dawned for both of them.

'Oh, for fuck's sake,' Danny said as he recognised the signs.

Like Nudge and Adella, the blonde girl was only barely avoiding fading into the background completely. A dim part of his brain chimed in that at least he no longer had to wonder what a person from the Georgian era looked like. What he'd taken as some sort of eccentric period costume was probably what the poor girl had died in.

She shot up from the chair. 'You can really see me, can't you?' She looked both terrified and excited at the prospect.

'Yes. I can,' Danny said, pinching the bridge of his nose and squeezing his eyes shut in frustration. 'What's your name?'

'Elisabeth, sir. Well, Lizzy is what everyone called me. Back when I was alive, I mean.'

'Who's she?' Nudge stuck his head around the corner, having heard the sound of voices.

'It's another bloody ghost,' Danny whispered back. 'Keep a lookout for the doctor.' He turned back to Lizzy. 'Hi. I know this must be exciting, to be able to speak with someone, but I really can't have you here while . . .' He trailed off as he realised something. 'Do you listen in on all of the therapy sessions?' he asked, scandalised.

Lizzy gave a good attempt at a blush, considering she looked like she'd been dead for over a century. 'Sometimes,' she said defensively. 'I don't have much else to do. There's Dr Reeder downstairs, of course. He's nice but I've never thought feet were that interesting and, well, I know it's snooping but I figured I was never going to tell anybody anyway. With me being dead and all.'

Nudge had walked into the room now and stood level with Danny. 'That actually makes a lot of sense,' he said, after thinking about it for a second. 'Hi, by the way. I'm Nudge. I'm a ghost too,' he added brightly.

'Please!' Danny said, trying to keep his voice as low and even as he could. 'Would you both mind stepping outside so that the nice doctor doesn't institutionalise me?'

Lizzy ignored the question. 'I know you,' she said, pointing at Danny. 'You were here last week. General Anxiety Disorder with secondary OCD, right?' she said in a disconcertingly upbeat tone. 'You couldn't see me then though?' she added.

'A lot has happened since,' Nudge said.

'You must be the friend who died,' Lizzy said in the same delighted tone of voice that was slightly at odds with what she was actually saying. 'And you're a ghost too. Brilliant! I haven't met a new one in years.'

'Please!' Danny managed to choke out. 'Can you just—'

He was interrupted by the sound of Dr Choi's foot-steps on the landing. Danny and Nudge looked at one another and then back to Lizzy, who had taken the opportunity to sit back down as she heard the therapist approach.

'Get her out of here!' he whispered to Nudge, and threw himself into the armchair opposite the door just as the doctor came in.

'Again. Sorry about that, Danny. I've had back-to-back sessions since eight and I haven't had a moment,' he said as he settled into his chair.

'No problem,' Danny said in what he hoped was a neutral voice as he studiously attempted to keep looking straight ahead.

Off to the therapist's right, Nudge and Lizzy were engaged in a whispered argument.

'C'mon. Let's leave them to it,' he heard Nudge say.

'But I want to see what happens. A session with someone who "sees things" that are actually there. It's fascinating.'

'Well, yes. I suppose it is,' replied Nudge in the tone of someone who'd actually quite like to stay, now he'd thought about it. 'But we need to respect his privacy.'

Danny thought that this was a little rich coming from someone who would regularly break into his flat even before they'd been supernaturally tethered to each other, but continued to give Dr Choi his full attention.

'So, how have you been?' the doctor asked.

'This is textbook,' Lizzy whispered. 'Give the patient the illusion that they are controlling the direction of the session but steer it in such a way that the conversation moves towards cognitive-behavioural patterns you want to work on.'

'I'm doing better,' Danny replied, trying to ignore the running commentary. 'The past week was tough. I still feel very raw, but you were right about the sleep. I felt more capable of handling things once I got a few nights' consecutively.'

'I'm glad to hear that,' the doctor replied, making a few notes on his pad. 'And have there been any more hallucinations?'

Danny didn't answer. He was distracted by the fact that Lizzy was leaning forward out of her seat to peer at the therapist's notes.

'I'm sorry?' said Danny, suddenly remembering himself.

'I asked whether you've seen your friend since we last spoke. Or had any other type of hallucination?' he repeated.

Behind his right shoulder, Danny saw Nudge try to gently grasp Lizzy by the arm to lead her away, only for his fingers to pass straight through. He turned to look at Danny and mouthed the words, 'What do I do?'

'No,' Danny said, after a pause to consider how well and truly fucked he was. 'You were right. It must have been the lack of sleep and the stress. I haven't had any hallucinations since.'

'Excellent news,' said the therapist, scribbling some more.

'He doesn't believe you,' Lizzy said, still looking at the notebook from her perch.

'You can read that?' Nudge asked.

'It's shorthand. I learned it from watching him transcribe his session notes,' she said proudly. "H/O EV DPS" means "history of evasion and downplaying symptoms". He doesn't think that Danny's being honest.'

Can't imagine why, Danny thought to himself.

'Say that you sometimes hear distant voices when you're half-asleep,' Lizzy offered. 'That's really common.'

Danny repeated this for lack of any better lie and was relieved to see the doctor relax slightly.

'This is a lot easier when you actually tell me the truth, huh?' he said, offering a reassuring smile. 'That's quite common. Particularly when someone is stressed. It's probably happened to you dozens of times before but you're only noticing now because you're focused on it.'

'They're called hypnagogic hallucinations,' Lizzy said to Nudge. She seemed to be enjoying having an audience to show off to.

Behind the doctor, Nudge was mouthing, 'Should I go?' and pointing towards the door.

'You're concerned that the more vivid hallucinations may return, however?' the doctor asked.

'Yes!' Danny practically shouted, taking the opportunity to answer both, and then when Dr Choi looked at him strangely followed it up with, 'But no sign of Nudge so far, so that's something at least.'

'It's progress,' the therapist agreed. 'You just need to recall what we spoke about last week. These stress hallucinations are happening, in part, because of the guilt that you are carrying over the events of the accident.'

Danny nodded in response as he watched Nudge unsuccessfully try to get Lizzy to follow him as he made his way towards the door.

'You just need to keep telling yourself that it wasn't your fault.'

'That's what I've been saying,' Nudge said.

'I know,' Danny replied. To both.

'And that it was your friend's own poor decisions that led to his death'

'Hey!' Nudge said, turning back into the room to defend himself.

'I think that's maybe a little bit harsh,' Danny started, trying to mollify him.

'Damn right,' Nudge said hotly.

'Danny, the more you defend your friend's actions, the more you unconsciously put the responsibility for events on yourself.'

'I see,' Danny said, hoping that his response might be enough to end this line of questioning.

'I think it might help to say it out loud,' Dr Choi said.

'Excuse me?' Danny replied, trying to give Nudge the nod to get out while maintaining eye contact with the psychiatrist.

'Saying things out loud is a useful way to reinforce cognitive-behavioural changes,' Lizzy added helpfully.

'You stay out of this, Downton Abbey!' Nudge said.

'By acknowledging the responsibility that your friend had in his own death, you will better be able to accept that it wasn't your fault,' explained Dr Choi.

Behind the doctor, Nudge's shoulders slumped. 'Just tell him what he wants to hear, Dan. He's right anyway.'

'The accident was not my fault,' Danny started. He made eye contact with his friend over the shoulder of the doctor. 'It wasn't Nudge's either. We just got unlucky.'

'That's a start.' Dr Choi said, smiling. 'I'm not trying to get you to demonise your friend, Danny. You just have to accept that people make their own decisions. You can't be responsible for them all.'

'He's very good,' Lizzy said.

Danny got the impression that she might have developed a small crush on the doctor.

'Okay, let's talk about alcohol,' Dr Choi continued.

'What about it?' Danny said, trying to keep the guilt out of his voice.

'In the aftermath of a traumatic event, it can be very easy to use alcohol as a coping method,' he said. 'Especially in this country.'

'What's that supposed to mean?' Nudge asked. He clearly did not share Lizzy's affection for the doctor.

'Dr Choi is from *San Francisco*,' Lizzy said in an awed tone, pronouncing the city's name like it was some fabled place, like Camelot or Oz.

'It's been tempting,' Danny said, cautiously trying to think through his sentence. 'I had a setback immediately after our last session.'

Admit to something small to pull focus away from the bigger issue that you don't want to talk about. Evading psychoanalysis 101. It really was all coming back to Danny.

'That's to be expected. Progress isn't always a straight line.'

'It's just been hard the last few days because I haven't had anything to distract me,' Danny said. 'I hope that when I get back to work that will help.'

'Distractions *can* be helpful,' Dr Choi conceded. 'They can keep us from dwelling on negative thoughts. What I don't want is for you to use work as a distraction from dealing with your recovery. That can sometimes be as harmful as alcohol.'

Danny figured that he couldn't just keep nodding silently, like the dog from that insurance advert. 'What do you mean?'

'It can be easy to treat our surface-level symptoms with distractions and fairly basic lifestyle changes but that's only a temporary fix unless you make the necessary behavioural changes to address the root cause.'

'So, more CBT then?' Danny asked, with a resigned sense of foreboding. Danny had never enjoyed the journalling and identifying thinking errors that went along with this. If he had his way, his own thoughts and emotions would be none of his business.

'That's cognitive behavioural therapy,' Lizzy said to Nudge.

Dr Choi smiled. 'I'm afraid so. Everything else – the medication, the distractions – is just a band-aid without significant changes to your thinking patterns.'

Danny was about to reply when the doctor interrupted him. 'How have your Intrusive Thoughts been since the accident?' Dr Choi asked. He managed to pronounce both capital letters. Danny wondered if they practised how to do that in medical school.

'Fine,' he replied simply. He could sense where this particular conversation was going and wasn't happy about it.

'Have you been experiencing any more suicide- or self-harm-related Intrusive Thoughts?' the doctor asked bluntly.

Danny avoided Nudge's gaze, focusing on the older man sitting opposite. His mind flitted back to his panic attack before the funeral and the sleepless night after the crash. 'Some, immediately after the accident,' he admitted. He was getting flustered now. It had been too long since he had talked about any of this openly and it was even more difficult than he remembered. He really wished that Nudge and Lizzy weren't there to hear this. Or even just Nudge. Lizzy had presumably been there the first time around.

He tried to make eyes at Nudge again to get him to leave but Dr Choi interpreted this as avoiding his gaze and pushed the topic once more.

'That's to be expected, Danny, especially in light of recent events. It's just important to remember that these thoughts are a distressing symptom of your condition. They don't reflect an actual desire to commit any of the acts.'

Even Lizzy looked a little abashed now. Danny guessed this part was less fun when the person in question was able to maintain eye contact with you.

'No, seriously. I've been okay since,' Danny said. It was the truth. His life had been so full of genuine, real-life catastrophes since he'd learned about Nudge that his brain hadn't needed to throw any completely fictional ones at him.

'I am not trying to open up old wounds,' Choi continued in a soothing tone. 'It can be easy to forget lessons learned. In light of a fairly significant trauma like the one you just had, we need to make sure that the same issues don't occur.'

'I understand,' Danny said, trying to shut down this particular line of conversation before it went any further.

Nudge's face was a mortified mask. Danny couldn't tell if he was shocked by what the therapist had revealed or just embarrassed for intruding. Either way, he silently mouthed an apology and backed out of the room.

Chapter 18

The rest of the session was uneventful in comparison. Lizzy had enough awareness to follow Danny out of the office afterwards. Both she and Nudge started apologising as soon as they reached the landing but Danny just tiredly put a finger over his lips and they held off until they'd escaped out onto the street.

He had intended to find somewhere quiet around the corner to talk to both ghosts, but Lizzy pulled up a few feet from the door and refused to go any further. He took out his phone and began the now-familiar process of faking a phone call.

'I'm so sorry,' Lizzy said. 'I should have left. I didn't realise that having an observer there would hinder your ability to be open and honest. I feel that I've set back your progress.'

She really had absorbed a lot of the lingo.

'It's fine,' he lied. 'I was just surprised to see you there. How long have you . . .' he searched for a better word than 'haunted' '. . . been there?'

'Nearly a hundred and thirty years. Girl and ghost,' she said. 'I started working for the Pembrokes in 1891 as a scullery maid and then I died in 1893. Complications of childbirth.'

Once again, it was difficult to reconcile Lizzy's bubbly tone with the actual content of what she said. 'And you've just been hanging around all this time?' Nudge asked, so horrified at the implications of this possibility that he seemingly forgot his own apology.

The former scullery maid nodded.

Danny made a mental note to double-check what a 'scullery' was later.

'Did you have unfinished business?' Nudge asked.

The large smile that he'd begun to suspect was a permanent fixture on Lizzy's face faded slightly. 'I suppose that's what you would call it. I'm a bit hazy on the details. I remember wanting to make sure that my baby was okay.

'The Pembrokes were good people, you see. They didn't send me away when I got into trouble and they said that they'd look after my baby, seeing as how Peter, he was their eldest, was the father. But the next thing I knew, I was a ghost. At first, I thought that I was in purgatory, and it was my punishment for having a child out of wedlock, but Mr Pullman said that's nonsense and that religion is just an opiate of the working classes and that I had nothing to be ashamed of. But I got to watch over Oliver, that's what they named my boy, as he grew up. Mrs Fitzpatrick, the housekeeper, raised him as her own, so he was able to grow up here. He got an apprenticeship as a cooper in the Guinness brewery. Mr Pembroke organised it for him, which I thought was very decent of him, all things considered. A cooper in Guinness's could make a good living at the time. Not that it mattered, since Oliver joined the Fusiliers in 1915 and was killed at Gallipoli. That's in Turkey.'

Both men blinked silently in reaction to both the entire Victorian-novel's worth of intrigue and the breathless, unpausing way that the former maid recounted it.

'I'm so sorry. That must have been terrible,' Danny said eventually.

Lizzy's eyes brimmed with emotion. It looked like that whole story had come from very far back and Danny got the impression that it had built up more momentum than she'd expected. He could sympathise.

Just as quickly as it had gone, her smile returned. 'Thanks. You mustn't worry though,' she said in her now familiar bright tone. 'It was a very long time ago.'

'Sorry. Who is Mr Pullman?' asked Nudge.

'He's another ghost. A groom in the stables up the road. Kicked in the head by a horse in 1902. Very clever man. Terribly interested in workers' rights. A good friend of that James Connolly, or so he claimed. This was pre-death of course. James Connolly isn't a ghost, as far as I'm aware, at least. I suppose he could be. If there was ever a man to have unfinished business—'

'—And is this Mr Pullman around?' interrupted Danny, sensing an opportunity to throw a verbal railway sleeper under the tracks of Lizzy's monologue.

For the second time in as many minutes, Lizzy's smile dimmed. 'No. Not anymore. I haven't seen him for the past couple of weeks.'

'You mean, he's moved on?' Nudge asked.

'No,' she said thoughtfully. 'I thought so at first. I heard on the radio that they might be finally raising the minimum wage and I thought maybe that's all it took, but I think it's something else.'

'Is it something to do with this pulling sensation I'm feeling?' Nudge asked

Her eyes widened. 'You can feel it too? I thought it might just be me but when Mr Pullman disappeared, I thought, well, he was never one to be tied down to one place. Not like me and here.' At this she placed one of her hands against the walls of the building as if to reassure herself. 'But if he didn't have anything to hang onto, then it might have taken him.'

'So that's why you won't leave the building? You're tethered to it?' Danny asked.

She nodded. 'I suppose you could call it that. I used to wander a bit. Down as far as the main street sometimes to talk to some of the other spirits that live, well, not "live" around here but they stopped showing up and now, I don't dare go too far.'

'When did all of this start?' Danny pressed.

The former maid thought about it. 'Perhaps a month ago? It wasn't so strong to start with. Just a vague feeling in the pit of my stomach. I didn't even mention it to Mr Pullman when I saw him last. Since then, though, it's grown much stronger. I've never felt anything like it.'

'Did you not think about trying to move on?' Danny asked, as delicately as he could under the circumstances.

The ghost looked uncomfortable. 'At one point, maybe. After I heard about Oliver, I thought about it, all right. I just didn't know how,' she said. 'Now? I'm not sure I could even if I wanted to.' She looked downcast, then brightened up once more. 'Plus, things are much more interesting since the therapy practice moved in.

Speaking of which . . .' The ghost nodded at a blonde woman walking up the path towards them.

Danny smiled and pretended to still be on the phone as he stood aside to let her pass. She was maybe in her late forties, with immaculate hair and make-up.

'Sorry, I don't want to miss this. She's my favourite.' Lizzy said hurriedly, or even more hurriedly than usual. 'Bipolar disorder presenting in kleptomania,' she added, as if this explained everything. Seeing their blank faces, she clarified. 'She's addicted to shoplifting. She comes here as part of her court settlement. I hope we can talk again soon. I promise to wait outside with Nudge next time.'

With that, she followed the blonde woman back up the stairs.

'I'd only been wondering what the Georgians actually looked like. This was a weird way to find out,' Danny said, to fill the awkward silence between the two men after she left.

Nudge looked confused. 'Georgian? As in the country? She sounded Irish to me. Although the accent was weird. I assumed it was just a time-difference thing.'

'No,' Danny said. 'As in the Georgian period, you know? In history?'

'What?'

'It was the period under King George. Or Prince George?' Danny said, rapidly losing confidence in what he was saying. 'One of the Georges. In the 1800s.'

'No, I know that, you dick,' Nudge replied indignantly. 'There were multiple kings called George during the Georgian period. Also a prince, but technically that's considered the Regency . . .'

Danny looked at him, mouth agape.

'I did history as part of my degree, remember? Don't act so surprised. She was from the 1890s though, so that makes her a Victorian.'

Danny was simultaneously impressed that his friend had managed to retain so much from his degree and also bizarrely disappointed that Lizzy hadn't actually been a Georgian.

They walked in silence for a moment.

'Did you really remember all of that from your lectures?' Danny asked. It seemed increasingly that anything he'd learned in college had leaked away.

Nudge smiled, embarrassed. 'Not really. No. My mum was a fiend for *Pride and Prejudice* when I was growing up. I must have watched Colin Firth jump into that fucking pond a hundred times. I guess I kind of picked it up by osmosis.'

Danny was relieved. He'd already had his whole concept of life and death shaken to the core. Nudge spontaneously being an expert on British history would have been too much. He glanced back at the door through which Lizzy had disappeared. 'I'll text Lucy on the way back and give her an update.' Although, how he was going to phrase this so he didn't sound completely insane, he had no idea.

*

Their journey back to the flat was conducted in tense silence. Danny could feel Nudge's desire to talk about what he'd heard in the session with Dr Choi but, while he was normally a sucker for an awkward lull in conversation, he resisted in this instance. Unfortunately, Danny compensated for this discomfort by taking repeated anxious sips of his flask throughout their bus ride and, by the time they'd reached home, he had drained it completely.

Danny stifled a deep, jaw-cracking yawn as they tramped up the stairs to the flat. He felt emotionally exhausted, completely wrung out. He'd often felt like this after therapy sessions, as if the effort of confronting his thoughts and mental intrusions had taken a physical toll on him as well as a psychological one.

Now his head felt as if it were stuffed with fibreglass and he could feel the start of a headache brewing. His mood wasn't being helped by the fact that Nudge had kept throwing him sidelong, worried glances the whole ride home. Danny knew it was just the stress and fatigue from the session that was making him bad-tempered but each sympathetic look irritated him further. The smartest course would be to excuse himself and take some time to decompress, he knew. But the thing about going to therapy, the smug, rational part of his brain recalled, is that, just because you know what the emotionally healthy option is, doesn't mean you'll do it.

'Oh for fuck's sake,' he said, throwing himself into an armchair in the living room. 'Just ask.'

'Do you want to talk about it?' Nudge asked, tentatively.

'Why? Did you not get enough of an earful at the session?' The drink had made him mean, he could feel it. He'd gone way beyond the minimum amount of alcohol that he needed to see Nudge, so he was in no state to talk about this sort of thing.

'I know that things like this can be tough,' Nudge started. 'I just want you to know that you can talk to me about it.'

'Okay,' Danny said, with a sudden burst of manic energy. *Uh oh*, the rational synapse said. 'What would you like to talk about?' he continued. 'How about the toilets in the old science block at school. Remember them? That's where I used to go to have my panic attacks.' He wasn't sure where the anger had come from but it was here now, engulfing him, dragging him along in its wake, all the stress and resentment of his circumstances boiling over.

'Dan, I'm so sorry,' Nudge said, with a genuine catch in his throat. 'I didn't know.'

He's just trying to help. Go easy, the rational synapse tried to suggest. 'Because I didn't fucking want anyone to know,' Danny replied. 'Least of all you.'

Nudge reacted like he'd been slapped but Danny kept going. 'You always do this,' he continued. 'Why do you have to stick your nose into every part of my life? It was bad enough when you were alive.'

Are you listening to me at all? his rational synapse asked politely.

'Why can't you just mind your own fucking business?'

I'll take that as a 'no'.

'Why couldn't you have just gotten out of the fucking car?'

The words, when they came, seemed to have fermented out of the mix of bile and whiskey in his stomach without bothering to consult his brain.

Oh, so that's what that was, the rational part of his brain chimed in, as two weeks of pent-up frustration that he'd carried around with him like a weighted vest was released with one sentence. Tears were streaming down his face now; he wasn't sure when they'd started.

'That wasn't your fault,' Nudge replied quietly. He was edging towards Danny's chair like someone approaching a flighty woodland creature.

'It should have been me,' Danny said. These words had been rattling around his brain for so long that it was almost startling to hear them out loud.

'No, it shouldn't have,' Nudge said softly but firmly. 'I made my choice that night. You tried to talk me out of it.'

'If I'd—'

'—If nothing,' Nudge cut in. 'I'd made up my mind to leave and there was nothing that you could have done to stop me. Truth be told, I was as miserable as you that night.' After a beat, he added: 'Maybe not quite as miserable. You've had more practice.'

Danny snorted a laugh through his tears and wiped his eyes. 'I need a cup of tea,' he said, staggering into the kitchenette. Therapy was all well and good but something deep in his Irish genes refused to deal with this kind of situation without a cuppa.

As the kettle boiled they stood in awkward silence, although the angry tension had drained out of it.

'Can we talk about it?' Nudge asked.

Danny waited until he had a steaming cup in his hands before answering. 'It's not what you think,' he said eventually.

'I don't think anything,' Nudge said, the picture of innocence.

Danny motioned at Nudge to walk back through to the living area and he lay back onto the couch. Dr Choi's office may not have one but he could at least use it here. 'Look, I've always been anxious about everything. You know that better than anyone.'

Nudge nodded.

'But I didn't think that there was anything, like, *clinically* wrong with me. Wrong isn't the right word but you know what—'

'—I get what you mean. Go on.'

'I just thought that I was a worrier. Honestly, I assumed everyone felt the same way, but they were just better at hiding it than I was. It wasn't just the anxiety though: when I was a kid I'd get these intense, graphic thoughts, fears that something terrible would happen to me or to someone in my family. And so I developed these habits. I'd have to flick the light on or close the door four times, or else the thoughts would come to pass.'

'I never knew that,' Nudge said.

'Yeah, well, I'd stopped by the time I got to secondary school. Compulsions, they're called. Basically, repetitive actions you do to sort of fight negative thoughts. That's what OCD is, really. It's not being super clean or organised. Although maybe it is for some people. It's having these upsetting thoughts that you can't get rid of and that you, well, *obsess* over.'

'So those were the intrusive thoughts that the doctor mentioned,' Nudge asked.

'Yeah, that's the thing, the compulsions are more of a symptom than the real issue. You'll have the thought, *What if something happens to my family?* or, *What if I get sick?* and they trigger the compulsions.'

'But you stopped doing them?' Nudge said.

'*Kind* of,' Danny said hesitantly. 'I stopped doing things in patterns of four, sure, but the thoughts never went away. Instead, I would just obsess over them internally.' He shifted his weight on the couch. This was the first time he'd talked about it to someone outside of his immediate family. If talking like this in Dr Choi's office had made him feel like a crab without a shell, now he felt like a crab without a shell dangling over a pot of boiling water.

166

'I feel like I'm not explaining it correctly,' he back-pedalled. At least with his parents he'd had time to pre-pare what he was going to say. 'You get this notion out of nowhere, like, *What if I hurt myself?* That's the intrusive thought. Now, that would be bad enough on its own but suddenly, you're thinking, *I can't believe I just thought of self-harming. That's awful!* which leads onto, *Do I actu-ally want to hurt myself?* and then suddenly it's 3 a.m. and you're dwelling on how upset your mum is going to be when she finds out you're suicidal.' Danny reached over and took an awkward sip of tea from his semi-prone position.

Nudge had stood up and was now pacing the room. 'When did you go through all this?'

'My whole life really but it came to a head in my final year in college.'

Nudge stopped in shock. 'But we hung out all the time. How did I not know?'

'I was very good at hiding it,' Danny said. 'Until I wasn't. Eventually, my parents twigged that something was up. The part where I wouldn't move out of the foetal position might have been a clue. They put me in touch with Dr Choi and he helped me through the worst of it.'

'With CBD?' Nudge asked.

'CBT,' Danny corrected. 'CBD is the stuff that's in weed, I think. Although, that might have also helped,' he conceded. 'It's therapist-speak for basically trying to bully your brain out of bad habits. I did a lot of journal-ing and identifying errors in my thinking.' Danny took a deep breath. He felt simultaneously a massive sense of relief and terribly exposed. Intellectually, he knew that there was no way for Nudge to tell anyone any of this, but he still felt strangely vulnerable.

Nudge, to his credit, merely looked remorseful. 'I can't believe I didn't know any of this.'

Danny sat up from his reclining position. 'Nobody really knew the whole of it, to be honest. Not even my parents. They just kind of caught the worst of things towards the end.'

'I'm really sorry. About all of it. I wish I could have been of more help. Or any help.' Nudge stood awkwardly a few feet from where Danny sat. 'I'm glad you had professional support. I hate to think of you suffering like that alone.'

'Thanks, man.'

The brief period of silent male awkwardness was almost a relief after the intensity of the conversation. Danny was more practised at talking about his emotions than most but even he had reached his limit. He needed a nap, a takeaway and possibly one of the *Paddington* movies.

'I still think that someone with OCD should have a cleaner bedroom,' Nudge said eventually and then ducked instinctively as Danny threw a cushion at his head.

Chapter 19

'And we'd get the movie channels with that as well.'

They were in Danny's parents' back garden. It was the morning of Buster's christening and Danny had escaped outside to take a discreet swig of his flask and also to escape the chaos that seemed to go hand in hand with getting a toddler ready to leave the house.

'For the last time,' Danny said firmly. 'We are not upgrading to Sky.'

Danny had started leaving the television on for Nudge, set to a channel of his choice, while he slept or hadn't drunk sufficiently to connect yet. The increase in his electricity bill seemed like a small price to pay for some much-needed alone time. Unfortunately, Nudge was no longer satisfied with Danny's terrestrial channels and wanted him to pay for the upgraded TV package.

'I bet Sven has Sky,' Nudge grumbled.

'Go haunt him then,' Danny replied. He sipped his whiskey in irritated silence. This had been happening more and more. Things had cooled down since they'd had their talk after the therapy session but there was a very good reason he and Nudge had never lived together while he was alive: they would have got on each other's nerves, like they were starting to do now.

'There you are!' Danny's dad said from the back doorway. 'Some godfather you are, hiding.'

'What are you doing out here then?' Danny countered, guiltily hiding his flask behind his back.

'Also hiding,' the older man admitted.

'How's it going inside?'

Joe sat down beside his son on the bench opposite the back door, Luna trailing after in case anyone spontaneously produced sausages. It had never happened before but the dog lived in hope.

'There's been some progress,' his dad reported. 'Steff has stopped crying and your mum is helping her get changed.'

The early morning sun was startlingly bright, and the two men watched their breath crystalise in front of their faces in silence for a moment.

'It feels as if her Communion was only last year,' Joe said wistfully. 'She was a demon before that as well,' he added, somewhat less so.

'I remember,' Danny said. Steff's Communion outfit had included a parasol, something he recalled vividly because he'd received a smack across the back of his head with it after making fun of her dress.

'You'll be sick of aul' fellas saying things like this, but you watch! You're acting as Buster's godfather today and, before you know it, he'll be starting school.'

Danny tried to imagine this. He hoped that Buster's rate of growth would have slowed down somewhat by then, or else they'd be escorting a seven-foot behemoth to the gate of the local primary. 'That kid is going to go through some amount of school uniforms,' he said.

'What I mean to say,' Joe continued, although Danny thought he saw a brief look of pain flash across his face as

170

he anticipated that particular expense, 'is that life moves on quicker than you think. A lot of the time, it's bittersweet, like when I watched you two grow up so quickly, but it also takes us further away from the bad times.'

Danny looked up. He hadn't expected this.

'You've had a lot of the bad, son,' Joe said. 'Especially recently. I know men of my generation—' He stopped and corrected himself. '—I know that *I've* never talked about it. About how to deal with grief. I've lost people. Friends, parents, a sister. I felt worse than I thought possible but, like I was saying, time moves on. And although it took me further away from those I lost, it can also bring hope and joy if you let it.' Joe turned to look at his son. 'But you have to *let it*, Dan.'

Danny was caught off guard. He and his dad never spoke like this. While Joe had always taken anything to do with mental health seriously, he'd never really confronted Danny about it before.

'Nudge is gone, Dan,' Joe continued. 'God rest him. You have to accept that and start moving on.'

'I know that,' Danny replied.

'Do you?' his dad pressed. 'Your aunt told me that you'd asked her about that medium she saw after Noel died.'

'That was just—' Danny started to say, reeling internally. He was used to being able to control these types of conversations with his parents, to steer them towards safer waters, but he was on the back foot now '—stupid,' he finished weakly. 'Wishful thinking.'

Joe put an arm around his son's shoulder. 'Look, this isn't an intervention, although at some point we may need to discuss what happened to all of my whiskey.'

Danny looked up guiltily.

'Watering down my Jameson didn't work when you were sixteen and it doesn't work now.'

Danny flushed. 'I'll replace it,' he started to say, but Joe waved this away irritably. 'I don't care about that, Dan. I care about you thinking you need to hide it from us. Do you think you're the first one to turn to drink after losing someone?'

Danny thought about lying but couldn't bring himself to do it. 'Does Mum know?'

Joe gave him a raised eyebrow in response and Danny nodded. Of all the stupid questions he'd asked in the last few weeks, this one took the top prize. She'd probably been the one to send Joe out here.

'I'm trying, Dad. I swear,' Danny said.

Joe's face softened. 'This isn't me giving out to you, Dan. I just want you to know that you don't have to go through this alone.'

'Thanks,' Danny replied, his voice thick with shame. He'd been so preoccupied with Nudge's dilemma that he hadn't thought about how all of this might be worrying his parents. He and Nudge made wordless eye contact over his dad's shoulder. The ghost looked as guilty as Danny felt.

Steff, of all people, rescued him from having to explain himself further. 'So, this is where you are!'

All of them, living, dead and dog, jumped to find her standing at the back door. She wore a modest blue dress with a green wrap covering her shoulders and an expression that was equal parts stress and fury.

'Oh, she looks nice,' Nudge opined. 'Very classy.' He sounded relieved to have a distraction from yet another heavy personal conversation he'd inadvertently eaves-dropped on. This didn't stop Danny from shooting him a poisonous look at his comments.

'Is everything in the car?' Steff asked them.

'Yes, love,' their dad replied dutifully.

'We need to leave in twenty minutes!'

Both Hook men looked at one another. 'We're ready to go when you are, Steff,' Danny replied cautiously.

'I still have to do my make-up and I can't find Brian's shoes and Connor's family are starting to arrive at the church already.' Danny went to speak but was pre-empted. 'And that reminds me. No farmer jokes today!'

Both Danny and Joe tried to protest but were once again verbally steamrolled by Steff: 'That includes Cork jokes, hillbilly-incest jokes, banjo jokes and any talk about EU farm subsidies,' she continued, ticking the forbidden subjects off her fingers.

'That covers most of your speech,' Nudge said.

Joe stood up to try and make peace, but Danny waved him back to his seat. He wanted to show that he could still step up and be a functioning adult. Plus, he was the godfather, after all. 'Steff, go back upstairs and get your make-up sorted. I'll make sure Bust . . . Brian is ready.' He gently steered her back inside. As the door closed behind them, he thought he saw his dad give him a wink.

'Is everything else okay?' he asked as they made their way to the stairs. Her phone was buzzing constantly.

Steff shook him off and sat at the bottom of the stairs. 'No, it's not fucking okay, Dan! Connor's family keep asking for directions every five minutes. Chloe just tex-ted me saying that Sarah won't be coming because James will be there and don't get me started with our family.'

This last sentence was muffled as she sank her face into her hands. 'It's all falling apart. I just wanted to show everyone that I'm not some disaster teen mom!'

'I mean, technically, she stopped being a teen mom on her last birthday,' Nudge said, having followed them inside.

Danny ignored the ghost and squatted down opposite her. 'Listen, don't worry about our family, or Connor's, right? I'll take care of them.'

She looked up at him. 'Like, as in a hit?' she asked, a little hopefully.

He pulled her up off the stairs. 'No, look, I'm the godfather, right? We're a team now. Team Buster!'

'Team *Brian*,' she insisted.

'Yeah, whatever. I'll keep an eye on the families, okay?' She still looked sceptical, so he continued. 'This isn't my first rodeo. I'll keep Uncle Barry away from your college mates and I'll keep Sharon from singing. Until the end of the night anyway. I'm only one man.'

She started with, 'What about—' but it was Danny's turn to do the interrupting.

'—Don't worry about Connor's family. Add me to the WhatsApp group and I'll start directing them. I'll make sure they don't act up at the afters as well. You can worry about keeping your UCD mates from drinking all the booze.'

Steff smiled. 'I think I'll worry about inducting my son into the Church, Dan.'

Danny gently shooed her up the stairs. 'Yeah. Of course.'

'A lifetime of guilt and sexual repression awaits,' Nudge announced happily. 'Go, team Buster!'

'Team Brian,' Danny corrected him absentmindedly.

'What?' Steff said, from halfway up the stairs.

'Never mind.'

*

After ushering Steff into the arms of their mother to finish getting ready, Danny had taken charge of Buster. His nephew had been dressed in a romper that looked like a miniature suit, complete with a little waistcoat and bow tie. A matching flat cap sat on the bed beside him and Danny resisted the urge to hide it. Steff had explained earlier that the frilly white christening dress that he'd been expecting was no longer mandatory. Danny wanted to ask why she had decided to go with something that was even more embarrassing instead but had held his tongue as part of his new, supportive persona.

'Sorry, buddy,' he said as he struggled to fit the soft white booties over the baby's feet. 'I want you to know that this wasn't my idea.'

He spent most of the drive to the church keeping the child from removing and eating any of his accessories and trying not to respond to Nudge's grumblings. With the whole family packed into the car, the ghost had to make space for himself in the boot. It had been that or run alongside like a flamboyantly dressed member of the Secret Service.

The car park was full, and Danny pushed down the feeling of déjà vu at seeing so many people in formal wear milling about outside a church. As they stepped out of the car, they were mobbed by the crowd. Danny surveyed them critically, as it was his job to keep them in line for the event. Firstly, there was Buster's dad Connor's side of the family. After seeing them in person, Danny finally understood where Buster had inherited his size. Connor was tall and wiry but Buster's grandfather, Sean, was a huge man, easily six foot three, with broad shoulders and a keg-shaped torso. He had been shoe-horned into a navy suit that looked like it had been fitted several years and about three stone earlier.

He swept towards the Hooks as they got out of their car. 'There he is,' he announced in a Cork accent so thick that Danny could have probably cut swatches of it and used it to insulate his house. 'The man of the hour!' With Steff's blessing he put a hand under each of his grandson's armpits and Lion-Kinged him into the air. The rest of the O'Riordan clan surrounded Sean as he proudly bounced Buster up and down. Danny mentally dubbed this group The Farmers. He was aware that this generalisation would have earned him a stern look from Steff, but he wasn't planning on saying it out loud.

He turned his attention to the other crowd of familiar faces surrounding Danny's parents. The Hooks were mostly tradesmen. Today, the assembled uncles included a plumber, a carpenter, two electricians and a painter/decorator. Danny mentally categorised them as The Cowboys. This, again, was slightly unfair but he blamed his mum for making him watch *Oklahoma!* over and over as a kid. The Farmers and the Cowboys should be friends. Indeed.

Steff's friends from school and college were a bit of a wild-card group but, luckily, most of those wouldn't be attending the actual ceremony, just the party afterwards, so Danny was able to focus on the families.

As they began to file into the church, a tall, blonde woman that Danny guessed to be in her early thirties emerged from the Farmers carrying Buster. She had the largest dimples that he'd ever seen on an adult before, and they were only exaggerated by her big, warm smile as she cooed at Buster who was perched on her hip.

Danny's mum provided the introductions. 'Daniel, this is Helen. She's Connor's cousin and the godmother. Helen, this is Steff's brother, Daniel.'

Helen awkwardly moved Buster to one arm and held out her other hand to shake. 'Nice to meet you! All set?'

Danny shook her hand quickly so that she could return the child to both arms. 'I think so. Are you okay to hold him?'

Helen smiled down at Buster as she readjusted him. 'If you don't mind? I haven't got to see him in ages.'

'Not at all. Just let me know if your arms start to get tired.'

Together they walked inside the church and made their way up the middle aisle to where everyone was taking their seats.

As they walked, Danny muttered to Helen. 'Who are the liabilities on your side?'

Helen looked at him, shocked. 'I'm sorry?' she whispered, struggling not to break stride.

Danny realised that he could have probably phrased that better. The responsibility, and the whiskey, had made him bold. *Could she tell I'd been drinking?* he worried briefly before realising that it didn't matter, he had made a promise and he would need his opposite number to be on the same page if it was to work. 'We're the godparents. Connor and Steff have enough to worry about today without any family drama. It's up to us to make sure we keep them onside. Now, who should I be keeping an eye on?'

Again, Helen just stared at him in confusion. They had reached the top of the church now but the grandparents, parents and the priest were having a brief chat off to the side, so they still had time to themselves.

'You need to volunteer some of your own intel,' Nudge said, sidling up to the altar beside him. 'As a sign of good faith.'

Danny sighed. There had been a classic spy movie marathon on TCM this week, and Nudge had picked up a lot of the lingo. He wasn't wrong though.

'Do you see the guy in the too-tight grey suit in the third row there?' Danny said, nodding his head in the man's direction. 'That's our uncle Barry. He got divorced two years ago and now he tries to chat up younger women. He was a menace at his son's twenty-first.'

He then turned and surreptitiously nodded towards a woman in her early sixties in the second row, who was deep in conversation with his mum. 'That's my mum's sister, Sharon. She used to sing with the Black sisters back in the day and once she has any amount of drink in her, she'll start singing and won't stop until closing time.'

Helen looked worried, and Danny briefly wondered if he'd maybe overdone it with the whiskey. It was getting hard to tell these days. She was probably terrified at what kind of weird family her cousin had got himself involved in. Thankfully, her expression changed to one of resignation. 'Okay,' she said. 'See the two fellas sitting at opposite ends of the second row?'

Danny scoped them out of the corner of his eye and indicated that he did.

'That's Liam and Thomas, Sean's brothers. They can't stand one another,' she continued.

Danny noticed both their resemblance to Buster's grandad and the dirty, sidelong looks they were throwing at one another. 'Really? Why?'

'I'm not sure. Some say it was over a woman. Others, the ownership of a particular field. Possibly both.'

Danny ignored Nudge's guffaw and counted to ten in his head so that he could keep his promise to Steff about rural jokes, as Helen continued. 'The "why" doesn't matter though. We just need to make sure that they stay away from one another once drink is taken. Usually, their wives would put manners on them but Auntie Sandra has shingles and wasn't able to make it, so Thomas will be the one to look out for. He's the one on the left . . . Now, my cousins are mostly fine, except for Daragh in the third row there. He got deep into that cryptocurrency thing . . .'

Danny listened and committed as much of it to memory as he could, while worrying about what kind of weird family his sister had got herself involved in.

Chapter 20

The ceremony had gone pretty much according to the steps that Danny had hastily googled the day before. The priest hadn't tried to catch them out with any trick questions regarding their commitment to Catholicism and Danny had, however dubiously, taken responsibility for Buster's spiritual and moral upbringing.

With all that pesky religion out of the way, the families were able to move onto the most important part of the christening, the afters, at The Farrier, a large pub located conveniently around the corner from the church. It was the *de facto* Hook family venue for these sorts of things, having played host to at least five funerals, half a dozen christenings, and Uncle Barry's ill-advised, post-divorce celebration.

Danny was about to head inside when he noticed that Nudge was hanging back, standing on the opposite side of the road, staring up at the pub, his brow furrowed in confusion.

Danny took his phone out of his pocket and pretended to receive a call, wandering back to his friend. 'Hey!' he said, snapping his fingers in front of Nudge's face. 'What's up?'

'I can't go inside,' Nudge said.

'Look, I get that they're an acquired taste but, once they get a few drinks in them, my family are actually—'

'—It's not that,' he insisted. 'It's like the opposite of the tether between me and you. There's something stopping me from going inside.'

'What? Like a force field?' Danny asked sceptically.

'Kind of.'

Danny turned to regard the pub again. It didn't look sinister. At least, no more so than any other gastropub. 'What do you think it means?' he asked.

'Fucked if I know,' Nudge replied.

Danny stared at the doors through which his family had just walked. 'Do you think it's safe?'

Nudge just shrugged in response.

Danny stood, feeling helpless, and, for the hundredth time, wished there was a supernatural 999 number he could call to deal with this sort of stuff. Before it occurred to him that there technically was. He scrolled through his contacts to find Lucy's, hestitating before dialling. They hadn't heard from her since the conversation after Adella's death, the previous week. He had been trying to avoid crowding her but figured that this counted as an emergency.

She answered on the fifth ring. 'Hello?'

'Lucy. Hey, it's Danny from . . .' *Killing your granny.* '. . . Adella's.'

'Danny. Hi. Is everything okay?'

She didn't exactly sound thrilled to be hearing from him but Danny took the fact that she didn't immediately hang up the phone as a good sign and soldiered on. 'I hope so. Something weird is happening. I'm outside a pub and there's something preventing Nudge from entering. Like a force field.'

'Tell her I said that it feels spooky as shit,' Nudge urged Danny.

'Nudge says that it feels unusual.'

'Where is this place?'

'Do you know The Farrier?'

'The one in Drimnagh?' She sounded surprised.

'Yeah.'

There was silence on the other end of the line for a moment. 'I'll be there in ten minutes,' Lucy said eventually.

Danny felt a millisecond of relief before panic took over again. Suddenly a vague supernatural danger seemed preferable to explaining Lucy to his family.

'Do you think it's dangerous?' he asked her.

'Better safe than sorry.'

The phone went dead. He stared at it blankly for a few seconds before making a decision. 'She says she's on her way,' Danny said to Nudge. 'Wait for her here. I'm going to head in.'

'What if there's something terrible in there?'

'There is,' he replied over his shoulder. *And if Buster's christening is ruined, she's going to be a nightmare.*

He edged cautiously inside. As often as he'd been here, he was still surprised when he walked in. Growing up, The Farrier had been the dictionary definition of a Dublin old man's pub. It had been bought by new owners a few years before, however, and they had gutted it. Now it was a bright, airy gastro affair.

Steff had booked out a series of tables in the far corner. There had been a definite swell in the party numbers since the church, mostly Steff's school and college friends but also a significant number of actual family members who had sidled in, muttering something about having got the time wrong for the ceremony. Danny could just about put a name to all of his cousins on a good day, but he drew the line at trying to keep track of their children. They seemed to increase exponentially with every family gathering and a gang of them were now doing determined laps of the tables, the guests and the staff.

Steff and Connor had set themselves up strategically at the nexus of two of the larger tables and their respective families colonised either side.

Danny waded his way through the crowd, scanning for anything that seemed strange or possibly supernatural. He did eventually see something that terrified him to his very bones: but it had nothing to do with ghosts. Nadine and Clark were there, chatting happily with his mum. At least, Clark was chatting happily. His mum wore the same politely baffled face she'd had when she'd brought Danny to see *The Matrix* sequels.

'The more you travel, the more you realise that almost every culture has some ceremony that they perform to welcome a child into the world and it actually has less to do with religion and more about gathering the parents' support network of family and peers so they are better able to—'

'—That's very interesting, Carl,' his mum interrupted, politely but firmly. 'When did you say you were going back to the States?'

'I didn't,' Clark said, a little wrong-footed.

'What a pity. Ah, Dan, there you are,' she said as he sat down opposite her.

Danny made a mental note to give her an extra special Mother's Day present this year.

'Hey guys,' he said, hoping that he was successfully hiding the mild hysteria in his voice. 'What are you doing here?'

'Steff invited me when we ran into one another at the funeral,' Nadine answered. 'The pictures you showed me were so cute; I had to see him in the flesh.'

They all politely ignored the words 'You have been avoiding my texts, so I am checking up on you' that were flashing over her head in giant, neon letters.

'It is weird though, when you think about it,' Clark said. 'We were at a funeral a few days ago and now, here we are, celebrating a new life.'

'Buster's not *that* new,' Danny said, looking over to where his nephew was diligently gumming Connor's iPhone while his dad was distracted.

'He does remind me of Nudge a little bit,' Nadine said, and Danny wondered just how far she'd gone with this New Age, hippy stuff. 'But mostly just the drooling and lack of object permanence.'

Danny laughed but her comment reminded him that he'd come in for a purpose. 'I was supposed to be chatting to the staff about the food. A godfather's job is never done,' he lied, standing up. 'Clark, have you told my mum about your podcast?'

The look of surprised betrayal on his mum's face as he hurried away would haunt Danny for some time.

When he emerged outside the pub, Nudge was trying to stop Lucy from coming inside. He was not being terribly effective at this as, unlike Danny, Lucy seemed to have no qualms about walking through him.

'Just hang on a minute until . . . Danny, there you are,' Nudge said, relieved. 'I was just trying to stop her from going in, all gung-ho.'

'This place has changed,' Lucy said, forgoing a hello and examining the front of the bar. She looked very different from the last time he'd seen her. She was still wearing her camel-hair coat but, instead of the mishmash of clothing she'd worn before, she had on a simple black dress. This piece also seemed authentically retro but had the benefit of actually fitting her. He'd guessed her age at their last meeting to be early thirties but now revised this down to maybe only a few years older than himself.

'It got bought out a few years ago,' he said. 'They did the whole place up.'

'And you can't go inside?' she asked, directing this to Nudge.

'No, it's really freaking me out. It's like I want to take a step towards it but then can't.'

Lucy nodded. 'Right, let's take a look,' she said, matter-of-factly.

'I'll just stay out here then,' Nudge said. 'On my own. In the cold.'

'You can't feel the cold,' Lucy reminded him.

'I can feel left out though.'

Lucy ignored him and disappeared through the front door. Danny glanced at Nudge, shrugged, and then followed. He almost walked into the back of her as she stopped just inside the lounge, looking around with disgust.

'Everything is too new here.'

'I know, it's pretty soulless all right,' Danny replied distractedly. He was keeping a close eye on the crowd in the corner. He didn't want to explain Lucy to his family. Or to Nadine.

'No. I mean there isn't anything that would be able to affect Nudge.'

'Oh, right,' Danny said, embarrassed. A thought occurred to him. 'Hang on, through here.'

He guided her to a door beside the bar. What she'd said about everything being too new had twigged a memory about this place. Plus, this had the advantage of moving them out of sight of everyone.

Danny pushed through the door to a narrow corridor where the toilets were located. 'So, the new owners replaced everything. Except . . .' he pushed through a door at the end of the hall.

It was like stepping back in time. The airy, modern feel of the lounge gave way to a dark, narrow bar. This was The Farrier he remembered. A quintessential Dublin old man's pub where things like cocktails, natural light and families were actively discouraged.

'. . . the front bar,' he finished. 'Originally, this was going to be torn out as well, but the regulars threatened to boycott if they did.'

The owners must have taken the threat seriously because it looked like not a plank nor stool had been touched since the early eighties. The one exception were the flat-screen TVs that were showing the racing. It was crowded and Danny was about to apologise for almost walking into the back of someone when he realised who it was.

'Dad?'

Joe Hook almost spat up his pint in surprise and looked guiltily at his son. 'Dan. The queue for the bar inside was terrible, so I thought I'd get served faster in here.'

'Really?' Danny said, pointedly glancing at the TV. 'Who have you backed?'

Joe's shoulders fell. 'Doesn't matter. Fucker fell at the second hurdle. Who's your friend?' he asked, noticing Lucy.

Danny felt his sense of panic rise slightly. 'Oh, this is Lucy. She was friends with Nudge. We just ran into one another. Lucy, this is my dad, Joe.'

Danny's dad reached out towards her and shook her hand. 'Nice to meet you. We were all very sorry to hear about Nudge.'

Lucy returned the handshake politely but she was staring around the bar, as if looking for something. Danny was about to fill the awkward silence that followed but Lucy got there ahead of him.

'Tell me, Joe. Was this pub ever haunted?' she asked.

Danny wanted to step in and make an excuse, but he couldn't for the life of him think of a way to spin what she'd just asked.

'Haunted?' Joe repeated. He looked like was about to reflexively answer 'no' before stopping himself. 'Now that you mention it. There *was* something with one of the regulars back in the day.' He turned to look over the bar, before saying, 'Paddy, you've been here since God was a boy, right?'

The white-haired man turned his gaze away from the racing long enough to reply. 'Away and shite, Joe. I'm not that much older than you.' Paddy was a gnarled old man who looked like he'd been carved out of the same wood that panelled the bar top. Danny wondered if there was some sort of tree under the Guinness Storehouse where they grew Dublin barmen like him.

'What was the story with your man who died at the bar?' Joe went on.

Paddy gave them his full attention. He was silent for a moment, as if dredging the memory from somewhere very far away. Eventually he said, 'Jimmy Nolan. He was an aul' fella here when I was still a lounge boy.'

'A regular, was he?'

Danny noticed that a couple of the other patrons were listening in now that the race had ended on the TV. Paddy seemed to be enjoying the attention. 'As regular as the seasons. He was in here more than some of the staff. Until one day, at closing time, Luke, Luke McCall, the owner back then, was locking up and went to move him along only to find that he had died and nobody had noticed.'

'He died sitting at the bar?' Danny asked, sceptically.

Paddy nodded. 'Right there!' he said, pointing to a stool in the corner. Its current occupant did not look thrilled about this.

'What happened then?' Lucy asked.

'Well, he had no real family to speak of so, as I recall, we had a whip-around among the staff and regulars to see him buried,' Paddy said. 'It wasn't until afterwards that things started to get strange.'

'Small things at first,' continued Paddy. 'Nobody could sit in Jimmy's stool for long. It felt wrong, they said. Like you were standing on someone's grave.

'Then the cleaning staff started complaining about stuff being thrown around when they came in each morning. Pint glasses smashed and the like.'

'So, Luke called someone in,' Lucy said. It wasn't a question.

'He had to,' Paddy replied. 'People were a lot more superstitious in those days. We were bleeding customers. Luke had us clear the whole place out one evening. Wouldn't tell us what was going on. There was a rumour he brought in a heathen priestess to do some voodoo.'

'Really?' Danny asked, intrigued.

'That's what people said at the time. Bullshit, of course. Unless voodoo priestesses drove Datsuns.'

'You saw her?' Lucy asked. She had been scanning the room, seemingly only half-listening to his story but she snapped back to attention at this.

'Just from behind,' Paddy said. 'Luke had us clear out, but I had to drop back to pick up my wages and I saw her through the window. Didn't look like any voodoo priestess I ever heard of. Looked more like a nurse. Whoever she was, we never had any problems with the dead again.'

He turned to look at two of the old lads sitting near the taps. 'Except for the Walking Dead there, of course.'

It was as if some spell had been broken and the sound bled back into the small pub as the two gentlemen in question threw their own abuse at Paddy. Danny noticed that the patron who'd been occupying the late Jimmy's stool made a point of moving himself elsewhere.

'Another one?' Paddy asked Danny's dad.

Joe looked down at his near-empty glass and then over at Danny, embarrassment flashing across his face for a microsecond

'I'll have a Lucozade, Dad,' Danny said, remembering their conversation earlier. He didn't need to know about the flask Danny had been working on all day.

Joe smiled in relief and turned to Lucy. 'Lucy, what will you have?'

'Oh, there's no need,' she said, but he pressed her. 'Do they have sherry?' she asked.

Both generations of Hooks looked at her for a beat. 'I could ask, I suppose?' Joe said eventually. 'Is this like a new, hip throwback thing? Is sherry the new gin?'

'Never mind,' Lucy said, embarrassed. 'I'll have a glass of wine, please. Red.'

Lucy slipped onto the stool in the corner, which had been recently vacated, as Paddy waddled off to start the pint. She seemed to be studying the wall behind the bar. It was decorated with foreign banknotes which had been out of circulation for decades, postcards sent from regulars long dead and bar mats advertising drinks that had been off the shelves since before Danny was born.

Paddy returned with the drinks and Joe passed the Lucozade to his son. 'I'd better head back.'

'I'll be out in a bit,' Danny said.

'Take your time.'

To Danny's horror, he said this with a wink before exiting to the lounge.

The intense way that Lucy was staring at the walls must have been a little off-putting because another patron decided to take his leave and Danny was able to sit on the bar stool beside her.

'What are you looking—'

'—There!' she interrupted him triumphantly.

Danny looked to where she was pointing but couldn't see anything beyond the usual Deutschmarks and ads for Harp. 'What?'

'There,' she said, practically leaning over the bar to point.

At first, Danny thought she was showing him a faded pornographic postcard from Holland that some prude had since censored with a biro. Eventually though, he saw what she was talking about: the yellowing slip of paper about the size of a Post-it that had been pinned underneath. A series of symbols had been drawn on it in red ink. They were unlike anything he'd seen before: it looked like something the Zodiac Killer would have doodled on his school notebook.

'What the hell is it?' Danny asked.

'It's a Spirit Lock,' Lucy replied. Seeing Danny's confusion, she continued, 'It's a rite, I suppose is the best word, one which can displace ghosts.'

'So that's why Nudge can't come in?' Danny asked, wondering if he could get one for his bedroom.

'Yeah, it keeps the dead from crossing the threshold.'

He squinted at the symbols. 'What language is that?'

'Some form of Phoenician. Nobody is quite sure of the exact origin.'

'As in, the city with the gondolas and . . .' Danny faltered '. . . Cornettos?'

'That's *Venetian*.'

'So, what? You hang one of these up and it keeps ghosts away?' Danny said, attempting to distract her from both his geographical and historical ignorance. *Why couldn't botany come up in conversation more often?*

'It's not that simple,' she said. 'Notice anything about it?'

Danny stared at the symbols again. They certainly gave him the heebie-jeebies but there was nothing unusual about them beyond that. The paper looked like it had been pulled off a notebook: it was barely legible because the ink had faded so much.

Red ink.

'That's not biro, is it?' Danny asked, as realisation dawned.

'Nope. The inscription requires a sacrifice. Blood. *Fresh* blood,' she said with some relish. Seeing the look on Danny's face, she continued hurriedly, 'Just a few drops. Usually.'

'So, is this like what Adella used to do?' Danny asked, thinking of the nurse that Paddy mentioned.

'No,' she scoffed. 'Adella would talk to the spirits and help them realise that it was time to move on of their own accord.' Her tone was dismissive, as if dealing with ghosts this way was like some ridiculous, New Age method of parenting. 'She didn't approve of this sort of thing,' she continued.

'Why not?'

Lucy had the same awkward look on her face now as his father had had when they'd had the birds-and-the-bees talk when he was twelve. Or their grief talk earlier that day. 'Remember how I said that some spirits, after long enough, become detached from reality?'

Danny nodded.

'Well, if they're displaced from wherever place it is they're haunting then this can happen a lot quicker. The further they are from the familiar, the more confused they get. They stop behaving like people, they become . . . *feral* is the best word to describe it, I suppose.'

Danny looked at the symbol and shuddered. 'So, the force that Nudge and Lizzy have been feeling. Could it be related to one of these rites?'

She shook her head. 'Everything I know about them . . .' She corrected herself. 'I mean, from reading about them, they only work on a small level. Rooms, a building, maybe a whole street. Nothing like we're seeing here.'

'There you are!' a voice from behind them said in an aggrieved tone. They both turned to find Steff standing in the connecting doorway to the lounge. 'I've been looking all over for you. They're about to cut the cake inside and it would be nice to have the godfather there for the photos.'

'Sorry, Steff, this is Lucy. She knew Nudge.'

Steff's stern look softened somewhat. 'Oh, I'm really sorry. Why don't you both come in? They're about to start serving the food.'

'I don't know if—' Danny started but Steff had entered mum mode now and practically herded them both back into the lounge.

They returned to find a much looser atmosphere. Jackets had been thrown over the backs of chairs and the second cousins had been corralled onto one of the tables in the corner with Tayto and fizzy drinks. As promised, there was a large cake waiting on the table in front of Buster. Buster's dad, Connor, was doing his best to keep him from sticking his entire face in it.

By the time the pictures had been taken to Steff's satisfaction – every possible combination of child, parents, godparents and grandparents – the lounge staff had begun to distribute platters of food.

Danny passed Buster to one of the circling aunts and set out in search of Lucy, who he had lost track of. The good news was that he found her relatively quickly. The bad news was that he found her talking to Nadine.

'Hey guys,' he said, utterly failing to act casually. 'Where's Clark?' he asked, scanning the pub for the American.

Nadine made a face. 'He decided to head back to the house.'

'Did something happen?' Danny asked. The two women looked like they were stifling laughs.

'Well,' Nadine started. 'After your mum gave him some *constructive* feedback on his podcast . . .'

Danny winced in sympathy

'We ran into Lucy here, who asked about his tattoos, specifically the one he got when we were in Peru.'

'I know a little bit about the culture and the mythology,' Lucy explained. 'Clark had a reproduction of one of the local deities on his arm. He thought that it was Ch'aska, goddess of beauty.'

'I assume he was incorrect?' Danny asked.

'It was actually a pretty well-known depiction of Axomamma, a goddess of agriculture,' Lucy said, nodding.

'Agriculture?'

'A specific type of agriculture,' Nadine added, suppressing a smile.

'She's the Goddess of Potatoes,' Lucy said and Nadine laughed again.

Danny felt bad for Clark. All that American self-confidence had met Irish women on their home soil and bounced.

'I take it he was not happy about this?' Danny asked.

'No,' Nadine said, through laughter.

'Not even after I explained how important pota-toes were to Incan culture,' Lucy said, trying to keep a straight face, and failing.

'I'd really better go after him. Last time he got a taxi, the driver practically took him back via Wexford,' Nadine said. She turned back to Lucy. 'It was great to meet you. Can you text me the name of that book you mentioned?' She looked over at him. 'Better yet, have Danny text it to me. At least that way, I'd know he was still alive.'

Danny tried to look suitably chastised and she laughed and gave him a hug. 'She seems nice,' she whispered before following Clark out of the pub.

What did she mean by that?

'The one that got away?' He whipped his head back. Lucy was staring at him, a small smile on her face.

'Something like that,' he replied, blushing. 'Sorry I had to rush off there,' he continued, to change the subject.

'No problem. You had family responsibilities.' She surveyed the rest of the room. 'I've always liked chris-tenings,' she said in a wistful tone. 'They don't have all the pressure that comes with weddings and, obviously, they're a lot more fun than funerals.'

The penny dropped for Danny with a clang. *The black dress.*

'Of course. I'm so sorry. How was the ceremony for Adella? I didn't mean to pull you away from—'

She held up her hand. '—It's okay. I stopped by the funeral home to pay my respects, but I don't really get on with the rest of the family. It's part of the reason I hur-ried over, if I'm honest. Good to have a distraction.' She glanced around and then reached into her coat pocket, pulling out a slip of paper. 'Here. I pinched this from inside while you were busy with the paparazzi.'

Danny glanced down at the symbols. 'How'd you do that without Paddy catching you?'

'I used my feminine wiles.'

Danny shot her a shocked look. 'Really?'

'Of course not. I waited until he went to change a keg and then I ducked under the serving hatch. I figured that your friend has waited out in the cold long enough.'

Danny turned the paper over in his hands. 'What about Jimmy Nolan?'

'That thing has been there for over thirty years. Whatever is left of Jimmy is probably long gone.'

Danny took a deep breath and then ripped the paper in two. He had half-expected the pieces to burst into flames but there was nothing.

'We'd better go tell Nudge that his ban has been lifted,' Danny said.

'Good idea. I'm gasping for a smoke. I miss when you could smoke in pubs.'

Danny was pretty sure that particular law had come in when he'd been about nine, so he wasn't sure what days she was reminiscing about, unless she'd been lighting up in primary school, but still, he followed her into the cold night air. Danny instantly regretted not stopping to pick up his jacket. He enviously eyed Lucy's coat for its warmth and then briefly eyed her everything else for less practical reasons before catching himself.

'It's about time.'

Danny nearly jumped out of his skin as Nudge appeared behind them. 'Fucking hell, Nudge, don't do that.'

'What took you so long?' Nudge complained. 'It's been ages. I'm sure I felt the tether weakening while you were in there.'

'Sorry,' Danny said. 'I got caught up with family stuff but Lucy worked her voodoo and you should be able to come in now.'

Lucy was watching them both silently, her face unreadable, as she lit up another John Player.

'I thought I felt something,' Nudge said. 'By the way, what happened with Nadine's new fella? He came storming out of there about twenty minutes ago with a face like a smacked arse.'

'Long story,' sighed Danny. 'I'll tell you about it when we get home.'

'Fair enough,' Nudge said. 'Who's your man?' he asked, pointing behind them.

'Who?' Danny turned to see an older man standing in the middle of the road. He wore a battered old raincoat over a check shirt and his bearded face seemed all but consumed by the neon sign above the pub's front door.

Danny shared a look with Nudge, who just muttered 'Pisshead.'

'Hey pal, come in out of the road,' Danny said as gently as he could, while scanning for oncoming traffic. He didn't want to get involved but the man was likely to get hit by a car where he was.

The old man slowly tore his gaze away from the front of the pub towards Danny. 'He barred me,' he said. The voice was so quiet that Danny barely caught it over the sound of the breeze. 'Thirty years, I've been coming here, and he just barred me.'

Danny recognised the signs quicker this time. The strange, almost inaudible voice. The way he nearly blended into the night behind him.

'Who is he?' asked Nudge.

'I think his name is Jimmy Nolan,' Danny replied.

Chapter 21

Both Lucy and Danny took a half-step back.

Nudge looked at them curiously. 'What?'

Lucy opened her mouth as if to explain and then gave up, at a loss to summarise the last half-hour's discoveries.

'He's the ghost of a punter who was exorcised from here about thirty years ago,' Danny explained. 'That's why you couldn't enter. How is he still here?' This last part was directed at Lucy.

'I have no idea. It should be impossible. To hang on all this time . . .'

From her tone, Danny inferred that this would not have been pleasant for the man.

The ghost of Jimmy Nolan was still staring up at the front of the pub. Danny guessed that he had been in his sixties when he'd passed. Then again, it had been the 1980s, so there was every chance that this was what a healthy forty-year-old looked like at the time.

'Can you try to get him to cross over?' Danny asked quietly.

'I wouldn't even know where to start,' Lucy said. 'It's incredibly delicate work. They need to be spoken to with extreme—'

'—Oi, Jimmy!' Nudge shouted to be heard above the wind. 'You're dead! Time to move on!'

'What the hell do you think you're doing?' Lucy hissed at him.

'What? Maybe he just needs some tough love.'

Luckily, Nudge's shout didn't seem to have fully registered with Jimmy. It was enough to shake him out of his reverie though and now he fixed the trio with a blank, confused stare. 'He barred me,' he said again, although this time a note of anger crept into his monotone. 'After thirty years of coming here.' Now his voice was a growl.

'They didn't bar you, Jimmy,' Lucy said.

The ghost ignored them and began to march towards the front of the pub. Out of pure instinct, Danny jumped in his path, arms outstretched, but the spirit just walked through him. As he whipped around, the ghost was looking at his hands in confusion. For a second, it seemed like he might snap out of whatever rage he was in and come to his senses, but he just turned his focus back to the pub. 'Luke!' he shouted and disappeared through the front of the bar.

'What the hell is wrong with him?' Nudge asked as they hurried after him. 'Does he have ghost dementia or something?'

Lucy's cigarette went flying as she gripped the handle of the door. 'He's confused. It can happen with some of them.'

They slammed the door open and bustled inside. Their rushed entrance caused some of the patrons nearest the door to turn and regard them. Luckily the christening party was far enough away that they hadn't noticed.

They didn't have to look far to find their quarry. Jimmy had stopped just inside the door and was searching around at the lounge with a face of mounting confusion.

'Why don't we just leave him?' Nudge suggested. 'Let him haunt the place. What harm could he do? It might give it some character.'

Lucy whipped around to whisper urgently to both of them. 'Listen to me. In this state, he could be extremely dangerous—' She was interrupted by the ghost staggering towards the bar.

'You. Gimme a pint,' he roared. The bartender, a young man in his twenties, didn't react. 'Don't ignore me, you little bollocks! You can tell Luke where he can stick his ban. I've been coming here since fifty-five.'

The barman, oblivious to the raging ghost only feet from him, placed a two-thirds-full pint down to settle and looked across at Danny and Lucy, who had followed the ghost to the bar. 'What can I get you?' he asked them.

'We're oka—' Lucy began.

'—Two pints of Guinness, please, pal,' Danny interrupted.

The bartender nodded and moved off to pull their pints.

'This is no time for a drink,' Lucy said.

'It's the farthest tap from where he's standing,' Danny explained, nodding at Jimmy.

The former regular had given up on getting the barman's attention and now decided to take things into his own hands by leaning across and grabbing at the settling pint. His red, gnarled hands passed through the glass, surprising nobody but himself. 'What nonsense is this?' he said, repeatedly trying to get a grip on the glass. 'Luke, is this you?'

Curiosity won out over Danny's desire to calm the ghost down. 'Who's Luke?'

'Do you mean Luke McCall?' Lucy asked the ghost. 'He was the barman who . . . found you.'

'He barred me,' Jimmy repeated.

'Jimmy, he didn't bar you. You're confused. Think back to what actually happened,' Lucy said. Danny was impressed by her calm manner.

The old ghost fixed Lucy with a strange look, as if only noticing her for the first time. 'I know you,' he said. 'You were there too. With Luke. You helped him kick me out.'

'No, Jimmy. You must be thinking of someone else. That was a long time ago. You're just confused.'

'Stop saying that!' Jimmy thundered. Behind the bar the mirrored shelves rattled as if a breeze had swept through the room. The bartender, who had been in the process of topping up the pints of Guinness now that they'd settled, glanced around, confused.

'How the fuck did he do that? Can *I* do that?' Nudge asked, glancing at the shelves.

Jimmy looked just as surprised. His own poltergeist activity, if anything, seemed to have shocked him into a state of calmness.

Lucy took the opportunity to step up beside him. In lieu of holding his hand, she placed hers beside his on the bar top. Danny stepped up to block her view from onlookers, so she didn't get thrown out for talking to herself.

'Jimmy, I know that this is scary. You were locked out for a long time.'

Danny expected another tirade, but the older man simply nodded and looked around the bright, airy lounge in confusion. 'I remember being outside,' he admitted. 'For so long. This, this was my place. Now, I don't even recognise it.'

'Well, I suppose a lot can change in thirty years,' Nudge said.

Danny could almost feel the tenuous connection that Lucy had forged with Jimmy dissolve with Nudge's unwise words.

'Jimmy. Don't—' Lucy started but she had lost him.

The ghost looked around and seemed to be understanding the significance of all the changes. 'No. Thirty years. I don't believe it.'

Once again, the shelves started to rattle. A bottle of Grey Goose, too tall to maintain its centre of balance, toppled off one of the higher shelves to the ground and smashed onto the floor behind the bar.

The barman swore and shot an accusing look to where Danny was standing. Desperately, Jimmy stumbled over to him and waved his hands in front of the man's face. 'Look at me, damn you. I'm right here.' The spirit's voice was almost pleading.

The barman simply bent down and, after reaching in for a dustpan and brush, began to sweep up shards of glass.

Jimmy looked around wildly and then staggered towards a high table a few feet away. 'Why won't you look at me!?' he roared. The occupants of the table, a young couple, looked down at their drinks in confusion. The woman moved quickly to stop her pint of Bulmers from vibrating off the table as the ghost passed by. The man stared through the ghost of Jimmy at Lucy and Danny, who had stepped over to them.

'Did you see that?' the man asked and then, as if his brain had caught up with events, 'Can we help you?'

Lucy shot Danny a look that said that she was going to make this particular explanation his problem. He grabbed a beer mat from their table. 'I was just going to say that the legs on that one are wobbly. It always rattles when the door opens. Stick this under the base and it should be all right.'

The man took the mat and looked as if he was about to say thanks, but Danny had hurried off after Jimmy, who had staggered into a clear space of floor in the middle of the room. Danny noticed with alarm that he was moving closer to the christening party.

'We need to do something about him,' Danny said, as Lucy appeared beside him.

'I know, I know. Just let me think,' Lucy replied.

'I don't know if we have much more time,' Danny said.

Unheard, Jimmy bellowed at the room. 'Why won't you look at me?'

'What about the Spirit Lock thing?' Danny asked.

'You tore it up,' she reminded him.

Her tone was a little bit accusatory, as far as Danny was concerned, but he ignored it. 'Can you make another one?' he asked. 'Do you know how?'

She bit her lip. 'Maybe? But . . .'

'But what?'

'I'd need to do it here. The ceremony to activate it is not exactly subtle. If someone tried to stop me in the middle then, well, it would be bad.'

'How long do you need?' Danny asked. Over Lucy's shoulder he could see Thomas, one of Buster's great-uncles, accepting a round of drinks. He flashed back to the dirty laundry that Buster's godmother had aired to him. Thomas and Liam, brothers who hated one another, and a terrible plan began to form.

'I don't know. Once I get set up, maybe ten minutes?'

'You get what you need. I'll distract everyone.'

'How?'

Danny glanced back over to the christening party. 'Family secret.'

She looked as if she was about to argue but Danny gave her a gentle push towards the bar. 'Go!' he said, before turning to Nudge. 'While I'm distracting them, I need you to distract him,' he said, nodding at Jimmy.

'How the fuck do I do that?'

'You're a human distraction,' Danny said exasperatedly as he headed towards his family's table. 'Think of something.'

As he approached, he studied the group again. The man who his eyes had fallen upon a moment ago, Thomas, was talking with Danny's dad. A brief search identified Liam, Thomas' brother and nemesis. As luck would have it, Liam had just been handed a fresh pint by his nephew.

Silently apologising to Steff, he strode over to where Thomas was chatting and scooted past him, unseen, swiping the man's pint off the table as he did so. He stepped behind a column and took a moment to catch his breath before setting the pint on a shelf. After some thought he picked it back up and took a deep swig, partly to strengthen his psychic powers but mostly to settle his nerves.

He glanced over to where Jimmy was still ranting in the centre of the room. Nudge was cautiously edging closer to the older ghost. 'How do I distract someone who's been dead for thirty years?' he shouted across the room. 'Hey, Jimmy. Women can vote now.'

They could vote in the eighties, you fucking idiot, he wanted to shout but Nudge just continued. 'All the bees are nearly dead,' he went on. 'And the Nazis are back.'

However inaccurate, Nudge seemed to at least have gotten Jimmy's attention. 'What in Christ's name are you talking about, son?' he asked.

Danny sighed and then ducked back around the pillar to where Thomas and Joe were standing. His timing was excellent as he arrived just as the older man had finished his drink and was bemusedly looking around for the other one. 'I definitely put it down there. Didn't I?' he was saying as Danny sidled up. 'I must be having one of those senior moments that Sandra is always talking about.'

'Are you looking for the pint that was there?' Danny asked, innocently.

Thomas turned to face him. 'I am, yeah. Did the lounge girl take it by accident?'

'Your friend over there picked it up,' Danny said, pointing over to where Liam was now sipping his fresh drink. 'Sorry, I saw him do it when you weren't looking but I assumed you'd bought it for him.'

'He did what?' Danny was shocked by how quickly the man's tone went from good-natured tipsy to one of drunken rage. Helen hadn't been lying about them hating one another. 'The dirty fucking langer!'

Danny began to rethink his plan of action. 'I'm sure it was just by accident,' he said, trying to walk things back slightly, but it was too late. Thomas had stormed through the crowd towards his brother. Buster's grandad, Sean, saw him coming and, to his credit, tried to step into his path but Thomas managed to do an impressive side-step for a man his age and get an arm around him to slap the pint out of Liam's hand. The resulting crash caused everyone to turn as the two men confronted one another, with Sean in the middle trying desperately to hold each of them back.

'What was that for, you fucking headcase?' Liam spat. Connor had hurried over at the commotion and was also restraining his uncle from retaliation.

'You know full well what it was for, you thieving bollocks!' his brother managed to choke out, despite having Sean's forearm across his throat.

'Who are you calling a thief!' Liam raged and renewed his efforts to struggle out of Connor's grip.

Danny retreated from the scrum of bodies and looked over to see where Lucy had run off to. She was now standing in the corner next to the bar with the small slip of paper in her hands. He was too far away to hear her, but he could see her mouth moving, as if she was reciting something. Luckily, the barman and the rest of the patrons were too occupied watching the brawl in the corner to notice her.

Danny wasn't sure whether it was Lucy's chanting or the fact that the fraternal spat had taken attention away from him, but now Jimmy seemed to become even more agitated. It was as if he were standing at the centre of his own personal hurricane. Around him, pints began to tumble off tables and people reached out to steady drinks.

'Dan, what's going on?' He turned to find Aunt Sharon beside him, watching the knot of men in the centre of the room. At this point, Danny's dad and uncle had also waded in to try and keep the two men apart and now a tall blonde woman was roaring at Liam to let it go.

'Connor's uncles have kicked off,' he said, hoping that he sounded just as surprised as everyone else.

Although the fight had briefly gained the attention of the barman, Danny could see him glance back towards where Lucy was standing, as the bottles on the shelf began to rattle again.

We need a better diversion. 'We need to distract them. Do something to cheer everyone up,' Danny said, once again silently asking Steff for forgiveness for what he was about to do.

'Well,' Aunt Sharon started, with faux-reluctance. 'I suppose a sing-song might work?'

'I think you're right,' said Danny and pulled over a chair. 'Hop up there, so everyone will see you.'

'If you think it will help?' Sharon said modestly, already climbing up on the chair. In fairness to her, when Aunt Sharon belted out the first line of 'No Frontiers' everyone did, in fact, stop what they were doing to look around. Unfortunately, after looking at her in stupefied silence for a couple of bars, Thomas realised that nobody was holding him back any more and used the distraction to plant a belt across the forehead of his brother. The brawl erupted once more although this time with a musical accompaniment. Aunt Sharon, for reasons only she knew, continued to sing as the two brothers once again started to trade blows. The barman rushed over to try and break it up.

Danny pried his eyes away from the chaos he had caused to find that Jimmy was no longer holding court in the centre of the room. Instead, he was advancing on Lucy, who was still methodically chanting.

'You,' he said. 'You did this to me.'

Nudge was hurrying alongside Jimmy, still trying to distract him. 'There's been, like, nine more *Star Wars* movies,' he said desperately.

Danny had no idea how much longer Lucy needed but imagined that Jimmy's intervention wouldn't help things. Glancing around, his eyes fell on a round of drinks that had been abandoned by a table's previous tenants as they struggled away from the skirmish, or possibly the sing-song. He snatched two pints from the table and, struggling not to spill them, threw himself into Jimmy's path.

'*Sláinte*!' he said, holding out a pint of Guinness to the ghost. Fortunately, all the attention was still focused on the fight and so nobody clocked him apparently talking to himself. Jimmy stopped short and recoiled from the offered drink as if it were a snake.

'I just spoke to Luke, and he said that it was all a big misunderstanding. So, this one is on the house,' Danny improvised. Out of the corner of his eye, he could see Lucy still chanting, a bar towel wrapped around the palm of her hand. "Fresh blood." That's what she had said. He winced in sympathy.

Jimmy was regarding him with suspicious, blood-shot eyes but he'd stopped advancing. Cautiously, he reached out an arm to take the pint. Danny pulled the glass back quickly; Lucy still hadn't finished. He could sense that it was building to some sort of crescendo, but not yet. 'Wait,' he said. 'First we should . . .' he faltered.

'We should make a toast,' Nudge said, having appeared at Danny's side.

'Yes. We should make a toast,' Danny finished, relieved. Over in the corner of the room the melee seemed to be dying down. He wouldn't have this window for much longer. 'To old friends, too long absent.'

Jimmy nodded with poor grace but seemed to accept the apology. Once again, he reached out for the drink and once again, Danny held it out of the ghost's reach. 'And to accepting apologies from those who made mistakes,' he babbled.

Jimmy seemed to realise that something was up. 'Enough!' he thundered and made to grab the pint. The glass passed through his fingers and tumbled to the floor.

Thankfully, this was at the same moment as Lucy was able to finish whatever she was doing with the Spirit Lock. Danny didn't understand the language, but she spoke the last lines emphatically. He was now close enough to see that, for a brief moment, the symbols on the paper in front of her glowed.

Jimmy let out a howl. It was too animalistic to be called a scream. The ghost of the elderly regular was pushed, as if by a hurricane-force wind, towards the nearest wall of the bar.

'Fucking hell!'

Danny whipped around to see that Nudge was being forced out as well. The Spirit Lock didn't discriminate, it seemed.

Lucy came around from the side of the bar, hand still bleeding and breathing heavily, as if she had just completed a marathon. There was silence as they regarded the wall through which both ghosts had just disappeared. The hush was only broken when the barman wandered over from where the brawl had been and regarded the spilled pint on the floor. 'Oh, for fuck's sake,' he said. 'What happened here?'

Both Danny and Lucy ignored him as they pursued the two ghosts out into the freezing December night.

Danny almost ran straight through Nudge, who had been standing directly outside the door.

'I *did not* enjoy that,' Nudge said, throwing a harsh look at Lucy. 'Some warning next time might be nice?'

The moaning reassured Danny that Nudge had not been permanently damaged by the experience, and he turned to search for Jimmy. He was on his knees in front of the pub, still letting out a low wail of despair. Danny took several tentative steps towards him. *Maybe, now that he's back outside, we can talk some sense into him,* he thought.

He was only a few feet from him when the ghost suddenly jerked his head up to face him. Danny had thought he'd looked worried before, but his face had taken on an entirely new dimension of terror. He managed to croak out the word 'No!' before an unseen force hooked him around the middle and violently yanked him across the road. His face was a frozen rictus of terror before he was claimed by the evening gloom.

All three stared in shocked silence at the spot where the older ghost had disappeared. Danny reassured himself that Nudge still seemed to be immune to whatever effects were claiming the other ghosts.

The moment was broken when the door clattered open. All three of them jumped in shock to see Steff march out, filled with self-righteous rage. 'Fucking Cork, culchie bastards!' she shouted. She regarded Danny and Lucy for a moment. 'Do either of you have a cigarette?'

Chapter 22

Uncle Thomas was escorted back to his hotel. Broken glass was swept up. Steff was given a cigarette and a double gin to calm her down and the night continued for those inside, albeit under the watchful eye of a bouncer who had been called in. Aunt Sharon was actually the saviour of the night in the end. Once the fighting had calmed down, it turned out that everyone really did enjoy a sing-song.

Danny had wanted to return inside immediately, to check that his family hadn't been irreparably damaged by his distraction, but he'd had to spend nearly half an hour around the corner from the pub trying to calm down Nudge first. Seeing Jimmy being abducted had only heightened his paranoia and it had taken all that time just to convince him that their tether still held and would continue to do so if he re-entered the Spirit-Locked pub.

Danny promised that he'd only be ten minutes and was eventually able to go back in and check on his family. At that point, they were making their way through 'Brown Eyed Girl' and Danny was able to pick up his nephew and whisper a promise to him that his birthday and Christmas presents would be outlandish for the next few years to make up for this disaster.

He was making his way back outside when he ran into Lucy near the door. He had left her to get cleaned up after her efforts with the Spirit Lock. 'Everything okay with the family?' she asked.

He glanced pointedly towards where Sharon was now leading them in a stirring rendition of 'Jolene'. 'Nothing that Dolly can't fix, apparently. What about you?' he asked, nodding towards her hand, which was wrapped tightly in her scarf.

'I'll be fine. I just cleaned it there. I used a shard from the Grey Goose bottle to make the cut. I reckon it was sterile enough.'

'I meant the Spirit Lock. It seemed to take a lot out of you.'

Her face was flushed, and she was still breathing heavily. 'I'll be fine. Things like that require a sacrifice. Not just the blood. There's a toll,' she said cryptically.

'What kind of—' Danny started but Lucy interrupted him.

'I need a drink.'

Danny wanted to ask more but figured she'd earned one after saving them from Jimmy. He let her lead him over to the bar to order from the now increasingly wary barman. 'Another red wine?'

'No,' Lucy replied, scanning the bottles that had survived Jimmy. 'Let's do shots!'

Danny turned to look at her in surprise. She seemed almost giddy, as if the adrenaline of the Spirit Lock had taken years off her.

'Do they have tequila? I've always wanted to try it.'

'Not unless we want to spend the rest of the evening with me over the toilet. Lucy, are you sure that—'

'—Okay, so no tequila. That's a shame. The salt-and-lemon thing seems like fun.' She steamrolled over Danny's concern. 'What about absinthe? Can we have any of that?'

'I'm pretty sure that's illegal over here,' Danny said. 'What about sambuca?' He figured that this looked like it was going to happen with or without his input, so he might as well aim for something he could keep down.

'Sambuca? Yes!' Lucy exclaimed. 'Two sambucas please,' she said to the barman.

He nodded and moved off to pour them. Lucy put her hands down on the bar in anticipation and then removed them with a look of disgust. She pulled out a hanky from the sleeve of her dress and wiped down the bar.

Danny couldn't help himself; he laughed.

'What?' she asked, trying to figure out what the joke was.

'Sorry,' Danny said, managing to get a hold of himself. 'It's just the mammy-sleeving. Caught me off guard.'

'Mammy— what?'

'Keeping a hanky up your sleeve. It's something that we always used to slag my mum for and it's something that Steff has found herself doing now that she's constantly having to clean up after Buster.'

'So, I'm a mammy-sleever!?' Lucy said, in faux-outrage.

'I'm afraid so, and you'd want to be careful. Family legend says that my nanny once caught her sleeve on a candle, and there were so many Kleenex in there that her whole arm went up like a firelighter.'

Lucy laughed and made a deliberate point of taking the handkerchief out of her sleeve and putting it back in her coat pocket. 'Better safe than sorry.'

The barman returned with two glasses of the viscous liquid. Luckily he didn't actually set them on fire and so they were spared Danny's nanny's fate. He looked over at Lucy and thought about Adella. *Grief presents itself in strange ways*, he reminded himself. He knew this better than most. He held up his glass in a cheers. 'Well, you're only young once, right?'

This elicited a snort of laughter from Lucy for some reason but she clinked her glass against his. They downed the liqueur. Danny simultaneously tried to repress bile and flashbacks to college. Lucy made a face and stuck her tongue out.

'Can we get two glasses of water, please,' Danny wheezed to the barman. He grabbed one when it was set in front of him and took a grateful slug. He slid the other towards Lucy. 'Look, I really can't hold the high ground when it comes to drinking through the loss of someone but what did you mean that there's a to—' He didn't get to finish his sentence because it's difficult to talk when someone's tongue has been unexpectedly stuck down your throat. His eyes were still open when Lucy had decided to lean across, grab him by the shirt collar and pull him into a deep, liquorice-flavoured kiss. He closed them as he instinctively leaned in.

His first thought was that this was probably the grief again. Actually, if he was being totally honest, this was about his eighth thought. Numbers one through seven hadn't been so much thoughts as a swirling cascade of guilt, worry and hormones. It was definitely in the top ten though.

Someone in the corner of the pub shouted 'Yeow!' and Danny opened his eyes, realising two things. One was that the barman was standing opposite them, holding out the card reader for the drinks they hadn't paid for yet and two, they were now kissing at the bar next to his family.

Luckily, the shout was just because the group in the corner were on Irish trad ballads now and a cousin had gotten a little too worked up during 'The Rocky Road to Dublin'.

It was enough to make Danny remember himself though. He pulled away and took a deep breath. 'Lucy, maybe we should . . .'

She took a step back and, if anything, looked more surprised than he did.

'Danny, I'm so sorry. I didn't mean to . . .' She looked over at the barman, turning red, and Danny quickly dug out a €20 note.

'Keep the change,' he said.

'I'm so sorry, Danny, I'm not sure what came over—' Lucy started again.

'It's okay,' he said. Luckily, nobody from the christening party seemed to have noticed.

'It was just the Spirit Lock and Adella,' she continued.

For once, it was Danny's turn to calm someone in an anxious spiral. 'Lucy, seriously. It's okay. I get it.' He passed her over the other pint of water. 'Just take a drink.'

She gulped down the water but did seem slightly calmer once she had. 'You're lucky, you know?' she said, turning to regard the christening party. They were still on 'Rocky Road'. The fact that half of them were singing a completely different verse to the other half didn't seem to be slowing them down any. He wondered if she'd missed the bit where he'd been able to provoke a mass brawl with just a few sentences but copped that this might be more about her family than his.

'Adella would have loved this,' she said, as the Hooks and O'Riordans tried to outdo one another in volume. 'She was a big fan of a sing-song.'

'How have you been?' he asked awkwardly. 'Since she passed?'

Lucy fiddled with a bar mat as she considered, folding it into smaller and smaller squares. 'I don't think it's sunk in yet. I never . . . I never thought about her being the one to go first. That I'd have to live without her.'

Danny shot her a confused look. It was a strange thing to say that you didn't expect to die before your grandparent but before he could probe further about what she meant, she continued. 'I wonder why the force was able to take Jimmy now and not before?'

Danny had enough experience in evading tough, emotional conversations, so he could recognise an amateur attempt when he saw one but figured it would be a little hypocritical to call her out on it.

He thought about Lizzy. 'He seemed pretty attached to this place. His connection, his tether, must have been too strong to break before now.' He shivered at the thought. 'Until we severed it by kicking him out again.'

Lucy leaned in closer and put a hand on his arm to reassure him. 'We didn't have a choice, Danny. A spirit as old, as lost, as that. He could have torn this place apart.'

Danny grudgingly nodded. 'Thank you,' he said eventually. 'For the help, for coming in the first place.'

'I lost one family member to supernatural nonsense this week. I wasn't about to see it happen to someone else.' She took a long pull of her drink and was silent for a moment. 'Would you think about severing the tether with Nudge? If you don't find something soon, I mean?' she asked suddenly.

'What?' responded Danny, caught out by the sudden change in topic.

The giddiness was gone now, replaced with the same intensity he'd seen earlier when she'd been chanting. 'Those rites, things like the Spirit Lock. They could sever the link between a ghost and a person as well as a building. You could be freed.'

'And what? Just leave him to become like Jimmy?' Danny said. The barman looked over and he realised he'd raised his voice.

'That might not happen. Severing the tie could force him to cross over,' she insisted.

'Yeah. "Might,"' Danny said. 'I can't risk that.'

'I've been watching you two,' she said, moving even closer to him. 'He's becoming too dependent on you.'

'He needs me,' was all Danny was able to reply.

'I've seen this happen before,' she continued, solemnly. 'With others who can see spirits. Some people get so caught up in talking to the dead that they forget to live their own lives.'

'*I am* living my life,' Danny protested.

'Really? I respect you for trying to help your friend but what are you going to do if you can't get him to move on?'

'We'll find something.'

'How long will you wait? Months? Years? Severing the tie might be the only chance that he has . . . that you have.'

'But there's no guarantee. What's to stop him getting sucked away as soon as the tether is cut, like Jimmy, like Adella?'

'We could try it somewhere further away from the source of . . . What do you mean "like Adella"?' Lucy said sharply and Danny suddenly remembered that they had never got around to telling her about what had happened after she'd become a spirit.

'After Adella . . . passed on. She appeared as a ghost. In the house,' he said.

Lucy nodded. 'You said that. That's fairly common directly after death. Are you saying that she didn't cross over afterwards?'

'Not *exactly*,' Danny said 'At least, I don't think so. She was talking us through the CPR and then, whoosh.'

Lucy waited a beat for him to continue. '"Whoosh"?' she hissed. 'What the fuck does "whoosh" mean?'

'She got pulled away. Like Jimmy did,' Danny said.

Lucy looked horrified and Danny realised how much he might have messed up by not mentioning this sooner. 'Why didn't you tell me!?'

Danny stuttered. 'I was going to but then, you could see Nudge and you were telling us about how everything worked and then you left without me getting a chance to say it. I'm really sorry. I kind of—'

'—You kind of *what*?'

'Kind of forgot you didn't know,' he finished, embarrassed.

Lucy looked at him as if she was deciding whether to cry, to scream or to savagely beat him unconscious with one of her shoes. Instead, she took a fourth

220

option and slammed her glass of water on the bar, abruptly about-faced and walked straight out into the night.

Danny hurried after her. 'Lucy, wait! I'm sorry!'

Outside, she looked left and right and then strode purposefully towards an idling taxi waiting near the front of the pub. She didn't slow down but he did hear her mutter, 'He's sorry? Well, that's okay then.'

'Look, this doesn't change anything,' Danny said as he tried to catch up with her.

That did make her stop. She had reached the back door of the taxi but at this, she whirled around on Danny so he had to take a step back to avoid accidentally walking over her.

'What do you mean, it doesn't change anything? My . . . Adella has been taken. How does this not change anything?'

'We still just need to find out what's causing the force and stop it. If we do that, then we can help Jimmy, Adella and anyone else who's been caught up in this.'

'Oh! Is that all?' Lucy said scornfully, pulling open the taxi door and climbing in.

Danny risked reaching out to her as she did so. 'What are you going to do?'

But she'd already slammed the door behind her, heedless to his fingers. He just about managed to get his arm out of the way as it closed, and the taxi pulled off into the night. Danny watched it go.

'What did I miss?' Nudge asked, walking up behind him.

*

'You're fucking useless,' Nudge said, after Danny had filled him in on what had happened.

'I know,' he replied. They had retreated to the safety of the flat after Danny had assured his family that he didn't need a lift, would text them when he was home safe and, grudgingly, had given them a rendition of 'The Aul' Triangle'. 'I'm sorry, I messed up our only lead on this thing.'

Nudge looked surprised. 'I wasn't talking about that. Although, I mean, yeah. You did,' he said. 'No, I'm talking about how you managed to talk yet another woman out of wanting to sleep with you?'

'What?' Danny raised his head from his hands.

'She kissed you, yeah?' Nudge said.

'Yes, but—'

'And then you stopped her.'

'She was grieving, Nudge,' Danny said. 'Not every problem can be solved by sex.'

'It might have solved the problem of you not getting the ride for over a year.'

'I could hardly *not* tell her about Adella,' Danny objected.

'You could have done it with a little bit of nuance.'

'Yeah, because you're Captain Nuance,' Danny replied. 'She was saying that I should cut you loose anyway. Exorcise you and risk letting you become like Jimmy,' he added, petulantly.

'The cow! And I thought she was warming to me as well.'

They sat in mutual misery for a moment before Danny sighed. 'Look, she can hardly stop looking into this. Especially now that she has skin in the game. I'll give her a little while to cool off and then reach out.'

Nudge nodded. Something seemed to occur to him. 'Any word from Sven by the way? He never showed. I thought you said he was coming today?'

Danny hadn't even noticed that Sven had been missing. It was understandable given the circumstances, but he still felt a flash of guilt. He fished out his phone and looked through his messages. They included a text from his mum, asking if he got home all right, another suggestion from Nadine that he and Clark would have a good time if they went for a drink together (Danny wondered if she was just trying to get rid of him for the night) and a novel-length rant from Steff about Connor's family, their family and the terrible potential the mix presented for how Buster would turn out.

He'd also received a text from Sven. It was brutally short.

Sorry I've been out of touch. Dad's taken a turn for the worse. They're telling us that we should start calling family members who live abroad. Not looking good.

Danny relayed this to Nudge.

'Fuck. Poor Ian. Poor Sven,' he said, summing up Danny's feelings. 'We should go and pay our respects if we can.'

'I suppose we can do it tomorrow. I'll give Sven a text to say that we . . . that *I'm* going to do a fly-by. That way he can tell me to fuck off if he wants to,' Danny said, after some thought.

'Cool!' Nudge settled back onto the couch opposite the TV. 'Can you throw on Animal Planet?'

'Again?' Danny asked. Nudge had requested the channel on the previous two nights.

'They do an omnibus of *Monkey Business* after 2 a.m.'

'The one about the monkey sanctuary?'

'Apes,' Nudge corrected him. 'Yeah, Frankie is gearing up for a coup against Bob for troop leader.'

'And these are . . . ?'

'Chimpanzees. Yes. I'm telling you Dan, there's more intrigue in this than anything on Netflix.'

Danny was prepared to accept him at his word and switched the TV over to Animal Planet, which was airing a show where two men were making a fish tank in the shape of a drum kit.

'Oh great! *Tanked*!' said Nudge earnestly and settled in for what was presumably his night. 'You'd better get to bed,' he said. 'Big day tomorrow.'

He wasn't wrong. Danny had been on semi-official bereavement leave from his job in the shop since the accident. The next day was supposed to be his first back at work. He couldn't exactly say that he was looking forward to it but even this short break, combined with his recent whiskey expenses, had severely affected his savings. Trying to solve the mysteries of the afterlife was all well and good but he still needed to pay the rent.

Danny said goodnight and withdrew to his bedroom. He threw the component parts of his suit in the direction of his desk and made a mental note to hang it up properly at some stage. He sank back on his bed and contemplated the ceiling. He could hear the faint noise of the television down the hall as Nudge broadened his zoological knowledge.

Against his will, his brain flashed back to what Lucy had said about cutting the tether. He had dismissed it as an option completely but a treacherous voice at the back of his brain asked what the alternative was. Would this be his life from now on, falling asleep in a semi-drunken haze as the spirit of his best friend watched telly in the next room? Waking up hungover every morning and grimly consuming spirits? How long could he keep that up?

He had hoped he would drift off quickly, but these thoughts stubbornly refused to be dismissed.

Chapter 23

Danny stood awkwardly in front of Sven's house. Awkward in the sense that he wasn't sure what the protocol was for this type of visit and also because he was struggling with the weight of two shopping bags and a cardboard tray of coffees.

After a few fitful hours of sleep, Danny had got up and prepared to drop by Sven's before work. He'd informed his mum of Ian's condition and his intention to visit, however, which is how he ended up in her car, stopping off at Tesco beforehand. He had followed her through the aisles as she filled a basket with what she called 'a few bits' but what looked to Danny like a week's worth of shopping.

'You've no idea how easy it is to forget about the everyday, practical things at a time like this,' she explained. 'You spend so much time looking after someone that you forget to look after yourself.'

The words had made him think of what had Lucy said the night before and he was avoiding eye contact with Nudge when Sven's mum answered the door. Although Danny had drunk enough to bring his friend with him, Nudge had at least agreed not to talk or distract Danny while he was on this particular errand. He had managed to keep things together while in the car with his mum but could feel the concern radiating off her in waves.

'Hi, Denise,' Danny said, wishing his mum hadn't left for this bit. 'I'm sorry to disturb. Sven said, I mean Steven said that I could . . .' He saw her take in his bags. 'My mum thought that maybe you might need some bits, like bread and milk. It's stupid now that I say it.'

He was reprieved from his anxiety spiral by a sad but genuine smile and her pulling the door fully open. 'Thanks, Dan. That's very thoughtful. I really appreciate it.' As she took one of the bags and he followed her through to the kitchen, Danny noticed how exhausted she looked. He considered himself to be a connoisseur of sleep deprivation and recognised the signs of someone who hadn't got more than a couple of hours in at least a week. He'd been chiding himself for bringing coffees on the way over, as if he were just stopping by for a normal chat, but now he thought that it hadn't been the worst idea.

They emerged into an airy, modern kitchen that looked out onto the back garden and deposited everything onto the counter.

'I'm sorry about the state of the place,' Denise said, and Danny almost laughed at the normality of the statement. She tugged open the dishwasher and began to grab at some of the random plates and crockery by the sink until Danny stepped up and held out the tray of drinks.

'Let's have our coffees first before they get cold?' he suggested, using the same soothing tones he'd come to hate from others in recent weeks. Short of anything else to say that wasn't a stereotypical platitude, Danny handed over a Styrofoam cup. 'Here, cappuccino, right?' She nodded and accepted it gratefully. He tried to determine the contents of the other cups by peering through the lids. 'That's Sven's Americano there. I wasn't sure what Lucia drinks, so I just got a latte and another Americano and I figured she could have whatever—' he stopped as Sven limped into the room with Lucia, Ian's homecare nurse, padding softly along beside him.

Sven, already pale at the best of times, was essentially translucent, apart from the dark circles around his eyes. He steadied himself against the counter and looked at the Tesco bags quizzically.

'My mum,' Danny said by way of explanation. He offered a coffee to Lucia, who took the Americano gratefully.

Sven accepted his coffee and an awkward hug from Danny consecutively before slipping onto one of the stools by the counter. There was another awkward pause while everyone sipped at their drinks before Danny decided to bite the bullet. 'How is he doing?'

Sven and his mum exchanged glances. 'It's not good. His lungs are getting weaker . . .' his friend couldn't bring himself to speak any further.

'He's alert at least,' Denise added. 'For the moment.'

There was another uncomfortable silence. 'Look, I just wanted to make sure that you knew that if there's anything that you need. I don't want to intrude.'

'Would you like to see him?' Denise asked.

Absolutely not! 'Yes. If that's okay?' Danny said out loud, because he wasn't a complete monster.

Sven rose from his seat. 'I think he'd like to see you.'

The words 'one last time' hung unsaid in the air between them as Danny followed his friend out of the kitchen, while Lucia moved to help Denise put away the groceries.

When it was just the two of them, Danny took the opportunity to stop his friend. 'How are you doing?'

Sven let out a sigh that seemed to go on for a full minute. 'We knew it was coming,' he started, choosing to look at the pictures lining the hallway rather than at Danny. 'I thought it would make this part easier, you know?'

Danny nodded, although he had no idea.

'It doesn't,' Sven said simply and moved to open the door they'd stopped in front of.

It gave onto what used to be called the 'back room'. Danny knew this because he had spent many an afternoon after school in there. This had been where Sven had kept his Xbox. It was where they'd watched movies on rainy Sunday afternoons. There was a couch in there that Danny had spent more nights on than the bed in his current apartment.

The couch was gone, as was the Xbox. Instead, there was a bed surrounded by machines, a dresser, a collection of chairs and a smell. The smell was hard to define. It was part hospital antiseptic, part the stale stench of a room that hadn't been aired in too long and the indefinable, but unmistakable, smell of illness.

Danny found himself taking in all these details. The click and whir of the machine that delivered oxygen. The way that the dresser lolled at a strange angle, as if it had broken in the journey from upstairs. The rumpled blanket in the armchair, where someone had been catching what little sleep they could. Anything to avoid looking at the occupant of the bed.

If Ian Kelly had looked seventy-five the last time Danny had seen him, at Nudge's funeral, then he now looked like the mummified remains of a 75-year-old. He sat in the bed, propped up by a homeware-department's worth of pillows, in a blue pyjama top that was at odds with his blotchy, yellowing skin. Danny would have thought that he'd arrived too late if it weren't for the terrible wheezing Ian was making with the help of the oxygen tube hooked up to his nose.

'Ah. Danny. Could you please tell my son that denying his father's dying wish for a proper drink will haunt him for the rest of his life?' His voice was a reedy gasp and each sentence was bookended by a deep, laboured breath, but he sounded surprisingly lucid.

Danny looked over at Sven.

'He wants a Guinness,' Sven explained.

'Or a whiskey. I've a cabinet full of the stuff not ten feet from here,' Ian said.

'It's not even ten in the morning, Dad.'

'I don't have many ten-in-the-mornings left,' Ian protested.

'At least wait until you've had breakfast,' Sven said. He picked up a plastic tumbler of water and held it out to his dad. 'Here. Get your lips around this instead.'

Ian took a slow, difficult pull from the straw. 'It's no Guinness,' he complained afterwards.

As Danny settled into one of the chairs by the head of the bed, the patient gave him a slow once-over. 'You look terrible,' he said.

Danny struggled for something to say, until he saw the twinkle in Ian's deep-set eyes and then he knew what was expected of him.

'You're one to talk, Iano,' Danny said with forced joviality. 'I knew all that cycling and running was bad for you. You should have stuck to takeaways and telly like me.'

Ian made a gurgling noise that alarmed Danny until he realised it was just him laughing. 'Cheeky git! I regret not throwing you out of the house when you followed Steven home like a stray. It would have saved me a fortune in crisps.'

'Someone in this house had to eat carbs,' Danny countered.

Sven smiled at their back and forth until his dad's gurgling laugh descended into a wracking cough. Danny instantly regretted everything he'd said but the fit passed after a few seconds.

Ian settled back onto his small mountain of pillows and went on to address Danny again, but something caught his eye. 'Paul?' he said, in a puzzled voice.

'What?' Sven asked his dad, leaning in.

'It's Paul,' Ian repeated.

Sven shared a worried look with Danny. 'No Dad. It's Danny. Paul had an accident, remember?'

'Paul, how did you get in here?' Ian asked, ignoring his son.

'This happens sometimes. He gets confused. I think it's the medication,' Sven explained quickly. 'I'd better get Lucia.'

Danny said nothing, partly because Sven limped out of the room before he could, but mostly because Ian was staring straight at where Nudge was standing in the corner of the room.

'What is going on?' asked Ian. 'My mind's been acting up lately but I'm fairly sure you're supposed to be dead.'

Nudge stepped closer to the bed uncertainly. 'Are you talking to me?'

'No, I'm talking to the corpse behind you,' Ian said bluntly.

Nudge looked at Danny, who was just as confused.

'He can see me,' Nudge said, redundantly.

'How?'

'It's very impolite to talk about someone as if they're not here, you know?' Ian said. He seemed to be enjoying this. Danny guessed, in his condition, any surprise besides the inevitable was a pleasant one.

Danny heard footsteps coming down the hall and made a decision.

'Ian, I can explain all of this, but you need to send the others away. Sven won't understand.'

Sven, Denise and Lucia entered, each wearing their own interpretation of the classic worried frown.

'How are you feeling, Ian?' Lucia asked in her soft Lithuanian accent, as she checked his pulse, followed by the tubes and finally the machines by the bed, with practiced efficiency.

Ian gave Danny a look that seemed to last a lifetime. 'Sorry, Lu, I think I had one of my senior moments there.'

Danny saw both Kellys visibly relax.

'Dee, love, could I have one of those horrible yoghurts please?' he asked his wife.

'They're not horrible. They're specially designed for—'

'—They taste like someone else has already eaten them,' Ian interrupted.

Denise smiled and promised to go and get one.

'Steven, go and help your mother.'

'She'll be fine, Dad.'

'Help her anyway. I can't tell Danny all your embarrassing childhood secrets if you're sat there eavesdropping. Lu, you go with him. We'll work on cutting them out of my will so that you inherit everything later.'

Danny got the feeling that this was a running joke, judging by the way both of them rolled their eyes, but after a few more Are you sures? and I'll just be outsides they hurried out, leaving Danny alone with Ian.

'So, what's going on?' Ian asked Nudge. 'Have you faked your death? Did you sneak into your own funeral? I have to say that it's something that I've given a lot of thought to.'

'It's overrated,' Nudge said, moving towards the bed.

Ian nodded, disappointed, as if he had secretly suspected as much.

'Nudge is a ghost, Ian,' Danny said and then, to stave off any protests, waved a hand through his late friend's head.

'Hey!'

'Oh, give over. It's not like it hurts.'

'It's rude though,' Nudge muttered. 'You don't see me waving my hands through your head. You probably haven't even washed them either.'

Ian looked on at this exchange with the expression of a small child witnessing a card trick.

'I know it's hard to believe,' Danny started softly, keeping an eye on the door in case anyone walked in.

'Makes perfect sense to me,' wheezed Ian.

This wrong-footed Danny somewhat. 'Really?'

'Well, considering the fact that I attended his funeral, nobody else in the room could see him and that he's currently standing with his foot passing through my medical waste bin. I'd say it makes the most sense out of everything.'

Nudge looked down and swore as he realised that he had inadvertently placed one of his feet through a yellow bin sticking out from under the bed. 'Gross. Is this for, you know?' He made a face. 'Poo?'

'No. It's for used needles and bandages and stuff like that,' Danny said, turning back to the bedridden man.

'Oh, well, that's much better then,' Nudge grumbled.

'So, Paul, what's death like?' Ian asked with remarkable directness.

'I would hold off as long as I could if I were you, Ian,' Nudge said, still inspecting his foot for any spectral needles. 'It's a bit of a mess at the moment. How can you see me? Are you drunk?'

'What does he mean, "drunk"?' asked Ian.

Danny tried to gather his thoughts to give an explanation, but he was interrupted by Nudge. 'Danny gets *Sixth-Sense* powers when he's pissed.'

Ian just nodded as if this made sense. 'No. Sober as a judge, I'm afraid. Not for lack of trying though.'

Danny surveyed the IV and tubes going in and out of the older man. 'Maybe it's the drugs he's on?' Another, bleaker thought occurred to him. 'Or else maybe . . .' he realised he was still speaking out loud and shut up.

'Maybe I'm so close to death's door that I can have a look through the window?' Ian finished for him.

'You're taking this remarkably well,' Nudge said.

'Well, I suppose that confirmation that there is consciousness after death is something of a comfort,' Ian replied. A thought seemed to occur to him. 'The

Christians aren't right, are they? Only my sister has been trying to get me to see a priest and I've been telling her to feck off.'

'Unconfirmed. It might do no harm just to cover your bases though,' Nudge said.

Danny and Nudge looked at one another. Without speaking they decided to hold off on informing him that the afterlife left a lot to be desired when it came to the whole 'eternal paradise' thing.

'I'm glad to see you again,' Ian said. 'Steven took your death very hard. I'm afraid I'm not about to make things any easier for him.' He looked up at Danny and beckoned him closer. Danny leaned in and the older man grabbed his hand. 'He's going to need you. After I go. Please look after him. He'll have his mum and my family but you two were like his brothers.'

Danny found that he couldn't speak and so he just nodded and tried to blink away the tears.

'Now, if you need alcohol to see Paul then that must mean that you have some on you,' Ian said, surprising them both and breaking Danny out of his emotional reverie.

'What?'

'Come on! Don't be stingy,' Ian rasped and started patting at Danny's jacket with his skeletal hands. 'Aha!' he said triumphantly, as his fingers struck the metal flask in Danny's inside pocket.

Danny took the flask out but hesitated. 'I don't know. If Denise finds out, then I'll be sharing that hospital bed with you.'

He looked at Nudge, who shrugged. 'Give the man some whiskey.'

Danny passed across the flask and helped Ian bring it to his mouth. He took a surprisingly long swig and then smacked his lips and sat back. 'Ugh. Still drinking the cheap stuff, I see.'

Danny took the flask back and drank a nip himself, to avoid being rude. 'Well, I've had to downgrade since I stopped stealing from your drinks cabinet.' He looked around the room. 'You know, I think we had our first drink in here,' he said to Nudge.

'Did you now?' Ian said, reaching for the flask again.

Danny handed it to him. 'Yes, it was while you and Denise were away. Nudge convinced Sven to let us try your whiskey.'

'I always suspected you were a terrible influence,' Ian said amiably, as he took another deep sip.

'We got quite a taste for the Black Bush, as I recall,' Nudge said, laughing. 'I'm surprised you never noticed.'

The bedridden man was chuckling now. 'Oh, I did. Did you really think you were being subtle? Topping up perfectly good whiskey with water. You should be ashamed of yourselves,' Ian said, grinning at the memory. The smile gave him the appearance of a skeleton who'd just been told a good joke.

Danny and Nudge looked at him in surprise. Sven's parents had always disapproved of him drinking, even after he turned eighteen. They'd thought it would set back his rugby career.

'I never told Denise, of course,' Ian continued. 'But every teenager needs to be able to cut loose occasionally.'

Nudge found his tongue first. 'So, you just kept letting us drink your Bushmills? We must have gone through a case of the stuff over the years.'

'Of course not,' Ian replied, through more gurgling laughter. 'I just started filling the Bushmills bottle with the cheap stuff.'

Danny laughed; he couldn't help himself.

Ian was doubled over in the bed, his narrow shoulders shaking with mirth.

'You crafty bastard,' Nudge said, joining in.

Ian didn't respond, shoulders still shaking. Something made Danny lean forward and gently push Ian backwards into the pillows. The older man was still wheezing but Danny realised that he wasn't laughing any more: he was genuinely struggling to breathe. He raced over to the door and called out for Lucia.

'What happened?' she asked, as she shot past him into the room. She was in full nurse mode now, urgent but calm. Sven and his mum had hurried in after her and stood hovering near the end of the bed as she worked.

'I don't know,' Danny said honestly. 'He was laughing and then he started gasping.'

'He can't catch his breath,' Lucia said, as she whipped the pillows out from behind Ian's head and expertly tipped the adjustable bed frame flat. Danny noticed that Ian was no longer gasping and felt hope surge for a moment before he noticed that he wasn't breathing at all now.

Lucia beckoned Sven and his mother over. She grabbed Denise's hand and placed it around Ian's. Sven grabbed his other hand and placed it against his forehead.

'What are you doing? We need to do CPR,' Danny shouted.

Lucia stepped around Denise and then gently but firmly led Danny out into the hall. 'There is nothing to do,' she said calmly. 'Ian signed a do-not-resuscitate order. He wanted to go on his own terms.'

'But—' Danny started.

'You need to let them have this time with him. To say goodbye.'

'I gave him whiskey,' Danny blurted out. 'Is that what . . . is that what did it?'

Lucia took his hand. 'You didn't cause this. It was coming regardless,' she said kindly. 'It's nice that he was able to drink with a friend at the end.' There was a look of genuine sadness in her face. She'd been working with Ian for nearly six months now and had clearly grown attached to the whole family. 'I need to telephone some people. Keep an eye on them, please,' she said quietly and made her way towards the kitchen.

Danny surveyed the scene from the doorway. Sven still had his head pressed against his father's hand, squeezed tightly between his own. His massive frame was shaking silently. Denise had her head bowed in what Danny assumed was prayer.

'Well, that was an anticlimax,' a voice said from behind him.

Danny turned and was totally unsurprised, though still deeply disturbed, to see Ian standing behind him. He was still dressed in the blue pyjama top and matching bottoms but his complexion and demeanour seemed much healthier, considering.

'Going out laughing,' Ian mused. His voice had returned to what Danny considered normal, no more wheezing or rasping. 'I had hoped for something more dignified. There are worse ways, I suppose.'

Danny shot a look into the room, but mother and son were both still too deep in grief to notice anything. 'Ian, are you okay?' Danny whispered, moving further down the hallway out of earshot.

'That's a bit of a stupid question,' Ian replied. He was holding up his hands in front of his face, as if he'd never seen them before. 'I thought I might be see-through,' he said in disappointed tones.

'I mean *obviously* you're not okay, but do you feel any pull?' Danny whispered more urgently. It had only taken a minute or so for Adella to be affected. He had no idea if they were within range of whatever had taken her spirit.

Ian was too distracted to answer, however. He was staring in at his wife and son, his new circumstances forgotten. 'I should have told them I loved them.'

'You did,' Danny said quietly.

'More often, I mean. Do you think? Could you maybe . . .' he jerked his head in their direction and waggled his eyebrows.

'Bad idea,' Nudge said.

'Yeah, it didn't really work out well the last time we tried that.'

'I heard about that,' Ian said sadly. 'I was just hoping that . . .' he trailed off again and Danny moved to comfort him. He held up a hand to pat Ian on the shoulder and then remembered himself and felt foolish. 'They knew you loved them,' he said.

Ian had stopped talking. But not because he'd been overcome emotionally. He stepped back and turned to them both. 'I feel strange.' He seemed to think about this and then added, 'I mean strange, considering everything.'

Both Danny and Nudge stepped forward. 'Try and link yourself to Danny,' Nudge said quickly. 'Think of him as an anchor.'

Danny reached out a hand towards the older man, just in time for him to be jerked back in the direction of the front door.

Like Adella and Jimmy, Ian was pulled completely off his feet, as if tackled by an invisible opponent. Unlike the others, he managed to get a word out before he disappeared through the door. Unfortunately, it was simply one long drawn-out 'Shiiiiiiiiiiiiiiit!'

Chapter 24

The next half-hour passed in a blur. Sven's aunt and cousins arrived and were ushered into the room. Neighbours gathered in the garden to pay their respects. Danny had the presence of mind to shoot Nadine and their other friends a message to let them know what had happened. Sven walked out into the hall in something of a daze. He seemed surprised to see that Danny was still there.

Danny grabbed his friend into a hug again. 'I'm so sorry, man,' he said, wishing he had something more profound or useful to say.

Sven nodded numbly. 'Thanks. Maybe you should head off? This place is going to be a circus for a while.'

Danny did want to get going, although not for the reasons that Sven thought. 'Are you sure? I can hang on for as long as you guys need?'

'No, you go ahead.'

Danny felt awful but he needed to get out of there. 'Okay, I'll call you later?'

He had his hand on the doorknob when Sven called out. 'Hey. What was he laughing about? At the end?'

Danny was glad that he didn't have to lie to his friend about this. He explained Ian's ruse with the whiskey.

Despite everything, this elicited a smile from Sven. 'That would do it all right.'

There was another beat of silence and, cursing everything that had happened to him in the past couple of weeks, Danny excused himself and slipped out of the house.

*

'What the hell are we going to do?' Nudge said, hurrying after him.

'I don't know,' Danny replied. He didn't bother reaching for his headphones this time to pretend he was on a call. Let people think that he was insane. 'But we can't just wait for Lucy to get back to us,' he added.

'We should call someone,' Nudge said. 'Are you sure Lucy didn't mention, I don't know, Jedi or something?'

'No.' Danny stopped in the middle of the path, so abruptly that Nudge almost bumped into him from behind. An idea had occurred to him. It was a bad idea but that was just par for the course these days.

They had reached the main road out of Sven's estate and, after a brief hesitation, Danny set off in the direction of his parents' house. He was due in work in about forty minutes but that could wait. He slipped a hand into his jacket pocket and grabbed at his flask. He needed to counteract the coffee.

'It has to be us,' he said finally.

'What do you mean "us"?' Nudge said. 'What the fuck are we going to do about it?'

'That time we were first talking to Lucy, you said that you could sense the pull coming from a consistent direction, right?' Danny asked, between sips.

'Yeah. So?' The penny dropped and Nudge shot him a look of panic. 'No! Absolutely not! Are you out of your mind?'

'We use you to follow the pull to its source,' Danny said, still power-walking in the direction of home, so that Nudge had to awkwardly jog along to keep up.

'And then what?' he asked. 'Ask them nicely to stop?'

'We'll find the place first and then . . .' In truth, he had no idea what they would do then, but he felt an odd sense of purpose for the first time in ages '. . . And then we'll improvise.'

Nudge managed to get in front of Danny's rapidly walking frame and block his path. 'We have no idea what we're getting into here. What if whatever it is gets stronger the closer we get to it?'

Danny glanced around and, seeing a laneway between two houses, ducked into it to avoid having this particular heart-to-heart on the main road.

'Whatever this is, it's happening to people all over the city.'

'We don't know that,' Nudge protested.

'Yes, we do. Adella, Jimmy and now Ian. They died miles apart, but they were all affected.'

Nudge went to speak but Danny kept going. 'And even if we didn't know that it was happening, it's Ian. We don't know where these people are getting taken but I'm guessing it's not good. I'm not prepared to leave Sven's dad to that. Are you?'

At this, whatever further protests Nudge had been about to vent died in his throat. He looked ashamed. 'I'm scared, Dan. What if it gets me as well?'

'We won't let it,' Danny said with more confidence than he actually felt. 'If the force of it starts to get too strong, then we'll stop and regroup, okay?'

Nudge swallowed and then after a beat, nodded.

'Good man!' Danny said encouragingly and resumed his walk back to his family home.

'So, what's the plan?' Nudge asked. 'Because you're not walking the right way, if you were wondering.' He gestured off to his left. 'It's coming from that direction.'

'We need to narrow down our search a bit. We'll be at it all day otherwise.'

'How are we going to do that?'

'I've got an idea. I just need a map,' Danny said as he turned into his parents' estate.

'You know they have them on your phone now?' Nudge replied, at least demonstrating that fear hadn't damaged his ability to be sarcastic.

'I need one that I can write on,' Danny explained as, practically jogging now, they reached his house. This time he didn't knock. He knew that neither of his parents would be home at this hour of the morning and, although Steff's car was parked out on the road, a brief search revealed that she and Buster were also out.

Danny made a beeline for the kitchen and opened the top drawer of the large sideboard in the corner. He pulled out, in quick succession: six separate sets of keys, four phone chargers, a sheaf of takeaway menus the size of a Russian novel and eventually, grunting with satisfaction, a stack of old maps. These he brought over to the kitchen table and began unfolding, casting each aside until he found one that showed the greater Dublin area in its entirety.

'I can't remember the last time I saw a real map,' Nudge said conversationally. 'At least not this decade.'

'Dad used to keep them in the car for work,' Danny explained as he scanned the map. 'Google Maps really was a game-changer for the taxi industry. Aha!' he finished, stabbing his finger down on the paper.

'Aha what?' asked Nudge excitedly.

'Well maybe "aha" is a bit strong,' amended Danny. 'I just meant that I've found where we are,' he said.

'Those years in the Cub Scouts clearly weren't wasted,' Nudge said snidely.

Danny ignored him and hurried back to the sideboard. After further rooting around in the Great Miscellaneous Drawer, he returned with a marker pen. After taking a few seconds to get his bearings again, he marked an 'X' at their location. 'Okay. Which way is the pull coming from? Exactly.'

Nudge considered it for a moment and then pointed towards the back of the house. Danny held up his hand to mark the direction and murmured to himself, 'Okay, so that's towards the roundabout, a bit off to the right.' With exaggerated care and the aid of the edge of a diary from 2015, also sourced from the drawer, he carefully drew a line with the marker until it disappeared off the edge of the map.

Nudge tilted his head to try and view it the right way up. It gave him the air of a curious pigeon. 'So what? We follow the line?' That's a lot of ground to cover.'

Danny held up a hand for Nudge to wait. After some more scrutiny, he drew another 'X' over Sven's house. 'Ian was pulled pretty much straight through the front door, right?'

Nudge nodded. Danny squinted down at the map; it lacked the detail of individual houses but, after consulting with Google Maps to get an approximate direction, he drew another line on the map. The two lines intersected on the north side of the city.

'Oh, I see,' Nudge said but Danny was already marking one 'X' in Harold's Cross and another in Drimnagh.

'Adella and Jimmy,' he muttered.

There was a brief interlude where Nudge and Danny consulted Google Maps, argued, staged a rough recreation of the events at Adella's bungalow and outside The Farrier, argued some more and then eventually came to an agreement on what direction the ghosts had been taken.

When Danny had finished drawing the third and fourth lines both men looked at where they intersected: somewhere on the border of Cabra and Phibsborough. Danny consulted his phone again with Nudge looking over his shoulder.

'It's a Tesco?' Nudge said, confused, after Danny managed to find where the lines overlapped. 'Is it an evil Tesco?'

'No,' Danny scoffed and then, remembering all that had happened in the last few weeks, he amended, 'Probably not'. He picked up the marker again and drew a circle around where the lines crossed. 'It's not exact. We'd need a compass and, I don't know, an astrolabe for that but this gives us an area to start with. We should be able to use you to get a more precise idea once we get there.'

Nudge examined the area he'd circled. 'And how do we get there?'

'Ah,' Danny said, his confidence disappearing. He hadn't thought about that. 'Bus?'

'More like two buses,' Nudge said, looking down at where they were heading. 'You're talking the guts of two hours to get out there.'

Danny swore. 'I can't afford a taxi,' he admitted. The past few weeks of not working combined with what he'd paid the psychics, his therapist and for his new whiskey overheads had drained his already pretty meagre savings dry.

'What about Lucy? Could she pick us up?'

Danny shook his head. He'd tried to get through to her a number of times already after Ian's death but there had been no answer. 'I think we can consider that particular bridge burned for the moment.'

'It's really annoying that you don't know how to drive.'

'I know,' Danny agreed.

They both stood in silence for a moment. Nudge's eyes fell on the detritus of the drawer that Danny had pulled out in search of the maps. In particular, he noticed a set of keys with a large Fiat keyring attached.

Danny caught him staring and, once the penny dropped, protested. 'No. Absolutely not!'

Chapter 25

'It's very simple. From left to right, you have the clutch, the brake and the accelerator, so just think, A, B, C,' Nudge explained, for the third time. They were sitting in Steff's grey Fiat Punto outside the house.

'You mean, C, B, A,' Danny said, trying to keep the lid on a rising panic attack.

'What?'

'You said it's clutch, brake, accelerator, so it's C, B, A,' Danny repeated, running his hands nervously over the steering wheel.

'No, it's right to left. A, B, C.'

'Nobody reads like that. It's completely backwards.'

'Well, somehow millions of fucking sixteen-year-olds figure this out every year anyway. Just remember that the brake is the one in the middle.'

'I can't do this!'

'Of for fuck's . . . We've been over this. You have your provisional licence. You've had lessons before.'

'Two years ago!'

'It'll all come back. It's like riding a bike.'

That was patently false, Danny thought. Riding a bike was intuitive. Driving a car involved learning an entirely new set of reflexive movements that were alien to him. It had taken almost fifteen minutes for Nudge to talk Danny as far as sitting in the driver's seat where they'd spent the past ten alternating between the basics of manual transmission and anxiety attacks.

Nudge tried a new tactic, outright abuse not having the desired effect. 'It's just gone eleven o'clock. The roads will be empty. You've done this before. We'll take things slowly and if you feel overwhelmed, then we can pull in.'

'Because that turned out so well the last time?' Danny accused. 'I've been drinking, I'm not supposed to be driving unaccompanied . . .'

'I mean, technically, you're not. I have my full licence,' Nudge interrupted. His brow furrowed. 'Or *had,* at least.'

'Cool, I'll just explain to the police that my invisible, dead friend is my co-pilot.'

'Look, you said it yourself; Ian, Adella and anyone else who's about to die in this city are relying on us. You're not the only one risking something here,' Nudge reminded him.

Danny sighed. It was so unfair when people used your own arguments against you. 'So, C, B, A?' he said wearily.

'If you like,' Nudge said. He had certainly warmed to this plan now, maybe because it involved torturing Danny. 'Now,' he said pointing at the gearstick. 'You need to be in first gear to move off after you stop. Second is the next one up and then third,' he said, miming where the gearstick should be positioned for each. 'Then you have fourth, fifth and reverse but, with any luck, we won't be needing them today. Do you have the route?'

Danny nodded and attached his phone to the magnetic holder on Steff's dashboard. He'd managed to find a route that both avoided the M50 and skirted around the city centre. He was pretty sure that this was all going to end terribly but knew the odds of success dropped to zero if they somehow ended up on the motorway or in the confusing warren of one-way streets in town.

'Right. This is going to be fine,' Nudge said and Danny wasn't sure which one of them he was trying to convince. 'Think of this as just the same as any other driving lesson.'

Danny gritted his teeth rather than bring up the memory of how his previous driving lessons had gone.

'I'll call out which lane you should be in and when you should upshift and downshift. Let's get this show on the road,' Nudge said.

*

On the whole, Danny felt that the next thirty-five minutes could have gone worse. After several, literal, false starts, he'd managed to coax the Punto out of the estate and get it pointed in the direction of the northside. The first half a dozen or so traffic lights had presented something of an obstacle in terms of the car cutting out but eventually he got to grips with the biting point so that, after a while, it was only happening every third or fourth time.

One repeated stumbling block was that Nudge tended to assume he knew far more about the rules of road and driving etiquette than he did. 'You're in the wrong lane!' Nudge would scold as they pulled up to another intersection, in Danny's opinion, a full ten seconds after this information would have been of use.

Nudge had been right, however, that they'd picked the perfect time of day to attempt this. The streets were mostly empty, so Danny wasn't causing too much traffic disruption. In fact, he was starting to notice a small but significant improvement in his driving by the time they approached Cabra. He had relaxed a tiny bit and now merely looked like someone who'd been told they had minutes to live as opposed to someone who was actively mid-heart attack.

This newfound confidence faded as their route took them off the main road and onto a much smaller, residential street. The narrowness of the road was exacerbated by cars parked on both sides and Danny drove down the centre holding his breath, praying that he wouldn't meet anyone coming the other way.

He was navigating the approach to a roundabout when Nudge suddenly jerked his head around. 'Hang on!' he said, as they edged out into the roundabout. 'Turn!' he shouted.

'Which way?'

'West.'

'What!?'

'That way. Right! Turn now,' Nudge shouted.

Danny gritted his teeth and kept the car going around the roundabout to take the next exit, much to the chagrin of a white-van driver coming onto the roundabout who had to slam on the brakes to avoid a collision. The sound of its horn followed them onto another residential road.

'West? *West?*' Danny yelled. 'Really? Who am I? Fucking Magellan!?'

Nudge wasn't paying attention. He had his eyes screwed shut tightly.

'What is it?' asked Danny, curious despite his frustration.

'I think we're close.' Nudge opened his eyes and scanned the road ahead. 'Take this next left.'

Danny did as he was bid. 'Are you going to be okay?' he asked as they pulled onto the new street.

He nodded. 'I think so. It's stronger here, definitely, but I don't think it can overcome the tether just yet. Turn right up here.'

They were deep into a housing estate now, driving past identical-looking terraced homes. Danny made a note to check where they were once they'd stopped because he wasn't certain he could find his way back out if he had to make a run for it.

'It's somewhere here,' Nudge said suddenly. 'Pull in.'

Danny had been dreading having to parallel park on one of these narrow streets almost as much as confronting whatever forces were behind the abductions. He clocked a space ahead that was large enough for two cars and, slowing to a crawl, pulled the Fiat into the kerb. It seemed to be going okay until a long-drawn-out scraping noise filled the car. Both men gritted their teeth and winced as Danny guiltily jerked the wheel away from the kerb and hit the brake, causing the engine to stall again. They were approximately parked at this point, so he didn't bother to restart it.

'How bad is it on your side?' Danny asked.

Nudge stuck his head out the window (without bothering to open it, naturally) and surveyed the damage. 'It's only paint,' he said, by way of explanation.

Danny looked around at the houses surrounding them. He had to admit that he was a little disappointed. In his head, whoever was behind this had been operating out of a castle on some sinister moor or a foreboding, Addams-family-style mansion.

'Can you tell which one it is?' Danny asked.

Nudge pointed at the opposite side of the street. 'I think it's the blue one.'

'How are you doing?' Danny asked.

Nudge shook his head to clear it. 'I'll be fine. It's really strong here but the tether seems to be holding. It just feels like, I don't know, vertigo, maybe?'

Danny patted the back of the passenger seat in lieu of his friend's shoulder. 'Let me know if it gets too much and we can pull back.' He shifted his focus to the house in question. It was three doors up from where they were parked. Nudge had called it blue but the peeling paint on the pebble-dash exterior was really more of a washed-out grey. Its narrow concrete driveway was separated from its neighbours by a short iron fence painted inexpertly black on one side and a hedge so large and thick that it was in danger of obscuring the second-floor window on the other. A large black Audi took up the rest of the driveway and most of the path in front of the gate. Between it and the hedge, Danny wasn't sure how anyone made it to the door. The car seemed out of place, sitting in front of the flaking green paint of the front door, shiny and new.

'What do we do now?' Nudge asked.

Danny had no idea. He honestly hadn't thought that they'd get this far. When he'd imagined their destination as a skull-shaped fortress he had assumed that they'd just break in. But now that they were faced with a normal-looking house, this seemed a lot harder.

'I guess we stay here and keep watch? See if anyone comes or goes.'

'Stake-out!' Nudge said with enthusiasm.

*

His enthusiasm lessened after another hour and a half. They used this time to lament Steff's lack of binoculars, parabolic microphones, or any other pieces of surveillance equipment. The only thing the Punto was equipped with was a CD player, a baby seat and an impressive number of fast-food wrappers and empty bottles in the passenger footwell.

'She could clean this out every now and again,' Nudge complained as he tried to place his feet in such a way that they weren't resting on a McNuggets box or an empty bottle of Diet Coke.

'Steff and Dad argue about it all the time but nobody else uses it these days, so—' Danny broke off as he noticed movement in the house they were surveying. 'Look!' he said, slouching down behind the steering wheel.

The front door opened and a man in his early thirties exited the house. He had a mop of sandy blond hair held back from his face by the pair of wraparound sunglasses resting on his head and he wore a tight white polo shirt that revealed a wiry, athletic body over tan slacks. As they watched, he awkwardly tried to hold the front door open with his shoulder as he pulled a set of golf clubs onto the front step.

Danny fished his phone out of his pocket and took a photo as the man fumbled with his house keys to lock the door behind him. Lacking a telephoto lens, the camera's built-in zoom did a good enough job of bringing into focus a clean-shaven, handsome face, whistling as he busied himself carefully loading his golf clubs into the back of the Audi.

As the boot slammed closed, he walked around to the driver's side door and then stopped. Danny hunched down further in his seat, worried he might have been seen but the man just leaned back and brought his shoulders up and down in a long stretch, working his neck over and back. He seemed very pleased with the results because he was beaming as he slipped in behind the wheel.

The Audi started and pulled out of the driveway. Luckily for them, it headed in the opposite direction so Danny didn't have to try and lean down any further. As the car vanished from view, he looked over to see that Nudge was also slouched down.

'What are you doing?' he asked. 'He wouldn't have been able to see you.'

'Oh yeah,' he said, embarrassed. 'I just kind of got caught up in the excitement.'

They sat back up straight in their seats. Danny looked down at the picture he'd captured on his phone.

'What now? Do we try and get in while he's gone?' Nudge asked.

Danny squinted across at the house, but the yellowing net curtains refused to reveal anything further. 'There's no way to know if there's anyone else in there or not,' he said. Plus, he still had no idea how to go about breaking into someone's house.

They looked over at the house again in silence for a moment.

'We're really bad at this,' Nudge said eventually.

Danny was about to agree with him when a banging on the passenger side window caused them both to jump in shock. They'd been so focused on the house that they had entirely missed someone walking up beside the car.

We really are bad at this thought Danny as he struggled to see around Nudge to confront whoever it was.

Their assailant was a pale brunette wearing a camel-hair coat and an expression that was equal parts weary surprise and frustration.

'What the fuck are you two doing here?'

'Hi Lucy,' Nudge said cheerfully.

Chapter 26

After they'd finished gawping at one another through the glass, Danny pointed to the back seat and Lucy, several choice curse words crystallising in front of her in the chilly afternoon air, opened the door. She was presented with Buster's baby seat and after staring at it for a couple of moments, swore again, slammed the door, and walked around to the driver's side.

'What are you two doing here?' she repeated as she threw herself in behind Danny.

'We're on a stake-out,' said Nudge. It did not sound as cool when he said it to someone else. It made them seem like a couple of kids playing spy.

'We used Nudge to trace the source of the disturbance,' Danny explained. He felt that this sounded a bit better.

'That's . . .' Lucy started before her brain caught up with the words, 'actually not a bad idea,' she finished begrudgingly.

'I'm sorry about how we left it yesterday,' Danny said. 'But a friend of ours passed away this morning and got caught up in all of this. We had to do something.'

'Another one?' Lucy asked, her frustration with them momentarily forgotten. 'Where?'

'Knocklyon,' Nudge said.

'That's . . .'

'On the other side of the city,' Danny finished. A thought occurred to him. 'How did you find us?'

'What?' she said, distracted. The news seemed to have shaken her.

'How did you find this place? Where's your car?' Danny repeated.

She stared at both of them as if she wanted to slap their heads together and then looked down. 'Am I standing in jellies?' she asked.

Danny twisted awkwardly around so that he could get a better look at the footwell of the back seat. 'Oh yeah, Percy Pigs. Bits of them anyway. Buster loves them but he has a tendency to throw them around before he's finished.'

Lucy gave him a look that told him she was adding this particular indignity to a long list of things she planned to hold against them at a later date. 'What were we talking about?'

'How you found this place.' Nudge prompted.

'Oh, yes. Well, after Tweedledee . . .' she jerked her thumb towards Danny '. . . told me that Adella had been pulled into all of this *a full week after it had happened,*' she enunciated these last words very carefully, 'I started asking some of the local spirits I know, and they eventually pointed me in this direction. I parked my car around the corner so I could scope it out on foot first.'

'Oh!' Nudge said, looking at Danny. 'That would have been clever.'

'And then I spotted you two, so I thought I'd see what stupidity you were cooking up. What *is* your plan?'

'We just saw someone leave,' Danny explained. 'And we were discussing our options for next steps.' This seemed like a better explanation than, 'We have no clue what to do now.'

He brought up the golfer's picture on his phone and handed it back to Lucy. 'This is the guy who came out. Recognise him?'

She studied the photo for a second and then handed the phone back. 'No, can't say I do.'

Danny was disappointed. He'd been half-hoping she would exclaim, 'It can't be. It's the evil Lord Macabre!' and then call in a hitherto-unmentioned team of supernatural Avengers to take over. He drummed his fingers on the steering wheel and peered across the road again at the house. 'I'm going to knock on the door. Maybe see if I can peek in through the window,' he said.

He felt a hand on his shoulder and turned. Lucy was looking at him with concern. 'Look, we don't know what we're getting into here. Maybe you guys should go home? I'll bring my car around and keep watch. If anything changes, then I'll call you.'

Danny was about to argue but the sense of urgency that they'd felt immediately after Ian's disappearance seemed to have ebbed away and left nothing but uncertainty in its place. Lucy was right. It didn't look like there was anything they could do at the moment. There was no harm in waiting another night to come up with a better plan.

This internal argument was derailed when Danny caught movement out of the corner of his eye. He leaned past Nudge to see an elderly woman coming out of the house that they'd parked in front of. She was waving at them with the righteous indignation that only a pensioner who has noticed a minor infraction could muster.

The new arrival was dressed in a long brown skirt over a pair of what looked like dinosaur-feet slippers. She accessorised both of these with a spectacularly pink housecoat.

Nudge tried to lean out of the way as Danny reached across to wind down the passenger-side window.

The woman reached the end of her driveway and stopped as Danny waved back at her. He put on his 'talking-to-old-people-and-children voice. 'Hello. Is everything okay?'

'You can't park there!' If her accent had been any more Dublin, then they could have mounted it on a plinth in the Guinness Storehouse. 'It's residents' parking only.'

This, as far as Danny was concerned, made the decision for him. He had been prepared to confront whatever paranormal force was causing the disruption to the spirit realm, but he wasn't crazy enough to take on a residents' association when it came to a parking dispute.

'I'm very sorry,' he said, still in a bright sing-song voice. 'I'll move it now.'

'Well, you'd better. Are you with the guards?' she asked suddenly, peering in at Lucy in the back seat.

'I'm sorry?' Danny asked.

'I've been watching you,' the old lady said with the same inexplicable anger. 'Sitting out here for hours. Did the guards send you here to silence me?'

Danny felt that he should have grown used to being wrong-footed by outlandish statements at this point. He'd certainly had a lot of practice recently. 'No,' Danny said slowly, looking back and forth between Nudge and Lucy for emotional support. He couldn't help but ask. 'Why would the guards try to silence you?'

The housecoat-clad woman had walked right up to them now and Nudge had to jerk back to avoid her as she thrust her face into the car. She looked around then seemed satisfied that the guards wouldn't be operating out of a Punto covered in quite so many mutilated Percy Pigs. 'Why are you sitting in the back, dear?' she asked. Ignoring Danny's question. 'Is this some sort of drug deal? We want none of that around here. You hear me?'

'No,' Danny said quickly. 'We're not guards or drug-dealers. We're . . .' he faltered. It might be easier to just admit to being some sort of police intimidation squad or heroin dealer. It would certainly be less tricky to explain than the truth.

She squinted at Lucy. 'Do I know you, love?' Lucy looked as if she was doing her best to hide behind Buster's car seat.

'We're journalists,' Nudge prompted suddenly.

'We're journalists,' Danny parroted before his brain caught up with what he'd just said.

Their interrogator's demeanour changed instantly. 'Why didn't you say so?' she asked, her hands automatically going to her helmet of grey curls as if they were about to stick a long lens through the window. 'I'm not ready. You should both come in for a cup of tea.' When neither Danny nor Lucy moved, she apparently decided that they lacked the proper incentive. 'They just delivered the shopping yesterday, so I have teacakes.'

She didn't seem like the sort of person to take no for an answer, so Danny decided to just go with it. 'We'll be one moment. Just let us get our gear sorted,' he said.

This seemed to satisfy her, as she retreated back towards the door leaving them to their whispered argument.

'Why did you say we were journalists?' Danny asked Nudge, keeping his smile pasted across his face as the woman waved at them from her front step.

'Never mind him,' Lucy raged quietly. 'Why did *you* say it?'

She did have a point.

Nudge showed little remorse. Instead, he pointed at a piece of paper that had been sellotaped to the pillar by her gate. Danny hadn't given it much thought when they'd pulled up. He'd assumed it had been some sort of planning permission notice. Looking closer, he saw that it actually featured a grainy photo of a young man.

'She obviously has some sort of story to tell,' Nudge said, stepping through the door and out of the car. 'Let's hear her out.'

'But what if she's mental?' Danny asked.

Nudge leaned back in through the window. 'What? Like if she thinks that ghosts are being abducted?'

Danny supposed he had a point. Their definition of 'mental' had become a lot more fluid of late. He hauled himself out of the driver's seat, relishing the opportunity to stand up straight. He walked around the bonnet so that he could get a better look at the sign that had been taped to the pillar. It was a simple sheet of A4 paper, clearly mocked up on someone's home computer. Written at the top in large black font was: **Missing: Anthony 'Anto' Sharpe**. Further down, the notice detailed that Anto was twenty-three years old, five foot seven and had been missing since 28 October. He'd been last seen wearing a pair of navy tracksuit bottoms and a Bohemians FC tracksuit top.

Looking up and down the road from his new vantage point, Danny noticed an identical sign taped to a telephone pole a few doors down.

Lucy walked up behind him as he made to approach the house. 'Where are you going?' she asked.

Danny shrugged. 'Nudge is right. She might know something we don't. Old people like this are terrible snoops. Plus, I've been sitting in that car for an hour and a half now and I really need to use the toilet.' With this, he walked up the drive to where the older woman was waiting, ignoring the many and varied whispered insults that followed him.

'Hi, I'm . . . Paul,' he said, figuring at the last minute that it might not be the best idea to use his real name.

'Nancy. Although, I'm sure you know that already,' the woman said, taking Danny's hand in both of hers. 'Now come in off the road. Some of the aul' ones around here are real busybodies,' she whispered conspiratorially. 'Which is ironic considering what some of them get up to.'

Danny just kept nodding as he was gently but firmly led into a narrow hallway. He wondered if all grandmothers of a certain era worked off the same template when it came to home decoration. Aside from a disturbing photo of a Siamese cat above the telephone table, Nancy's hall was almost exactly like his own late granny's house had been. The same carpet of undistinguishable colour, the same textured wallpaper from the early nineties and the same portrait of Padre Pio looking beatifically constipated hanging at the bottom of the stairs.

Danny followed Nancy as she bustled into the front room. It was furnished with a surprisingly new-looking black leather two-piece suite, although the spot in front of the TV was still dominated by a floral-patterned arm-chair. It was the type of overstuffed fire hazard that was only keeping its shape through the structural integrity of the thousands of boiled sweets and tissues stratified in its recesses. Like Adella's, the floor space that wasn't taken up by the chairs and TV was monopolised by more end tables and a large bookshelf that contained dozens of family photographs and also a slightly alarming amount of cat ornaments.

'Sit down. Sit down,' she urged as she walked through to the kitchen out the back.

'Would I be able to use your bathroom, Nancy?' Danny asked.

'Of course. First door at the top of the stairs,' she shouted back.

Danny called out his thanks and moved to make his way back out into the hall, but he was blocked by Lucy. She looked as if constantly being surprised by the new ways in which he managed to piss her off.

'What are we doing here?' she asked quietly.

'We are keeping a nice old lady company,' Danny replied and then, when his sarcasm didn't go over well, 'We're keeping an eye on the house somewhere nice and warm that has teacakes, okay? Now, keep watch while I go see a man about a dog.'

He arrived back down in time to relieve Nancy of a tea tray that she was carrying in from the kitchen. He placed it down on the coffee table and slipped onto the two-seater sofa beside Lucy. Nudge stood in the door-way, where he could keep a wary eye on the golfer's house across the road.

'So,' Nancy opened as she sat down in the armchair and got herself settled. 'What paper did you say you were with?'

Lucy seemed prepared to leave him be the one to gaslight a pensioner, so Danny cleared his throat. 'We're actually with a local news website.'

Nancy seemed disappointed at this at first but rallied somewhat. 'That figures. I've been ringing the papers for weeks now but they've no interest,' she said scornfully.

'Nancy, maybe you could tell us the whole story. From the beginning, I mean? In your own words.' Danny said.

The older woman nodded and took a deep breath before beginning. Danny got the sense that she had rehearsed this. 'It's my grandson, Anthony. He's been missing for over a month now.'

'Okay, and he was living here with you?'

The old woman nodded. 'Ever since his mammy passed away, yes.'

'I'm very sorry,' Danny said, and meant it. 'Was his mother your—'

'She was my daughter, yes. The dad was never in the picture really, so it's been just me and him ever since.'

'And you reported him as missing?' Lucy asked, invested despite herself. 'To the guards, I mean?'

Nancy's look of sorrow and worry twisted to one of anger at this. 'Oh, I did. Not that they took it seriously. They *said* they'd look into it, but I haven't seen a single guard around here since.'

'Why did you think that they were out to silence you?' Danny asked, thinking back to her bizarre accusation earlier.

'They say that I've been harassing them,' she said indignantly. 'Just because I figured out that they're not doing a tap for my Anthony. They asked me to stop contacting them so often. That they'd call me when they had something. I said that I was going to report them to the papers—'

'—Why do you think that they're not taking this seriously?' Lucy interrupted, as if she'd sensed the beginnings of a rant and wanted to try and head it off.

Nancy looked uncomfortable at this. 'Well,' she started reluctantly. 'Anthony had a history. It was all behind him though,' she insisted.

'Was it drugs?' Danny asked.

She nodded. 'When Trish, his mammy, passed away, he fell in with a bad crowd. Got in trouble with the guards a couple of times and . . .' she trailed off, as if still overwhelmed by the memory.

Lucy reached out instinctively and grabbed her hand.

She nodded in thanks. 'He ended up doing two years in Mountjoy.'

'So the guards think he might be up to his old habits?' Danny asked.

'Yes. But even when he was on the gear, he'd still check in with me every few days. He would never leave for this long!'

Nancy obviously felt that they weren't taking her seriously because she leaned forward and repeated. 'He got himself clean in prison. He started going to meetings twice a week ever since he got out. He even got a job.'

She looked over at the cabinet by the wall. Framed photos covered its shelves in between yet more cat ornaments.

'Do you mind?' Danny asked, standing up to take a better look.

She waved at him to continue, and he stepped closer to examine the photos. They showed Anto's journey from pink-faced baby to toddler to gangly teen. He picked up one in a brown wooden frame. It was the same one that featured in the flyer outside. Danny assumed it must be the most recent.

Anto had dark brown hair that was styled into spikes down onto his forehead. He was skinny and seemed to share Danny's condition of having a head that was slightly too big for his body. What had been cropped out of the picture on the flyer outside was the fact that he had an arm wrapped around Nancy. It looked as if it had been taken on the very couch where Lucy was still sitting. As he smiled shyly, Nancy's face beamed out of the picture. Danny really wished he could help her find him.

'What was the job?' he asked.

'He said it was just gofer work. Off the books, you know? But he was learning a trade and his boss was helping him get set up with something more permanent,' she said.

Something caught Danny's eye: an older picture buried in the top corner of the cabinet, almost hidden behind a picture of Anthony playing football as a child, decked out in another Bohs jersey.

'When was this taken?' Danny said, reaching up and carefully removing the old silver frame and tilting it towards Nancy. It was a black-and-white photograph of about ten people standing outside what were still recognisable as the houses on this street. The men wore suits and carried pints in their hands; the women wore dresses and mostly carried babies. They smiled awkwardly out of the frame.

Nancy reached out and took the picture carefully. 'August 1958,' she said softly. Danny was pretty sure she would be able to provide the exact date and time, if asked. 'That's when the corporation finished this part of the estate and we were able to move in. That's my Henry there.' She pointed at a large, barrel-chested man with his arm draped over a young, smiling Nancy. She'd been quite the looker. What surprised Danny, though, was that she wasn't the only person in the picture that he recognised straight off.

Standing to their right, his tall frame languishing on the garden wall behind them, was a man with a mop of long hair that Danny knew was blond, despite the monochrome photo. In his lap, a chubby smiling baby was reaching out to grab at the pint he held in one out-stretched arm. He was the spitting image of the golfer, the man they'd seen pull out half an hour before.

'Who's this?' Danny enquired, trying to keep his voice neutral.

'That's Mr Brooks,' she said. 'He took one of the houses across the road.' She gave Lucy another strange look. As if she was trying to place her. 'You look so like—'

'—You must have seen the neighbourhood change a lot since then,' Lucy interrupted.

Danny shot her a confused look at the sudden change in direction of the conversation.

Nancy made a face. 'Gone to the dogs, more like. Kids on those scramblers going up and down at all hours of the day and night.'

Danny saw the method in Lucy's seemingly random question. 'Cars driving recklessly?' he chimed in, as casually as he could.

'I'm afraid to cross the road most days in case one of those boy racers runs me over. It would serve the little gurriers right, of course.'

'We were almost hit by one while we were parked up outside,' Danny said, matching Nancy's tone of moral outrage. 'This big black Audi nearly took the door off my car and then just drove off without even a second look.'

'Oh, don't get me started on him. He keeps parking it so that it blocks the footpath as well. I'm always telling him he should put it in his garage, or he won't have it for very long.'

'Oh. So, the driver lives around here?'

'Yes, Mr Brooks across the road bought it last month.'

Danny frowned. 'So, this is the son of the Mr Brooks in this picture?' he asked, pointing to the golfer's doppelganger.

Nancy nodded and then, after looking left and right as if to check that there weren't any eavesdroppers lurking in her house plants, she leaned in and whispered. 'It was a bit of a scandal,' she said, in the tones of someone pleased to be imparting gossip. 'He had a son out of wedlock. No one knew, of course. Not even his poor wife. Kept him a secret his whole life. They only reconnected earlier this year. Of course, you only have to look at him to see that he's the spitting image of his father.'

'So, the son lives with him now?' Danny asked.

She half-nodded and then stopped. 'Well, not *with him*. Not any more. Apparently, the father had to be

moved out to some assisted-living place a few weeks ago.
It's terrible the way some children just lock their parents
away. Although, I suppose that if anyone ever had cause
to resent a father, it's young Raymond.'

The rational synapse of Danny's brain, which had been
dancing up and down with its hand raised for the past
few moments, finally pointed something out. 'Did you
say a garage?' Danny asked, interrupting her monologue
on how terribly the elderly were treated in this country.

'Yes, he has one out the back. A lot of houses on this
street do. Henry always used ours for his homebrew. I
used to tell him that if he wanted to make beer, then he
should have taken that interview with Guinness's when
he had the chance.'

Danny placed the picture back on the shelf and took
the opportunity to look through to the kitchen. Out the
back window, he could indeed see a surprisingly long back
garden that ended in a dilapidated garage. A narrow pas-
sageway ran between the outbuilding and the side wall.

'Excuse me, Nancy,' Danny said, interrupting her
reminiscing. He clutched at his pocket and took out his
phone. 'I'm just getting a call.'

'Of course. Go ahead.'

Danny gave an encouraging look to Lucy as he stepped
outside and received a death glare in return. As he left, he
heard Nancy whisper, 'So, are you two together then?'

In the hall, he brought up Google Maps on his phone.
After finding their location and zooming in on the satel-
lite view, he was able to confirm that there was indeed
a narrow laneway that ran behind the houses opposite.

'What are you thinking?' asked Nudge. The ghost
had followed him out.

Danny showed him the phone. 'That might be our best way in. If I can climb over the back wall, there might be a window or something open?'

'You want to break in?'

'"Want" isn't exactly the right word but I suppose we're not going to get a better chance. How long does a round of golf take?' Danny asked.

Nudge shrugged. 'Couple of hours maybe? Longer, if you're bad at it.'

He checked the time. They'd seen the golfer pull out a little under half an hour ago. That should, theoretically, give him at least an hour to check it out. The longer he left it, the more chance there was of him getting caught in the act.

He popped his head around the door into the living room. Nancy was in full flow giving Lucy the ins and outs of the surprisingly intricate neighbourhood political landscape.

'. . . he doesn't think I can see him, but I know that he's been putting his bottles in my bin!'

Danny interrupted. 'I'm sorry, that was the office, I forgot something and I'm going to have to fly back and get it.'

Lucy stood up, a little too quickly. 'That's a shame. Nancy, it was so nice meeting you.'

Danny steeled himself for a bollocking and then happily exclaimed. 'Oh no, I'll only be fifteen minutes. Our editor asked you to stay here and get more details on Nancy's story. I'll swing by and pick you up after.'

If looks could kill, then Danny would be sharing the afterlife with Nudge. 'I don't want you going out of your way,' she said icily.

'No trouble at all,' he replied.

Lucy managed to keep her face neutral. 'Of course. Nancy, just give me a second.'

The older woman waved them away. 'Pay me no heed,' she stood up and began painstakingly putting the mugs back on the tray.

Danny knew it was coming but still only managed to half-parry Lucy's punch in the shoulder once the living room door had closed. 'What the fuck are you doing?'

Danny explained his plan. 'I need you to stay here and be lookout. If whatshisface returns, then you can shoot me a text and I'll make myself scarce.'

'You can't break into someone's house,' she said.

'I'm only going to break into his garden. We'll see how we get on from there.'

Lucy began to protest further but he pushed on. 'Look, *we don't have time!* Whatever is going on in there, it's got my friend's dad, it's got Adella, Jimmy and God knows how many others. We need to do this. *I* need to do this! You were right. I should have told you about Adella earlier. Let me try to make this right.'

Lucy's face softened. 'Please don't.'

Danny was touched by her concern. Obviously, she wasn't quite as mad as he had previously guessed. 'I'll be in and out before you know it,' he said, with rather more confidence than he felt.

Before she could argue any further, he slipped out the door with Nudge in tow.

Danny stopped at the end of the driveway and stamped his feet in the cold. It still hadn't turned two o'clock yet, so the street was empty. He rubbed his hands together as he acclimated to the chilly air, looking left and right. Figuring that there had to be an entrance to the lane somewhere along the street, he turned left and started walking. He clocked the golfer's house number as he passed by. Number thirty-eight. That side of the road was evens so he kept an eye on the numbers as he briskly walked. He finally came upon a way behind the houses between numbers sixty-eight and seventy.

There was a set of staggered railings in front, presumably there to dissuade the owners of the scramblers that Nancy had mentioned, and Danny slipped through them. Jogging slightly now, he found himself in the laneway that ran parallel to the street in front. He moved quickly back the way he had come, trying to count the houses as he did so. This was a little more difficult than he'd originally thought. Not all the houses had garages and occasionally he would pass a batch of three or four that offered only a featureless brick wall. He eventually reached what he was reasonably sure was the back of the golfer's house. He could see that the window fixtures had the same flaking green paint as the front and, more helpfully, someone had drawn a large 38 in faded white paint on the garage door.

The door was a single sheet of corrugated iron, designed to swing upwards, with a metal handle set into its centre. Danny reached down and gave it an experimental pull. It was, unsurprisingly, locked. He moved to examine the smaller gate immediately to its left, set into the brick wall. It was made of thick wrought iron, painted with the same black as the main garage door. Another optimistic push revealed that, this, too, was locked. This left Danny one other option.

He carefully raised his hands and rang them along the lintel above the gate. His parents' house backed onto a lane so he knew how broken glass set into cement was a low-cost, common burglar deterrent. His fingers brushed only damp concrete so he stepped back to judge the height of the gate properly.

'Any chance of a boost?' he asked his friend in jest but then saw his expression. 'Are you okay?' he asked, more urgently.

Nudge's face had paled, which was impressive considering, and he looked like he might throw up.

'Whatever we're doing, we need to do it fast. I don't think I can be this close for long.'

Danny nodded and looked at the gate again. Before he could overthink it, he took a step, planted one foot against the wall and threw himself up to grab the top of the gate. His recently cracked ribs screamed in agony as he dragged himself over but, eventually, he landed heavily on the other side. After catching his breath and checking that Nudge was still with him, he edged cautiously along the side passage.

The garage was a lot deeper than he had expected it to be, taking up more than a third of the long back garden. The rest of it was taken up by a short jungle of a lawn that was bisected by a rough path leading up to a cracked flagstone patio outside the back door.

The back of the house had been renovated at some time in the past to install a large sliding glass door that took up half the house's width and allowed Danny to see directly into a small kitchen-slash-dining area. It was mercifully empty. The other side of the house simply had a single, small window on this floor. Neither the window nor the patio door were open.

He began to pad softly through the garden towards the back of the house when Nudge called to him. He turned around to see his friend staring at the garage.

'What's up?' Danny whispered.

Nudge took a step towards the garage and held a hand to the door. 'The force, whatever it is. I think it's coming from in there.'

Danny walked up to join him. 'Are you sure?'

Nudge took a couple of steps towards the house with his eyes closed and then retraced them. 'Yeah, it's definitely there.'

Danny looked at the garage. The window had been covered with some sort of wood panelling on the inside of the glass, preventing them from seeing inside. The door was another iron lump of a thing painted the same black as the other side. It looked like something taken off a Cold War bomb shelter.

Danny reached out and gave it a careful tug, but it was, again, locked. He looked over at Nudge. 'Can you . . . You know?' He made a walking gesture with his fingers that he hoped was the international symbol for 'phase through the wall with your ghost magic'.

Nudge shook his head violently and took a step back. 'I can't.'

'I'll be right here,' Danny said in his best reassuring voice.

'You don't understand. Whatever is in there is the *source*.'

Danny looked at his friend. He might have been imagining it but Nudge seemed like he was becoming harder to see. He had spent the time at Nancy's sipping at his flask as well as her tea so it couldn't be that he was sobering up. Proximity to whatever was in the shed was having some sort of effect on him.

Danny looked around the garden with a renewed sense of urgency and his eyes fell on a trio of flower pots beside the shed door. He looked at the window again. It was boarded over but they seemed to just be thin plywood. He imagined that it wouldn't be too much work to pop them out once the glass had been broken.

He reached down and lifted the smallest of the three pots. If the miniature ecosystem of worms, earwigs and spiders that fled the resulting sunlight were any indication, then it hadn't been moved in decades. He hefted the pot's weight experimentally and then raised it to head height in preparation to smash against the window.

'Danny?' Nudge said.

He looked over at his friend who was pointing down to where the pot had rested. Something glittered in the dirt. Danny carefully put down the flower pot and, trying to ignore Nudge's smug look, leaned over to pick up a rusting key ring. There were a number of keys on it. All of which were the old type that Danny mentally associated with haunted houses in computer games. Only one was the approximate size to fit the garage though so, praying that the elements hadn't rusted it beyond use, he fitted into the lock and, with surprising ease, turned it.

He took another glance at Nudge. 'Maybe you should stay out here and keep watch?'

The ghost nodded enthusiastically. 'Good call.'

Danny pulled on the handle and the door swung outward. He stepped back a little but Ark of the Covenant ghosts failed to emerge. The house blocked most of the direct sunlight to the back garden at this hour of the day so the interior remained ominously shrouded in darkness.

He took a tentative step inside and swatted his hands at the wall to the right of the door. His fingers touched metal and, he pulled back, a loud clang caused both him and Nudge to jump. A long, thin pipe, maybe an inch in diameter, rolled into the shaft of weak light offered by the open door. Danny sighed and tried to get his heart rate down below hummingbird levels as he ran his fingers along the other side and was rewarded with a panel of switches.

He had been expecting a lone, flickering bulb to reveal a collection of torture devices and trophies from previous victims so was pleasantly surprised when overhead strip lights filled the entire garage with a clean, bright light.

'Garage' was the wrong word though, it looked part workshop and part laboratory. Danny picked up the pipe that had fallen to the floor and, after inspecting it, replaced it in a recess between a workbench and the door with what looked like a dozen others of differing lengths and thicknesses. The bench took up the whole front of the shed under the window. Danny could see that it was blacked out because a wooden peg board filled with tools had been hung across it. These *did* look like torture implements. Pincers, shears, trowels and hooks of all different shapes and sizes covered the rack.

The wall immediately to his left had a large metal locker and a long, ancient chest freezer against it but he moved away from these to examine the opposite wall. Or at least the massive iron contraption that obscured it. Danny didn't think he'd ever seen a furnace before but it was the only word that leapt into his brain, unbidden, when he spotted the soot-stained machine. The grubby, grey extension cord that ran from it looked out of place. It looked like the sort of thing that should have been kept stoked with coal, logs and the sweat of Victorian orphans. He glanced around the small space. The heat must have been hellish when it was switched on.

He turned to focus on the last wall. This, at least, provided some much-needed context for the rest of the room. This side of the garage had originally been the door out into the back lane, but it was obviously not designed to be opened any time soon. A series of steel and wood racks had been installed across it instead and on them sat a collection of glass objects.

There were vases and bowls of all shapes and colours, ornaments where horses or dolphins leaped and flickered in the overhead light. Bottles and flasks with curved, elongated necks sat beside egg-timers and lampshades. Danny was no judge of glassblowing but whoever used this workshop seemed to have some serious talent. The glassware wouldn't have looked out of place in the houseware section of some upmarket boutique.

His eye was drawn past all this though to a gap in the centre of the collection. One of the shelving units had been ripped out, leaving a space about five feet wide. In it sat something covered in an old drop-sheet. As Danny stood in front of it, he estimated it to be maybe four feet wide and well over six high.

'What the fuck is that?' Nudge asked.

Danny nearly vomited his oesophagus in fright. He whipped around to see that his friend had poked his head cautiously over the threshold.

'I think it's whatever you've been sensing,' Danny replied.

He grabbed a hold of the drop cloth and pulled. The tarp came away revealing . . . Danny had no idea what it revealed.

It looked like an hourglass for counting down to the death of planets. It looked like a desk ornament in Satan's office. It looked like the bastard offspring of an enormous hourglass and a mobius strip.

It looked fucking weird.

Nudge and Danny stared at it in awe for a few moments before Nudge broke the silence. 'What the hell is it?'

Danny didn't answer; he was too entranced by the glass structure. It was contained in a dark wooden case about six and half feet tall and maybe three feet wide. The frame supported two enormous glass bulbs, one on top of the other, which is what had put Danny in mind of an hourglass. However, rather than a simple opening connecting them, the top bulb descended into a swirling vortex of intricate tubes that wrapped around each other in a way that made Danny's brain ache. It looked as if the twisted glass passageways *should* terminate in the bottom bulb but, for the life of him, Danny couldn't figure out how. The centre mass of glass conduits coiled around one another, and through one another at certain intervals, to the point that anything dropped from the top seemed just as likely to end up back there as it did on the bottom.

Looking closer, Danny could see that the frame and, indeed, the glass itself was intricately carved with markings. Danny couldn't be sure but they seemed to be the same symbols that had been on the Spirit Lock.

A swirling, grey mass passed from one bulb to another through the pathways. At first, he thought it was some sort of dark smoke or perhaps the viscous liquid they put into lava lamps. Danny noticed part of a tube that ballooned out, magnifying the contents as they passed through, and leaned in for a better look.

He jumped back as the glassware enlarged a terrified face.

It was full of souls.

Danny backed away from the monstrosity in horror. He glanced over at Nudge, who, for some reason, was focused not on the giant ghost prison but on a picture that hung over the chest freezer near the door.

'Danny,' he said urgently, but Danny had turned back to the writhing mass of spirits winding their way around the glass channels and culverts. He could make out individuals now, within, looking not small, but somehow a long way off.

'Danny!' Nudge said again.

How many people die in Dublin every day? Dozens? Was this confined to just the city or was it pulling in people from further out? 'A month,' Lizzy had said. How many hundreds of souls were trapped inside this thing?

'DANNY!' Nudge shouted but it was the creak of the door and the sound of footsteps that finally caused him to turn around.

He saw the determined look on Lucy's face.

He saw the pepper-spray canister. It hung on a keychain. The same keys she'd presumably used to let herself in through the house.

Over her shoulder, he saw the picture Nudge had been looking at. A black-and-white photograph of Lucy and the golfer smiling at the camera.

Then he didn't see much of anything at all.

Chapter 27

Danny dabbed the milk-sodden cloth gingerly against his eyes. This was a little awkward with his wrists zip-tied securely around the leg of the workbench, but his vision was starting to clear now that the best part of twenty minutes had passed since Lucy had maced him.

She had been kind enough to fetch him a damp cloth and some milk to wash the residue from his face. Granted, this has been after she followed up the chemical attack with a kick to his groin. He hadn't been in much of a position to resist when, afterwards, she'd grabbed a zip tie from one of the workshop's drawers and secured him to the bench. Such had been the pain in his face that he had barely noticed the kick. He felt as if someone had taken a belt sander to his eyelids and sinuses. Danny had all but poured the entire pint over his face when she'd brought the carton out. This had helped with the worst of the burning but his eyes still streamed and the skin around them felt raw.

He regarded his captor through capsaicin-ravaged eyes as he tried to wipe his nose. It had been running constantly since the macing. Danny was worried it was part of his frontal lobe that had liquidated.

Lucy was pacing near the door, alternating between smoking, checking her phone and turning the canister of pepper spray nervously around in her hands.

'I've always wondered what using this would be like,' she said. Then she noticed something as she turned it around. 'Oh, this is expired,' she said, squinting at the bottom of the can.

'I can confirm it still works,' Danny croaked. 'Nudge, are you okay?'

'I'll live,' he replied grimly.

Nudge had spent the immediate aftermath of the macing watching helplessly and subjecting Lucy to a lengthy and creative masterclass in verbal abuse as Danny writhed in pain, but had since fallen silent.

It seemed stupid to say that a ghost looked unwell, but that was the only way Danny could describe it. Nudge looked paler, not in skin tone, but as if his very substance itself was being leached away. Whatever the hell that glass monolith was, Danny didn't think that Nudge would survive being around it for much longer.

He turned his attention back to the picture that hung by the door. With his eyes starting to finally clear after the pepper-spraying, he was able to get a better look at it. Danny kicked himself for missing it on the first survey of the room but he'd been too busy expecting a knife-wielding psycho to jump out at him to notice the decor. It was a black-and-white print that showed Lucy and the golfer on some beach, smiling at the camera. His hand was around her waist, and she was leaning into him comfortably. Something about it didn't add up though: both Lucy and the Golfer looked different. Older. Danny was bad at judging these things but he guessed around their mid-forties.

Lucy copped him staring at it and turned to look at the photo. 'Rosslare, 1976,' she said eventually. 'Our twentieth wedding anniversary.'

'You're not Adella's granddaughter,' Danny said.

He thought about the picture he'd seen in Adella's kitchen. The two young women in their nursing uniforms. 'Two nurses in the family.' That's what Adella had said. When they'd first met, he thought Lucy's face had been familiar because of one of the pictures of the grandchildren but, seeing her in black and white now, he realised that he'd recognised her from where she smiled out of that photograph, standing behind her younger sister.

'No. I'm not,' Lucy said sadly.

'Just how old are you, exactly?' he asked, looking between her and the picture.

'I'll be eighty-six in March.'

'I fucking knew it,' Nudge exclaimed, causing both Lucy and Danny to jump in shock. 'Vampires! Danny, protect your neck.' To Lucy, he shouted. 'He's anaemic, you know? There'd be no nutritional value in him.'

'Can you get him to be quiet?' Lucy asked Danny.

'Honestly, I've been trying for fifteen years,' Danny replied. 'It was you who made the first Spirit Lock that exorcised Jimmy, wasn't it?'

'I'd forgotten about it until you called me,' she admitted.

'Lucy, what the hell is going on? What is that thing?' Lacking available hands, he nodded toward the glass construction.

Lucy sighed and checked her phone again before throwing it on top of the chest freezer in frustration.

'Things like it have had many names throughout the years but we've been calling it the Soul Mill,' she said eventually, looking over at it with seeming distaste. 'It's . . . It works by . . .' Words failed her, and she took a deep breath before starting again. 'Have you ever seen a water wheel?'

Danny nodded slowly, not seeing the connection.

'The water turns a big wheel, which, in turn, powers whatever you need it to. That thing does the same but with souls.'

There was silence as Danny and Nudge took the enormity of this in.

'You're using ghosts like—' Words failed Danny.

'—Like hamsters running in one of those wheel things!?' Nudge finished for him.

'What is it powering?' Danny asked.

Lucy looked up at him. 'Us. I suppose. Ray and I.'

'Ray?' Nudge asked.

'Mr Brooks,' Danny said, remembering what Nancy had told them. 'He wasn't put into care by his son. He *is* his son.'

Nudge made a face. 'Sounds like a Greek play.'

'He's the one who got it working,' Lucy continued. 'He had to piece together the ritual from the fragments of writings from half a dozen ancient cultures. It took him years. Decades.'

'And, in that time, you never questioned whether this was the right thing to do?' Danny asked.

Lucy blanched. 'It's not like that; we were living apart by then. I only learned about it last month when he called me up out of the blue.' She looked at the mill again. 'I didn't even know he had a mobile phone,' she said softly.

'How come you separated?' Nudge asked.

Danny felt that they should be focusing on how they discovered the secret of eternal youth, but he'd be lying if he said he wasn't a little bit curious himself.

'Life got in the way,' Lucy replied but there was something in her voice, the way she refused to look at them, that told them something else.

Danny thought about the smiling baby he'd seen on Ray's lap in the picture at Nancy's house. 'You lost someone, didn't you?' he asked.

It was a complete guess but, from the look on her face, an accurate one.

She nodded, walking slowly over to the metal locker beside the chest freezer and opening it. The inside of the door was covered with old pictures. She ran her fingers over a faded photo of a smiling young woman with long black hair. Taken in the eighties, if Danny was any judge.

'Our daughter, Valerie,' Lucy said, so quietly it was almost a whisper.

'I'm sorry,' Danny said.

'She was only thirty-one,' Lucy said, not taking her eyes off the picture. 'Breast cancer.' She closed the locker door. 'Raymond was never the same. Not that you'd expect him to be, of course. Eventually, I just couldn't live in a mausoleum anymore. With a husband who wouldn't talk to me for weeks at a time and memories of our daughter in every room. I left and went to live with Adella.'

Mentioning Adella seemed to awaken something in her. She turned back to them urgently. 'It wasn't supposed to be like this. It's not supposed to . . . We're going to fix it.'

'Oh, so that it only pulls in the spirits of people that aren't related to you?' Nudge scoffed.

'He's right, Lucy,' Danny said.

'You don't understand, you've been able to see ghosts for all of five minutes. You've no idea what it's like to live with it all your life.'

'Enlighten me,' Danny replied. He wasn't going anywhere and every minute she talked was another minute she wasn't contemplating the large tool rack full of sharp, pointy things behind her.

'When your family heard about you talking to someone who wasn't there, they sent you to see a doctor, right?'

Danny nodded mutely.

'Things were a little different in the 1940s. Our dad would lock Adella and me in the attic for days. He would wash our mouths out with holy water. "For telling lies." So, we pretended we couldn't hear the lost souls that we saw every day, lonely and looking for help. It nearly broke Adella.

'When our father died, we could finally stop hiding it. Funnily enough, that turned out to be almost worse. I think Adella felt guilty for ignoring them for so many years. She spent more of the rest of her life talking to the dead than she did the living.'

Danny thought back to the numerous pictures of family, all those grandchildren. 'She had children of her own though. The pictures?'

Lucy's laugh came without any humour in it. 'What you saw was the over-correction as she got older, when her gift started to fade. Her over-compensation for all the time she'd lost. By then, her husband had left and the kids weren't speaking to her. It was only fair: she had barely spoken to them growing up. It was too late for the husband, but she did manage to patch things up with her children eventually.'

'"Some people get so caught up with talking to the dead that they forget to live their own lives,"' Danny quoted. 'That's what you said last night? You were talking about Adella.'

Lucy nodded.

'There's living your life, and then there's stealing it,' Danny said.

'We're not stealing anything. Remember the background echoes I told you about? All those untethered spirits? No form. No purpose. It's only supposed to pull them in. And even then, just the ones in the immediate area. They're too far gone to be helped now but the *power* they can generate,' she whispered. 'It could light up a city.'

'And it allowed you to turn back the clock?' Danny asked.

'I believe "renew vitality" was the literal translation.'

All three of them jumped at the new voice. A tall, blond man in a white polo shirt walked into the shed and examined the scene.

'Where *the hell* have you been?' Lucy asked.

Ray, to his credit, seemed to take finding his wife conversing with a ghost and a tied-up, half-blind man covered in milk in his stride. 'I was at the club,' he said, as if that explained everything. He took a step into the workshop and surveyed things.

'I've been trying to get through to you since last night. I left you a dozen messages.'

'You know I can't work that bloody thing,' Ray responded calmly. 'Who do we have here?' he said, striding across the floor to loom over Danny.

It took all of his willpower not to shrink back. The fact that his bound wrists didn't allow him to move any further also helped.

'We're here to stop you,' Nudge said.

Ray glanced from where Danny was hog-tied, smelling of yoghurt, over to Nudge, who now looked as if a stiff breeze would disperse him completely, and nodded. 'And how's that going?' he asked.

Lucy moved beside him and grabbed him by the arm. 'Ray, the mill. It's pulling in fully manifested ghosts. Maybe even anyone that crosses over. From all across the city. It has Adella.'

Ray looked up sharply at this. 'That's impossible.'

'I saw it take a spirit from all the way over in Drimnagh with my own eyes, Ray. It's far more powerful than we thought. We need to turn it off,' Lucy urged.

He shook his head and stood between her and the Soul Mill protectively. 'Hang on, just slow down. This isn't a light switch, Lucy. I can't just flick it on and off. There's no telling what impact that might have on us.'

Lucy looked at him, aghast. 'Did you not hear me? It has Adella. We can't just—'

Ray reached out and put a hand on each of her shoulders. It's possible that he'd meant it as a reassuring gesture but it just seemed possessive to Danny. '—I'm not saying we'll do nothing. Let's not rush into things. How do you know it has Adella?'

'These boys, they were there when she died. They saw her get taken.'

'You're prepared to throw away everything we built based on what these two idiots have to say?' Ray snapped defensively.

'I thought you said *he* built it,' Danny chimed in, ignoring the jibe. He wanted to keep them talking as long as he could. From his vantage point on the floor, he could see something at the back of one of the lower shelves. A hoodie, or a jacket of some kind, pushed back so far that it was out of sight of anyone standing up. Making sure that Ray and Lucy only had eyes for each other, Danny managed to snag the corner of it with his outstretched fingers. It fell onto the floor beside him. He looked up sharply to see if anyone had noticed but the happy couple were still talking.

'She's being too modest,' Ray said expansively. 'I admit that it was me who built and activated it but I couldn't get the blasted thing to do anything useful until Lucy helped me to translate some of the more obscure writings.'

Lucy looked down at this, ashamed. Ray noticed this and put his arm around her shoulder. 'I couldn't bring Valerie back but I could give us a second chance,' he said.

Lucy flinched at this. 'It's clearly not working the way we thought it would. Maybe we should—'

'—Should what?' Ray challenged her. 'Should give all of this up? Just because some drunken idiot and his spastic, dead friend think that there's something wrong?'

'Hey,' Nudge protested. 'Watch it, Grandad.'

For once, Danny was grateful for Nudge's attention-seeking while he worked on pulling the piece of clothing closer to him. It was a tracksuit top. After establishing that it didn't have a pair of bolt cutters in either of the pockets, he frantically tried to locate the front of it so that he could find the zip.

An incident where an eleven-year-old Danny had accidentally pulled one tight enough around his finger that it had swollen to the size of a plum tomato had taught him a little bit about zip ties. After he'd gone crying to his dad, Joe had patiently explained that they had a tiny plastic locking bar that allows them to get tighter but not looser. A small piece of metal jammed into the head of the tie could lift up the bar and let it slide free. He also explained that the trapped-finger incident was the sort of thing his mum didn't need to know about.

Danny was pretty sure that the pull tab on a zip would do the trick. He flipped the top around to its front, revealing a Bohemians FC crest.

'I'm not saying we take it apart,' Lucy was saying, 'Just shut it down while we figure things out. We might stay as we are now.'

'And what if you're wrong?' Ray countered. He changed tack softening his voice. 'I will figure it out. We'll be able to keep it running without it . . . upsetting anybody else. I just need some time.'

'And what about the hundreds of poor bastards you have running on your little afterlife hamster wheel?' Nudge asked. 'Are they supposed to just hang about?'

Ray ignored Nudge. He knew that the only person in the room he needed to convince was Lucy. 'We have a second chance. I, *we've,* done the impossible. Are we going to back down now?'

Lucy shook her head. Danny managed to jam the thin metal pull-tab of the zip into the head of the plastic tie and felt it loosen enough to slip his hands free. He kept them where they were: he wasn't sure what he was going to do yet. Seeing the Bohemians top had given him a horrible suspicion.

'So, let's not throw the baby out with the bathwater because we're having a few teething problems,' Ray continued.

Lucy seemed convinced. In her defence, Ray seemed particularly good at manipulation. 'What about them?' she asked, looking over at Danny.

Ray continued to keep his voice low and steady. 'I'll take care of it.'

She looked shocked. 'What are you saying?'

Ray kept his arm on his wife's shoulder, preventing her from pulling away. 'You go back inside and forget about this.'

Lucy looked aghast at her husband, but he pressed on. 'We deserve this. We deserve to live our lives again. Valerie, Adella. They would want that for us. For you!'

Fuck, he's good, Danny thought as he surreptitiously tucked his legs underneath him.

'You're talking about killing someone,' she said.

Danny saw his chance. 'It wouldn't be for the first time, would it, Ray?' he interrupted.

The blond octogenarian turned to look at him, his face an unreadable mask.

'What are you talking about?' Lucy asked.

'Look around, Lucy,' Danny said. 'That thing is the size of a fridge.'

'Now you just shut up,' Ray growled.

'So?' Lucy said, still not following him.

'You're saying a what, 86-, 87-year-old man put it all together by himself?'

'Eighty-eight,' Lucy said softly, turning to look at her husband.

'I said shut up!' Ray shouted, taking a step towards their captive. 'Don't listen to him, love.'

'Think it through,' Danny retorted. 'Each of those bulbs must weigh as much as he did. You had a gofer, didn't you?' He flicked the tracksuit top onto the floor in front of them. 'How *is* Anto?'

Lucy bent down to run her hands over the crest of the sweatshirt. 'Ray. Tell me you didn't.'

'You needed someone to do the legwork you were too old to do,' Danny continued.

'Shut the fuck up, you little bollocks!' Ray roared.

'What happened, Ray? Did he ask too many questions?' Then Danny looked over at the Soul Mill, a creeping suspicion forming in his mind. 'No,' he said slowly. 'That wasn't it.' He thought about what Lucy had said after she'd performed the Spirit Lock. 'Things like this, they need a sacrifice,' he said now, repeating what Lucy had told him, and glanced at the enormous Soul Mill. 'More than a few drops of blood this time, I'll bet.'

'He's talking shite, Lucy,' Ray shouted. Seeing the horrified look on his wife's face, he softened. 'I mean, he's right that I used Anto to help me out a bit at the start, but I didn't do anything to him.'

'Maybe tell that to the dead body in this freezer?' All three of the living turned to find that Nudge had edged further into the garage and was now sticking his face into the locked chest freezer beside the wall.

Danny was able to see Ray's patience snap. Something about the eyes. Maybe it was the rush of being young again, maybe he thought that he could still make up with Lucy afterwards. Either way, he was evidently fed up with the softly-softly approach. He grabbed a lump hammer from where it hung on the wall beside him and, intent on adding at least one more departed soul to his collection, charged at Danny.

Chapter 28

He was more than a little surprised when the prisoner met him halfway.

Danny had intended to hit his captor with a classic rugby tackle around the midsection but underestimated the impact that sitting cross-legged on a cement floor for half an hour would have on his legs. Instead of exploding from his position, like he'd intended, he half-tackled, half-fell into Ray, taking him around the knees instead of the torso.

It was enough to propel them both to the floor, however. In the shock of tumbling backwards, Ray let go of the hammer and tried to break his fall. After their bone-jarring impact against the concrete, Danny rolled away from the bigger man and tried to get his bearings. They'd ended up lying, almost side by side, in the narrow aisle between the workbench and the Soul Mill; Ray was now crawling to where the hammer lay, closer to the door.

Danny gave him a kick from his prone position to delay him and also on general principle. His blow glanced against Ray's hip, mostly ineffectually, and caused the bigger man to let out a noise that was closer to a snarl than a curse as he wriggled away. There was a short *détente* while both men pulled themselves to their feet, but Ray didn't even wait until he was fully upright before throwing his larger frame into Danny's.

The blond man threw himself forward and managed to slip both of his hands under Danny's arms and around his throat, pushing him back over the bench in front of the window. Danny threw wild, untrained punches at his opponent's head, but Ray just tightened his grip and Danny suddenly had to stop attacking and claw at the hands around his neck.

'Raymond, stop!' Lucy screamed. She had watched the initial assault, seemingly too stunned to move, but now she hurried over to grab him by the shoulder. Ray briefly let go of Danny's throat with one hand and shoved her. She flew against the metal locker with a crash and fell to the floor.

Danny bucked against him but, even with only one of Ray's hands around his throat, he was too exhausted to break Ray's grip. He turned his attention to the rack of tools behind him and tried frantically to grab one of them but his body position wouldn't allow him to reach.

A voice broke through the rushing sound in his ears.

'Oi! Benjamin Button!' Nudge had run forward into the room when the fight had begun but had stopped when he realised there was nothing he could do. *Almost* nothing. 'Did Lucy tell you that she kissed Danny last night?' he shouted, trying to cut through the man's bloodlust.

Danny wasn't entirely sure how this was supposed to *stop* Ray from strangling him but, to Nudge's credit, the man's grip slackened somewhat as he turned to face the ghost.

'What?'

The lapse in concentration gave Danny an opening. He managed to shift his weight so that the small of his back was on the bench, then raised both legs and planted them as hard as he could in his attacker's mid-section. Ray rocketed back and slammed into one of the shelving units beside the Soul Mill. Glass ornaments tumbled off the higher shelves and crashed into fragments around him. Danny gasped for breath and then decided that discretion was the better part of valour here. He made a bolt for the door, but Ray recovered quickly and tackled him from behind.

They hit the floor hard, with Danny bearing the brunt of it. His ribs screamed at the impact, but he didn't have time to devote any attention to them. He managed to twist around from where he was lying face down, but this just allowed Ray to grasp his throat with both hands again, this time using the full force of his weight to push down.

Danny glanced around wildly. Lucy was still in a heap beside the locker. Nudge was looking on in horror. He could see the lump hammer that Ray had dropped an ice age ago and flailed his arm to try and reach it. His hand came up a few inches short and he returned it to try and loosen Ray's grip, but the bigger man had all the leverage. He was straddling Danny now, using all his weight to wring his opponent's neck.

'Let him go,' Nudge shouted. From the corner of his rapidly darkening vision, Danny saw the ghost run around to where the hammer lay and unsuccessfully try to pick it up. His vision began to tunnel. The edges of his world turned a familiar shade of dark purple. It was not unlike the night on the canal.

'I said, LET HIM GO!' Nudge roared. There was a strange, extra harmonic to it now. Around them, the tools on the racks rattled and several fell from their hooks.

Ray's grip slackened slightly in shock, and he looked over to where the ghost had bent down again for the hammer. This time he didn't bother to try and pick it up but just swept his hand across it as if he was trying to slide it towards Danny.

It moved. Danny and Ray watched as, at Nudge's touch, the hammer skidded across the concrete.

Unfortunately for Danny, it was moving in entirely the wrong direction.

Danny had gone to a calm place now. *Well, that's it. At least my spirit won't have far to travel.*

His thoughts were interrupted by a sound like a gong. Or, more accurately, the sound of a large lump hammer striking the bottom of an enormous glass bulb.

Both strangler and stranglee turned their heads to look at the spiderweb pattern of cracks that radiated out from where the hammer had hit the mill. Ray let go of Danny's throat and pushed himself up, stumbling towards his creation. 'No, no, no, no, no!' the man repeated. He held up his palms to the side of the glass as if he was about to try to hold it together with his bare hands.

Danny glanced over to where Lucy had been thrown. She was conscious and slowly pulling herself up against the locker. 'Are you okay?' she asked.

Danny nodded and turned his attention back to Ray, who was still fussing with the Soul Mill. 'Maybe we should get out of here?' he croaked. He had no idea what would happen when hundreds of trapped souls were freed from their prison, but he figured they wouldn't want to be around.

Lucy seemed to be in agreement and reached across to help him to his feet, but they had only taken a couple of steps towards the door when the network of cracks in the Soul Mill reached critical mass. Danny had a split-second of warning as he saw Ray take a step back, covering his eyes.

'Get down!' he said, pushing them both to the floor.

On the surface of things, the explosion was fairly unspectacular. There was no bang, no sonic boom, just the sudden rattle of glass fragments hitting the walls and furniture. The way it felt, however, was something else entirely. Danny squeezed his eyes shut at a sudden pressure in his ears, as if he'd somehow risen thirty-six thousand feet then dropped again, all in a split second. His stomach turned itself in knots that had nothing to do with his recent diet of frozen pizza and whiskey. He rolled on his side and tried to focus on Lucy. From the look on her face, she was experiencing it too.

It made the macing feel like a refreshing spray of perfume.

'Are you two okay?' Nudge asked.

'Yeah. You?' Danny replied automatically, then felt foolish. His mouth had filled with a metallic taste and he couldn't tell if he'd bitten his tongue or if it was some side effect of the mill explosion.

'It's just lucky that ghosts can't shit themselves.'

They looked across the workshop. Ray had been in the direct path of the explosion. Danny could see that his entire left side glittered with broken glass and blood.

'Ray!' Lucy called. She went to move towards him, but Danny gripped her by the elbow.

'No. Look,' he said, pointing at the remnants of the mill.

The bottom bulb had shattered completely and the top one now lay in its remnants, cracked open like a chocolate egg halfway through Easter Sunday. But this wasn't what drew Danny's attention. It should be impossible for anyone to appear only inches tall when stepping out of the bulb, only to be fully grown when their feet touched the concrete of the workshop, but this is what happened to the young man who now stood over Ray's prone form. Danny got the sense that he hadn't grown, rather that he had just taken a single stride from a long way off. He was, or had been, a wiry man in his early twenties, dressed in navy tracksuit bottoms and a red T-shirt. Danny was pretty sure that he'd recently used the new arrival's tracksuit top to extricate himself from the zip ties. 'Anto?' he called out.

The young man didn't react, his focus entirely on the groaning Ray on the floor. Anto looked different to Nudge and the other ghosts he'd seen so far. He was barely an outline, as if the time spent in the Soul Mill had drained him of whatever gave spirits substance. Danny could make out the partially smashed figure of a glass ballerina on the shelf by looking through the man's head.

Anto was suddenly joined by another man, this one tall and bald, dressed in a black suit. Then, a red-haired woman in nurse's scrubs; a little boy no older than eight, in his pyjamas. Then, another young man, this one in a hospital gown. The room rapidly began to fill up with incorporeal bodies. They didn't bother with the niceties of observing physical space. As more and more of them arrived, they stood with the top halves of their torsos sticking out of a workbench or with one side of their bodies hidden by the wall of the garage. As they continued to fill the room, it became increasingly difficult to tell where one ghost ended and another began.

As the space filled up, Danny, Nudge and Lucy backed away towards the open door.

'Raymond!' Lucy called out again.

They could barely see Ray now through the thickening fog of spirits surrounding him. But Lucy's shout seemed to wake him from whatever daze he'd been in following the explosion of the mill because he pushed himself up with his good arm and surveyed the crowd of spirits around him in horror.

Danny wanted to run, to leave all of this behind, to move to some foreign country and never to speak of any of it again for the rest of his life, but he couldn't tear his eyes away. Lucy made another attempt to move to her husband's side, but Danny kept a grip on her arm.

With grim determination, Ray managed to pull himself to his feet, using the rack beside him for leverage. The crowd of spirits was so thick now that Danny felt as if he was watching it play out underwater, like they were at the bottom of some terrible sea. Ray looked like hell. One side of his face was a ruin of gashes and embedded shards of glass. He held his injured arm to his side as he surveyed the throng.

Danny hadn't known what to expect from his attacker. Bargaining maybe? Pleading for mercy? He certainly hadn't expected rage.

'Well!?' he roared at the assembly of the dead. 'What are you waiting for? An apology?' He laughed mirthlessly. 'As if any of you wouldn't have done the same thing, or worse, given the opportunity to get a few more *years*.' This last word was angrily hissed, as saliva and blood flecked from his lips. He somehow managed to stand up to an approximation of his full height. '"For the living know that they will die; But the dead know nothing, and they have no more reward; For the memory of them is forgotten,"' Ray recited.

Danny was fairly sure that this was a quote from somewhere but whether it was from the Bible or some old movie he didn't know.

Ray raged on. 'That's you. The forgotten. The departed. Nothing more than names on stone.' He whipped around to focus on where Danny and Lucy were still huddled. 'I refused to become one of them. Another sad old fart who rotted away slowly. *I beat death!*' This last statement was bellowed but it seemed to use up the last of his righteous energy and he slumped back down as blood continued to soak into his white polo. 'So, you can all just get fucked.'

Danny wasn't sure which of them moved first, or if it was some sort of unspoken group effort, but the mass of spirits closed the gap around the Soul Miller. Unfortunately, their washed-out transparency still allowed Danny and Lucy to witness what happened next. Danny had seen the part in the *Indiana Jones* film where the Nazi scientist chose poorly, his face melting like candlewax. This was nothing like that. In fact, any film or TV show where a character aged rapidly seemed to have several glaring, factual errors as far as he was concerned.

For one thing, they didn't include the grinding, popping noise of a skeleton experiencing six decades of arthritis and osteoporosis at once. The scream that they overdubbed didn't suddenly lower in pitch as the vocal cords atrophied. Most of all, Hollywood had failed to accurately capture the look of horror in the suddenly rheumy eyes of the victim.

The ghostly mob drew back suddenly. Danny didn't know how Ray had looked immediately before he'd switched on the Soul Mill, but he guessed that it wasn't like this. Nobody could look like this and still be walking around. The newly freed souls had returned his stolen decades with interest. His blond hair had disappeared entirely, except for a few colourless wisps that clung on at the sides. The process hadn't given him any of his weight back, but this just served to make his frame seem even more skeletal. It did seem to have healed the lacerations from the glass explosion but, while they were no longer bleeding freely, they now presented as a patchwork of pockmarked scars that ran down the entire side of his face and arm.

Lucy screamed. Danny didn't blame her. He was just about clinging to his own stomach contents. The noise caused her husband to turn his head towards them but, even at this distance, Danny could see that his eyes were shrouded in the near-total milky film of cataracts.

The skeletal figure of Raymond Brooks took one hesitant step forward on shaky legs and then, letting out a last rasping sigh, collapsed forward onto the cement floor of his workshop.

Danny was mildly surprised that he didn't crumble to dust upon impact.

'Jesus, fuck!' Nudge said, accurately gauging the feeling in the room.

Lucy called her husband's name again but there was little doubt that he hadn't so much shuffled off this mortal coil as been fired off it out of a cannon.

Danny had really hoped that the ghostly horde would move on once they'd gotten their revenge on their jailer, but the room still heaved with them. It was very difficult to tell since he couldn't make out individual faces, but they seemed to have turned their attention to the two remaining living people in the room.

Lucy was still fighting to get to her now-late husband and Danny whispered urgently in her ear. 'Lucy, they're not finished yet. We have to get you out of here.'

At this, she seemed to finally grasp the danger she was in. They turned towards the door, only to find that there were more spirits behind them. There were hundreds of them now, radiating from where the Soul Mill had stood. Danny could see them out in the garden, the weak winter sunlight warping and flickering through them as they moved.

'Try apologising,' Danny whispered urgently. His throat felt like it might seize up.

'What?'

'Tell them you're sorry,' Nudge urged.

'But I didn't know?'

'Good. Try starting with that,' he said.

'I'm sorry! I didn't know what it was doing!' Lucy yelled tearfully at the assembled masses.

There was no reaction. Danny realised that he was shivering, and not just from fear. It was suddenly freezing in the small workshop. Lucy was trembling too.

'What is happening?' Danny had never felt this cold, not even the night on the canal. It felt like his bones had been replaced by bands of freezing iron.

'I think it's them,' Lucy said.

Danny realised that their breath wasn't crystalising in front of their faces, as they spoke. Whatever he was feeling it had nothing to do with the actual temperature.

If it feels like this now, what will happen when they actually swarm us?

'What now?' Nudge asked.

'I don't know,' Danny stammered back, through chattering teeth. 'You're free!' He shouted at their silent audience. 'You can cross over now.'

'That's not how it works,' Lucy said.

'Well, why the fuck not?' Danny asked petulantly. 'The stupid fucking mill thing is gone. They can go wherever they want now.'

'They're too far gone to understand. They're hardly more than echoes of themselves.'

'I thought you said that that process takes years?' Nudge said, panic edging into his voice.

'It does. Whatever that thing did to them seems to have accelerated it. I'm not sure they even know how to cross over anymore.'

'Is there something you can do?' Danny asked.

'Like what?'

'What about a Spirit Lock?'

'There's too many of them and not enough . . .' she trailed off and whirled suddenly towards Nudge. 'You could do it!'

'What!?' Danny and Nudge replied in stereo.

'The Spirit Lock, the spell, it's not the blood or the writing, not really,' she said hurriedly. 'That's just a way to make the words have an impact on the other side. It's the words, the sacrifice that matters.'

'I can't bleed,' Nudge said.

'It doesn't need to be that kind of sacrifice.' She was speaking more quickly now. 'By performing the ritual, you would essentially be locking them out of the spirit realm; it would force them to cross over but . . .'

'But what?' Danny asked. His head felt like it was filled with snow. The conversation seemed to be happening a long way away.

'Because he's a spirit himself. It works both ways. They would be locked out and Nudge would be locked in. He wouldn't be able to cross over. At least, not naturally.'

'What!? Fuck that!' Danny said. He eyeballed the distance to the doorway. It was only a few feet away but there were dozens of ghosts in the intervening space and God only knew how many in the garden outside. 'Nudge, don't listen to her. We're going to make a break for it,' he said.

'Are you out of your mind!?' Nudge asked.

Maybe if we move fast enough then we can escape the worst of it with only a decade or so piled onto us, Danny thought. He ran his hand through his hair reflexively. *Might as well kiss the hairline goodbye now.*

'What happens to these people, the ghosts, if I don't show them how to cross over?' Nudge asked.

'Nudge, don't even think about—' Danny started.

'—What happens?' he insisted.

306

'I don't know,' said Lucy, in a small voice. Shivering, in her camel-hair coat, she suddenly looked much younger. 'They're so far gone already. I don't know if they could ever find their way back.'

Nudge nodded once, face set. 'Let's do it.'

Danny stepped forward, suddenly heedless of the press of spirits. 'What are you doing?'

'It's like she said,' Nudge told him. 'It's the only way to make sure you're safe and that these people can cross over.'

'But you'll be stuck here. Maybe forever,' Danny said.

'We'll burn that bridge when we come to it,' Nudge replied. 'Ian is in there somewhere. So is Adella, Anto, Jimmy and maybe hundreds of others. I can't leave them like this.'

'It doesn't have to be you—' Danny started.

'—Shut up and listen!' he interrupted. 'I can never begin to repay you for how you've helped me these last few weeks. But I'm the one who got us into this and I'm going to be the one to get *you* out.' He turned to Lucy. 'How do we do this?'

Their circle of ghost-free real estate had rapidly dwindled to the point that Lucy and Danny looked as if they were trying to occupy the same space. She poked her head around Danny's shoulder. 'Just repeat after me.'

He nodded and she started. Danny wanted to interrupt, to keep them from doing this, to suggest some alternative. But he had none. The surrounding press of ghosts seemed to be leaching away his ability to think and Lucy was already chanting. Nudge was repeating everything she was saying phonetically. Phoenician didn't seem like the easiest language – very few vowels – but she wasn't correcting him, so clearly Nudge was doing okay.

The ghosts stopped mere inches from them as they stared. Danny could make out individual faces now, but none had any expression. Not anger, not sorrow, just blankness. Danny shivered and turned his attention back to Nudge and Lucy. They seemed to be working faster than she had at the pub. *Maybe the ritual was more potent in the spirit realm?* he thought. Whatever the reason, they were soon reaching a crescendo. Lucy shouted the last few words, her voice cracking with the strain and Nudge repeated them at a yell.

For a beat, there was silence. There didn't seem to be any noticeable difference to the horde of ghosts.

'Lucy? Why aren't they leaving?' Danny asked softly, afraid that any sound might cause them to surge.

'I don't know,' she replied. 'Maybe we did it wrong.'

'Hey, what's this "we" business? I just repeated after you,' Nudge protested with his usual lack of a sense of priorities.

'Right. Okay,' Danny said hollowly, 'We make a break for it.' He pushed down the gnawing thought that Nudge may have just sentenced himself to an eternity as a ghost for nothing. 'On the count of three,' he said, bouncing on his toes trying desperately to get some life back into his dead limbs.

Lucy looked as if she was about to protest but then simply nodded.

'One,' he said.

Had Lucy left the back door open? We don't want to be slowed down once we get out there.

'Two.'

If we have to, we could dive through the sliding glass door.

'Danny, wait!' Lucy shouted.

He was snapped out of his planning and looked to where she was pointing. It took him a second to figure it out. More and more space was opening up between them and the front ranks of ghosts. Danny thought that they were retreating at first, but, after a moment's inspection, he saw that wasn't the case. Those closest to the front were just disappearing. It was difficult to see at first, because of how densely they were packed, but the more he looked, the more he saw that, like some sort of supernatural chain reaction, the spirits closest to them were thinning out and eventually disappearing entirely.

'We did it!' Lucy exclaimed.

'Again with the "we",' Nudge said, although there was a relieved smile on his face now.

The radius around them now extended almost to the walls of the garage and Danny stepped carefully into the doorway to see the last of the souls disappearing from view.

There was silence in the middle of the garage.

'I think that's all of them,' Danny said finally, after what felt like an hour but was more likely only a couple of minutes. 'You really did it, Nudge,' he added, laughing despite himself.

'Paul Nugent. Ghost wrangler,' he replied, smiling.

There was a beat as both men considered the sacrifice he had made. Danny's whole body felt like it was filled with pins and needles but the nerve-deadening cold he'd felt earlier was starting to dissipate.

They glanced over to where Lucy was kneeling by the mummified remains of Ray. Danny walked up beside her and placed a palm on her shoulder.

'He wasn't always like this,' she said quietly.

Danny was prepared to believe that. He also knew that people changed. Sometimes for the worse.

Lucy wiped the back of her sleeve across her eyes and nose. 'I'm sorry for pepper-spraying you,' she said finally.

'It's okay,' Danny replied.

'*And* for kicking you in the bollocks.'

Danny said nothing as he inspected the debris covering the garage.

Lucy was examining herself critically in the reflection cast by a glass lampshade. Unfortunately, its bulbous shape was causing her image to warp like in a fun-house mirror. 'How do I look?' she asked. 'Am I still young?'

Danny looked at her. The past half an hour had aged him by about twenty years, but she seemed still relatively untouched by the ravages of time. 'I think you're okay.'

'For the moment anyway,' she said wistfully. 'What do we do now?'

'I don't know,' Danny said, looking at the corpse of Ray Brooks, the Soul Miller. 'But it's going to involve explaining away a dead body.' He glanced at the chest freezer. 'Excuse me. Two dead bodies.'

'Oh,' Lucy said, surveying the carnage around them. 'Shit.'

Epilogue

'How have you been since our last session?' Dr Choi asked.

Danny glanced around the office as he leaned back into the armchair. Lizzy appeared to be keeping her promise to wait outside.

'I feel a lot better.' He saw the psychologist open his mouth to form a question, but he held up his hands and kept going. 'I know I say that every session, and half the time I'm lying, but I really do feel good. I have a sense of . . .' he frowned. 'What's the therapy word for finishing something but, like, in a good way?'

The doctor smiled. 'Closure?' he suggested.

'That's the one, yeah,' he confirmed. 'I feel a sense of closure and, I don't know, achievement. Like I've done something worthwhile.'

Dr Choi leaned forward slightly in his chair, scribbling something into his notebook.

Maybe it would be no harm to have Lizzy in the next session to give him the director's commentary, he thought.

'That's good, Danny. What, specifically, do you feel you achieved?'

Well, I saved my best friend and half of Dublin's recently deceased from a hellish afterlife, I defeated what was essentially a necromancer and I like to think I brought some amount of peace to Nancy and justice for Anto.

'I recently took a driving lesson,' he said, aloud.

*

Their session ended half an hour later. Danny had mostly been treading water, but he made a mental note to give it a proper go next time. He always made this vow at the end of an appointment, but it never hurt to have good intentions.

He stepped out of the office and clocked Lizzy loitering in the small waiting area outside. He was gladder than he thought he'd be to see her. He had been half-worried that she might have been pulled into the spectral gears of Ray's Mill, but she had been waiting demurely outside the office when he arrived. He gave her a wink and jerked his head in the direction of the stairs for her to follow him.

They walked in silence until they reached the cold December air outside. This time, Lizzy didn't hug the building as closely and followed him down the steps to the footpath. Danny ducked into a nearby doorway, out of the wind.

'I'm sorry about your friend's father,' she said softly. 'I'm sure he's in heaven now. Mr Pullman said that heaven and hell are arbitrary, man-made concepts that the church uses to impose its own agenda upon the working man but, I like to think . . .'

Danny grinned, despite himself. He had mentioned this in his session to the doctor. Lizzy's promise not to stay apparently didn't extent to not listening at the door.

He tabled this particular argument for now though and weathered Lizzy's trademark opening verbal salvo for a few more sentences. 'I'm glad to see that you're still knocking around,' he said when she offered up a rare moment for him to interject. 'You'd be a loss to the psychiatric profession.'

She smiled. 'I felt the pull, whatever it was, fade earlier this week. What happened?'

Danny gave her a condensed version of what had happened the previous Monday. She listened with rapt attention and even teared up a bit when he described what Nudge had sacrificed to allow the others to cross over.

'It sounds as if he was very brave. You, too, of course.'

'You're right. He was,' Danny agreed, pulling out his phone. He hesitated for a moment: he'd spent a few nights of the previous week awake in the early hours, contemplating life and death. He'd decided to use one of the sleepless nights to do a bit of research. Now that he was here though, he was having second thoughts.

'What is it?' Lizzy asked.

'Listen,' he started self-consciously. 'After we talked last time, I had some time on my hands and I did a bit of digging.' He stared down at the notes on his phone rather than have to confront her huge blue eyes any longer. 'Private, First Class, Oliver Fitzpatrick. That's the name you said he was raised under, right? Your son?' He briefly panicked that he'd picked the wrong person.

How many Oliver Fitzpatricks could there be in the Royal Fusiliers who had died at Gallipoli?

He soldiered, for want of a better word, on. 'Well, they have these family research websites now and I looked into him.'

He glanced up again, but Lizzy was uncharacteristically silent.

'Before he left for Gallipoli, he married a Dolores Fitzpatrick, *née* Douglas,' he said, double-checking the details on the phone. 'She gave birth to a daughter not long after, in 1916. A little girl named Bridgit.'

'A little girl?' Lizzy repeated quietly.

'Yeah,' Danny said. 'Bridgit left for Birmingham in . . .' he swiftly checked his phone again '. . . 1933.'

Five years before Lucy was born, he thought, but pushed it down for the moment.

'She died in 1956 but not before having four children under her married name, O'Brien. Three boys and a girl. Oliver, Stephen, Michael and Alison.' He powered onto his actual point. 'Alison moved to America in the fifties and had two kids, one of whom is now Dr Patricia O'Brien, Head of Psychotherapy at the UCLA Medical Centre. That's in Los Angeles.'

Danny turned his phone screen to show Lizzy a photo of an expensively dressed woman in her mid-fifties. Her hair was greying slightly but otherwise she looked the tanned picture of Californian health. 'Apparently she's a leader in her field.'

Lizzy's eyes shone and she brought up her hands as if she was going to take it from him. She remembered herself. 'Thank you,' she said, her voice thick with emotion.

Danny felt embarrassed but he was glad he'd gone to the trouble now. 'No problem. I just thought you might want to know that it's kind of a family profession.'

She smiled at this and wiped her eyes with the corner of her apron. 'I'd better get going,' she said hoarsely. 'Dr Choi's three o'clock is couples therapy and that's always good value.' She made her way back to the steps but turned when Danny called out.

'Would you ever think about it?' he asked. 'Crossing over?'

She cocked her head to one side as she gave this some thought. 'Someday, maybe,' she said eventually. 'At first, I was here because of unfinished business, then I think I hung around out of fear . . . but now? I'm enjoying my afterlife. One day at a time.'

Danny nodded and watched her disappear through the door of the clinic.

He glanced at the time on his phone screen and smiled. He had one more appointment today.

It took him the best part of an hour to reach Sandymount. He'd had to walk up to Dame Street and then catch a bus. He was still short of funds for a taxi, and he'd had enough driving to last him a lifetime.

He hopped off the bus and wandered along the seafront until he found her, sitting on a bench, staring at the Poolbeg chimneys. In Danny's opinion, it was way too cold to be outside like this, but he sat down beside her anyway. They both regarded the red-and-white-striped pillars quietly for a few moments.

'How'd it go with the guards?' he asked eventually. He'd read about the discovery of Ray's body in the paper, but had still spent the last week worrying that he would have avoided death-by-mallet only to have the Murder Squad kick in his door.

'Open-and-shut case apparently? Anto had Raymond's, what do you call it, DNA. He had it under his fingernails, from fighting back, they said.'

'And Ray?'

'Cardiac arrest is what they told me. They said it looked like one of the bulbs in his contraption shattered and the fright caused him to have a heart attack.'

'What did they make of the Soul Mill?'

'Satanic rituals,' Lucy snorted. 'They found all of his books and I guess it must have looked like some sort of devil-worshipping sacrifice thing.'

That wasn't much stranger than what had actually happened.

'And your new identity. That held up?' he asked. This was the thing she'd been worried about the most. They had decided to wipe off their fingerprints and allow Ray to take the rap for Anto's murder, but it meant that Lucy had to risk revealing her newly acquired passport, PPS number and birth certificate to the scrutiny of the guards.

'I don't think they looked into it particularly hard,' she said. 'Once they found everything in the garage anyway. Why suspect the granddaughter?'

The story that they'd come up with while they'd frantically cleaned away all evidence of them being there, was that, after Ray failed to show up at his sister-in-law's funeral, his granddaughter got worried and called around to the house to make sure he was okay.

'They questioned me for a couple of hours, but I think they had everything they needed.'

She took out her brand-new passport and flicked it open. 'It feels strange, to be posing as my own grandchild.'

Danny had to admit that that must be pretty weird all right.

'Valerie never got to have children in the end,' she said, more to herself than to him.

'Where did Ray get all the documents?'

'I'm not sure,' she admitted. 'He got me to take a picture for this when we reconnected.' She held up the passport. 'He must have been preparing for a while.'

They had removed Ray's new passport and documents along with everything else that suggested that a younger man had lived there, however briefly.

'So, what now?' Danny asked.

She held up her hands in front of her, looking at their smooth, pale skin. 'Whatever the mill did, it seems to be permanent, but I suppose the clock is running again now that it's broken. I guess I'll need to find a job.' She reached into her coat pocket and Danny was surprised to see her remove a vape pen instead of her trademark John Players. She saw him raise an eye at this. 'I've been given a second chance and this time, I'm going to look after myself.' She reached into her purse. 'That's not the only thing. Look.' She removed a brand-new Android phone from the bag. 'I picked it up during the week. It's got the internet on it and everything.'

Danny smiled at how proud she was. 'Very impressive!'

'I'm still trying to figure everything out,' she admitted. 'What *is* Twitter?'

'It's like teletext but everyone's angry and racist.'

Lucy wrinkled her forehead at this. 'What about you? Any fallout on your end?'

He shook his head. His job had been understanding about him missing his first day back, once he'd remembered to call them. Not understanding enough to actually give him any bereavement pay, but he was still employed.

Danny had acted as pall-bearer for Ian's coffin a few days later. He was happy he'd been able to do right by him in the end. He had managed not to cause any scenes at that particular funeral, which he considered progress.

Nadine had also shown up, without Clark. Apparently, he'd spontaneously decided to go travelling again.

She was still texting him and, now that he wasn't as distracted, he'd actually started responding. He liked to think that he had too much decency to pursue someone who had *just* come out of a relationship like she had. Although this did not stop him from regularly sending her cute pictures of Buster. He idly wondered if he could borrow his nephew for an afternoon. *Perhaps Nadine would like to meet in person? Just for a walk. Totally not a date.*

Lucy checked the time on her new phone. 'He's late.'

'In every sense of the word,' Danny agreed.

'I have to go. Would you mind?' she said.

Danny shook his head and, after securing the details of her new phone and a promise she wouldn't do any more necromancy, he let her disappear into the rapidly darkening evening.

He sat on the bench and decided that he would be the one to pick the rendezvous points from now on. Nudge may not feel the cold, but he certainly did. He was about to move on when a voice from behind him made him jump.

'Sorry, I'm late. It's a little hard to catch public transport like this.'

'Next time, we're meeting indoors,' Danny said with faux irritability. He was more pleased than he was willing to admit to see his friend. The mill's absence meant that he no longer needed to adhere to their tether and after the initial joy of having some much-needed alone time faded, he'd felt an acute sense of loneliness in Nudge's absence.

Danny reached into his jacket and removed the flask. He gave Nudge a sardonic 'cheers' before taking a swig. 'We are going to have to come up with some sort of signal for when you want to talk to me,' he said. 'I'll be doing Dry January.'

Nudge looked out at the smokestacks. 'We'll figure something out.'

'How are your parents?'

Now that he no longer had to remain close to Danny, Nudge had been enjoying his freedom. This had included visits to his parents' house. 'About as bad as you'd expect,' he said. 'I'll keep checking in though.'

Danny hadn't spoken to Nudge's parents since the funeral. He had been meaning to mend that particular fence, but with everything that had happened, he wasn't sure he was up to facing them just yet.

'I'm thinking of haunting somewhere,' Nudge said conversationally.

'Oh, really?'

'Not full-time,' he amended. 'I enjoy getting out and about now and then, but it would be nice to have somewhere as a base.'

'Where were you thinking?' Danny asked.

'Well, there's a few old buildings in Trinity,' Nudge mused. 'A ghost could build quite the reputation somewhere like that.'

'A bit of class.'

'Exactly.'

'Not a lot of entertainment for you, though?' Danny said thoughtfully. 'Just a bunch of students. *Trinity* students as well.'

'Well, I have also been considering the strip club on the Quays,' he said.

'I can't say that it has no appeal,' Danny said, after considering it for a while. 'But do you really want to spend the rest of your days surrounded by English stag dos?'

Nudge shuddered at the thought. 'Christ! I hadn't thought about that. Back to the drawing board, I suppose. What about you? What are you going to do now that you're not babysitting me?'

Danny smiled and retreated further from the cold into his coat. 'I suppose I'm going to have to get a life.'

Acknowledgements

It's very easy not to write a book. So easy in fact, that I spent thirty-plus years not writing one despite the fact that 'writing a book' has been a lifelong dream. I have so many people to thank for helping me make this a reality.

First and foremost, my wonderful girlfriend Shell. She's the reason this book exists. She was my first reader and the person I couldn't wait to bounce ideas off of every night. I'm incredibly lucky to have you in my life. This genuinely wouldn't have happened without your constant support.

At a certain point, someone had to read this that wasn't in a long-term romantic relationship with me. Huge thanks to my test readers Adam Dunne, Maggie O'Connor and Joe Orr for reading a much longer and worse version of the story and providing valuable feedback. I now owe all of you one favour, up to and including hiding a body.

I can't thank my incredible agent Beth Ferguson and the rest of the great folks over at Kate Nash Literary Agency enough for being the first ones in the industry to show some enthusiasm for my writing. The rejection and apathy of querying and submission can really be a drag, and your interest and passion for the story carried me through this whole process.

I also need to thank Deirdre Nolan, Leonie Lock and everyone at Eriu for getting behind this book and helping me make it everyone's problem; and Alison Walsh, my editor, for putting some semblance of order into a manuscript that looked a little like a serial killer's manifesto when she received it.

I'll probably never be able to thank my family enough for everything they've given me. The life I'm living now is a direct result of the sacrifices they made and the love and encouragement they constantly provided. My dad (Give it fifty pages), mum (Sorry for all the swearing) and sister, Amy (No, Steff isn't based on you) have always been there for me. In the process of editing this, I got the best gift ever in the form of my nephew, Finn. Love you Finn, you're not allowed to read this until you're at least thirteen.

To my bonus family, Graham, Dermot, Louise, Conor and Aisling. Thank you for all the encouragement over the last few years. You're stuck with me now.

I'm tremendously fortunate in the people I'm able to call friends and their support has been incredible. Whether they be Flamers, Whiskey Pals, Eden Grove Roomies or Best Buds, I love you guys. I've promised so many of you a free copy that it might not actually be financially viable for the publisher so I hope this paragraph is enough.

Finally, Rio, who is sitting immediately to my left as I type this. Waiting impatiently for her walk. Thank you for being my emotional support Border collie through— Okay! Fine. I'm done. Go get your lead.